BROKEN PLACES

BY BRUCE RYAN

First published in 2025 by BLIR Publishing
© 2025 Bruce Ryan
All rights reserved.

ISBN (paperback): 9781764086806

This is a work of fiction. Names, characters, places, and incidents are either products of the author's imagination or are used fictitiously. Any resemblance to actual persons, living or dead, events, or locales is entirely coincidental.

Printed in Australia

Cover design: Melinda Childs
Layout and typesetting: Katrina Burge

I dedicate this book to my mother, Hirell, and sisters, Lyn and Janet, my three greatest supporters.

Special thanks to my wonderful editor Katrina Burge, and cover artwork by Melinda Childs.

Chapter 1

Now let me make this perfectly clear: I do not see dead people.

I am, at heart, a sceptic. I don't usually believe something just because it is the norm or because some self-important, supposed expert, man or woman, tells me they know. Usually, they don't know. Often, they are on some ego trip and don't believe what they are saying any more than I do.

But here I sat, in the corner of this cell because of my own actions. I had plenty of time to think, and that was dangerous for me. The cold, hard truth about my predicament was terrifying.

In my early teens, I was hit by a car. When I woke from a week-long coma, everything was different. I had feelings of self-harm, a total lack of self-worth – indeed, a total lack of feeling that I even knew who I was and why I was here.

The prevalent information on how to treat me went from psychiatry to religion and everything in between. None helped much. I was truly aimless for the next few years.

My parents were, to their credit, supportive and paid for a university education and three years of bumbling through many jobs, trying to find anything I could stick at for more than five minutes.

Eventually, I found work with the department that handled social security. I was really a glorified office boy, though the independence it afforded me was a whole new world. Suddenly, I could get my own house – admittedly, a rented house in a very low socio-economic community. I knew almost all of the people in my street before I moved in, and they knew me.

It didn't cause any real problems, though sometimes I would be consulted on the street, and that can be less than enjoyable.

During my time in the department, I assisted a man in claiming unemployment and soon after, he opened his own business. Though I would never have guessed it, he was a genius with computer software and was soon very successful.

About a year ago, I had needed to see a doctor and I met Bob in the waiting room. He surprised me by saying that he had now opened two more shopfronts. One was in the suburb near the coastal town where my parents lived.

I was surprised that he even remembered me, to be honest, let alone attributed his success to the help I had given him. He talked about the difficulty he was having getting staff he could trust and joked that if I weren't in such a good job, he would ask me to manage the newest branch.

I told him that I certainly wasn't married to my job, and soon, I was managing the branch. The money was not much more than I had been earning, but the work was much less confrontational and more rewarding.

Life was working itself out, without any real input from me. The main problem I faced now was some terrible feelings of violence. Not violence from me or to me, but violence – terrible, unbelievably blood-curdling violence.

I'll try to explain; in some places, like the one near the highway, where tragic accidents had occurred or in one case, a house where a double murder had been perpetrated, which I viewed with an eye to rent, I would become extremely distressed.

This was something new. I had had a fairly strong panic attack when entering the house, and though I had not been informed of the murders, I felt them. The hackles on my neck rose immediately on entering the front door, but I was able to keep it together until I entered the kitchen. I couldn't see the blood and yet I knew it had been there, there in this dark place. My stomach churned, and I had to make an excuse to leave.

It was some time after this that I was told about the deaths, and that a man and his wife were shot to death by their son. In, yes, you guessed it, the kitchen.

My first response was, 'Bullshit.' But I was assured that the event was real, and on further investigation, on the internet, I found the story to be not only true but even bloodier than I had thought.

There seemed no way I could get away from these thoughts, feelings; I thought I would go mad. Then I thought, if I were already mad, things were explained.

I visited doctors and specialists, and nothing helped. Then one day, I decided I was going to take on my demons and confront things face to face. I drove to our local cemetery and with great trepidation, got out of the car to find a completely serene if not tranquil place. I walked every row waiting for something to happen, but nothing out of the ordinary occurred.

I began to question my every feeling of doom and despair, and then it hit me. It was the places that were damaged by some terrible event. An echo of the past. None of those now dwelling in the cemetery had met with a traumatic death where they now lay. The tragedy had occurred elsewhere.

Yes, it is hard to take these sudden feelings seriously, the pain and fear of the person who had passed traumatically. I continued to try to put it out of my mind, but every time I would travel by car or train, I would have these feelings, sometimes dozens of them, open places crowding in on me. It became so unpleasant that I had to stop travelling anywhere by train. At least if I got totally despondent, I could stop if in my own car.

I felt I couldn't tell anyone, and where had that got me? Locked up, again. Yes, it had happened before.

The reason for my incarceration was my own fault. I was on a long walk from one lookout to another. I had arranged to drop my car off at the second and got a lift from a friend the six kilometres or so back to the first. The walk was wonderful. I had done it once before but this time, I took more notice of the surrounding scenery. Cliffs and the ocean in the distance to my left and the road and the higher parts of the mountain to my right. I loved every part of the walk and arrived a little thirsty, having run out of water along the way.

I knew there was a small picnic hut with four individual table settings and a water tank that contained the water from the building's roof. I stood filling my bottle and the accursed feeling crept over me, then I felt the need to scratch with my foot to the side of the tank. With only a few rakes of my shoe, I uncovered a bone. *Bloody hell, a bone.* The area crowded in around me. I dropped my bottle and backed away quickly.

What could I say to the police? 'I just felt like scratching next to the tank.' They would have me committed.

I stumbled back to the car and sat thinking what to do. I could say that the bone was uncovered and I just noticed it. Oh god, I felt sick.

Eventually, I thought I had to ring the police. I had my mobile phone with me and at first, I thought I could ring anonymously but quickly realised that they would be able to trace the call. I could go to a phone box, but I couldn't remember where I had seen one. Another car pulled into the area and a family got out. I couldn't let them stumble across the remains, so I walked over to the male driver and asked if I might speak to him for a moment. He followed me to the building, and I pointed out the bones and said I was just about to ring the police.

He agreed that it was strange to find bones so close to the building, and he stayed with me as I rang. He yelled to his family to get back into the car.

I am no doctor; I couldn't tell one bone from another but to me, the most visible one looked like a finger.

The police duly arrived with sirens and flashing lights, considering the phone message told them the bones were buried. I thought that was overkill, no pun intended.

After stumbling around the area, the two young policemen came to talk to us and take statements. The man with the family was told he could leave after giving his details, but they asked me to stay due to me being the one to find the bones. They knew better than to disturb the site of the bones in case it was a crime scene. They set up barrier tapes accordingly.

It was difficult, waiting for almost forty-five minutes, and I began to get cold. I asked if I could get a jacket from my car and was given permission.

I took off my damp shirt and undershirt and replaced them with a new t-shirt and my jacket, and though that made things a little better, I still felt cold as I started the car and turned on the heater. One of the officers came bounding up to the car and ordered me to get out.

'What's the problem?' I asked, surprised.

'I asked you not to leave,' he said bluntly.

'But I wasn't leaving; I just got cold, so I put the heater on,' I explained with a smile.

He reached in, turned the keys and removed them. 'You're not going anywhere,' he said angrily, and I noticed he reached for and undid the press stud on his gun holster. 'Get out of the car.'

I reached down and opened the door. When I got out, I was pushed toward the police car and loaded into the back seat. I was too dumbfounded to speak. He slammed the door behind me.

I sat there stewing. What had I done but try to get some warmth, and what right did he have to take my keys, and what right did he have to force me into his car? Was I under arrest? True, he had not read me my rights and he had not handcuffed me. Still, I was furious.

Another police car arrived and a tall, important-looking man alighted. The young officer was soon at his side, pointing to the building where the bones were located and then pointing toward me, all the time delivering his report.

The other man was obviously a detective and the officer's superior. He muttered a few words and then walked over to where I was sitting and opened the door.

'I apologise for the brashness of my young and very inexperienced officer,' he said, and I felt the weight of suspicion lift off my shoulders.

'All I did was start my car as I had got cold,' I explained.

He nodded. 'So, it was you who found the, err, body?'

'Yes, I went to fill my water bottle, and it was there next to the water tank,' I answered.

He produced a notebook and, after taking a pen from his inside jacket pocket, he began to write. He took my name and address and the rough time I found the bones. Seeming satisfied, he reached out a hand and shook mine and then helped me out of the car.

'It is procedure to keep witnesses at the scene. Is that alright?' he asked and then as I nodded, he added, 'You can wait in your own car if you like.'

Stepping out of the car, I asked if I could use the toilet and he said, 'Sorry, that will be a part of the crime scene.' Then, realising that the toilet block had not been taped, he went over to the young officer and said, raising his voice so I could hear, 'Why have you not taped off the toilets?' Before the young man could answer, he blurted, 'Bloody incompetent. Where would a person wash up after digging in the dirt?' The younger man knew this to be a rhetorical question and so turned to leave and do the task. I sat back in the police car.

The officer now introduced himself as Detective Tim Marsh and we shook hands again.

'What made you find this body really?' he questioned quietly.

'Well, as I said, I was getting water from the tank and just noticed a finger bone sticking out,' I answered but felt sure he would not believe me.

He nodded and then stood thinking for some time before asking, 'I wonder why other people would not have seen it?'

'I really can't say. Perhaps it had been recently disturbed by animals, or I may have disturbed the dirt as I approached,' I answered, feeling uncomfortable. This man was a professional interrogator. What would give me the ability to fool him? Nothing.

He looked at me for what seemed like ages and then asked unblinkingly, 'You didn't know that there was a body there before you broke ground?'

'Of course not. How could I?' I asked back. I always seem to answer a question with a question when I am being less than truthful – I think most people do.

'Oh, I don't know. People do funny things, Mr...?' he answered, obviously acting as though he had forgotten my name, and I nodded.

'James Fitzpatrick,' I answered.

'Ah, yes, that's right,' he concluded. This was the little game these professional men play, as if getting you to tell them a truth, if they thought you had told them a lie.

I must have passed the test as he said, 'I will let you go as soon as we find out what we have.'

This conversation had taken place through the open squad car window and as he turned to walk away, I asked, 'Could I go back to my own car?'

He turned back toward me, walked to my door and opened it. 'Certainly,' he answered and as I exited the car, another car arrived. It was the Crime Investigation Unit's van. Two young-looking men alighted and after showing their identification, they were admitted to the area.

I walked along with Marsh over to the tape and waited for several minutes until one of the young men came into view. Seeing Marsh, he walked over to us and said, 'It's a bloody dog.'

No sooner than he had uttered the words, his partner shouted for him to come back.

I knew that what I had felt was not the death of a dog. I thought that I must have had my messages confused.

'Maybe they have found something else,' I said foolishly.

Marsh gave me a glare, obviously unimpressed.

Another few minutes passed and then the young man again approached us. 'There is a human body under the dog. We wouldn't have noticed it but there was one finger sticking up.'

Marsh again swung toward me and asked, 'Isn't that what you said you saw?' He glared at me as if he had stumbled on a murder case.

'Yes, it was. There was a bone sticking up and I thought it looked like a finger,' I answered.

The young man also now stared at me and shook his head. 'That is not possible. We couldn't see it until we removed the animal.'

They were still both staring at me open mouthed.

'Oh, it may have been a piece of the dog that I saw. I am no doctor,' I said. I was digging myself into an ever-deepening hole.

'No, the bone that could be seen was part of the skull,' he answered.

Marsh added, 'What did you see, Mr Fitzpatrick?'

'As I said, I thought it was a finger,' I answered, and I knew I sounded as though I was dithering.

Marsh crouched under the tape. As he walked toward the body, he said without looking back, 'Don't go anywhere, Mr Fitzpatrick.'

I paced up and down for another ten minutes or so and was relieved as I saw that he had a wry smile on his face.

'The bones speak. The man's legs were shattered,' Marsh said then added as he neared, 'I think you have more to tell me?'

'I don't think so,' I answered shakily.

'We might just take this back to the station, then,' he said, sounding me out.

'Whatever you like.' Though I had regained my composure somewhat, I still felt like Marsh was looking right through me. 'The car. Can it be brought down as well?' I asked.

'Yes, I will have one of my officers drive it down if you like?' he answered. I thought that I was allowing him access to my car. I had nothing to hide and so I agreed readily.

'You can have it searched if you like,' I said.

'And why do you think I would need to have it searched?' he asked, nodding at me, and I thought how stupidly I was handling this. I should just let him get on with his investigation, and soon enough, he would learn that I was not involved. I shrugged as an answer.

'What will be found in your vehicle?' he persisted.

'Absolutely nothing,' I answered confidently.

'We shall see,' he said, still glaring into my eyes. I suddenly found him threatening.

I was under some cloud and after thinking for a moment, I said, 'I think I need a lawyer.'

'Why would you need a lawyer?'

'I'm sorry but you are treating me like some kind of criminal. I will answer no more questions till I have a lawyer.' I was probably digging a bigger hole for myself, but I thought I needed to have someone speaking for me.

'Why, certainly, I can arrange that if you like,' he answered in a sly-sounding tone that made me feel even more uneasy.

Chapter 2

Now, at the station, I sat waiting to be interviewed. I was basically in a cell. I could see that it wasn't physically possible for me to see a finger, well, not exactly. I had said that they may have found something else when they had almost given up digging, and how would I have known that?

I had seen a finger but not really. Yes, that was weird, to say the least, but I couldn't just say I 'see dead people'. I don't see dead people, but I had seen the bones, the finger, at least, in my head.

I know I sound like a complete lunatic. I have often questioned my own sanity, but I could feel the terror, the violence, the uneasiness of the place, the broken place. This cell was one of those places and the walls seemed to be closing in on me. There had been a violent death here, right here.

Some time had passed before I was led into the presence of Marsh in an interview room. He sat with another detective, and I was positioned opposite them still with no lawyer.

The body language of Marsh looked more like one ready to back down. He had been all big and in my face when we had arrived at the station; now, he was more pleasant and almost looked apologetic somehow.

'Through a wristwatch on the remains, we have an identity. This man has been missing, along with his dog, for over twenty years. As you are too young to have been driving the car that killed him, you are no longer implicated in his death,' he stated.

I sat for a moment then let out a deep breath. I was relieved but I was also still angry at my treatment.

'I bloody told you I wasn't involved,' I said and thought how clumsy that sounded. I often sounded like that when I was under pressure; it was almost as though I was taken over by someone who only had a primary school education.

'Yes, well, you must understand the fact that you knew there was a human body there and the mention of seeing a finger was suspicious. The finger was not visible until the dog's skeleton was removed from the grave,' the second detective said.

I shrugged my shoulders and said, 'I'm no doctor. I saw bones and thought one was a finger, that's all.'

'Yes, and you say you just happened to scrape the soil when you went to get water?' Marsh said almost accusingly.

I shrugged my shoulders again, not immediately thinking of an answer.

'I understand, Mr Fitzpatrick, that you are not old enough to have killed the man, but our forensic investigator said that the bones were more than six inches under the ground. How do you explain that?' Marsh asked.

'I don't know. Perhaps an animal had scratched around it. I don't know.' Another problem I have is repeating myself to try to get my point across.

'Yes, well, you *are* old enough to have been in the car when it killed the man,' the second detective said, leaning forward to emphasise his point.

'Oh, if this is going to continue, I want the solicitor I asked for,' I said, feeling very uncomfortable.

'No need for that. You are not being charged with anything,' Marsh said.

'Then I can leave?' I asked, and both men nodded. Marsh got to his feet and opened the door to let me out.

I walked to the front desk where a uniformed officer got me to check and sign for my personal items and car keys.

Marsh followed me out of the building and as I was unlocking my car, he said, 'Sorry to have bothered you with all this, but you must understand that in many cases a criminal will try to become involved in a case.'

'I suppose that is a kind of apology,' I said, not making eye contact.

'Indeed, it is,' he said. I found my eyes lift to meet his and I thought they could see right through me.

'If there is nothing else?' I asked as I sat in the driver's seat and fumbled with my seatbelt.

'Nothing else for now,' he concluded and stepped back as I began to reverse my car out of the narrow parking slot. I turned the vehicle to exit, and as I looked up, Detective Marsh gave me a knowing nod. He knew something. He didn't know what he knew, but he knew something.

On my arrival home, I hurried to get inside and away from the world. I knew that Marsh was not the kind of man to let this go, to walk away. I had met his kind before.

I thought I should pack everything and leave, run away again. I could think of no other way to get away from his knowing eye.

I spiralled into a depression. I could feel it. What would I do? Where could I ever go that this kind of thing would not haunt me?

For hours I just sat on the couch with a blanket over me. It wasn't cold enough to need a blanket but somehow it seemed to help.

After what seemed like a lifetime, I forced myself to get up and take a shower. This often helped when I was in worry mode. The hot water pouring onto my face would often make me see sense, to stop panicking, to settle down, but this time that was not the case.

I had an almost sleepless night. Every direction I took in my thoughts seemed to come back to Marsh. He knew something.

When I finally did sleep, the alarm almost immediately rang and I needed to get up and go to work. I didn't have the luxury of ringing in sick; I was the only one rostered to work that day. I had a hurried shower and dressed and after a somewhat slower than usual drive, found myself in the small car park behind the shop.

I sat for several minutes. I didn't want to do this. I didn't want to face people, face the world when it came knocking. I dragged myself to the shop entrance and unlocked it. I turned the 'closed' sign on the inside of the door to show the open sign on its reverse.

The morning was uneventful. There was only one customer, a teenaged boy who, probably spending his dinner money, wanted to buy a computer game. He didn't have quite enough money but I let the fifty cents go, telling him he could catch me up next time. He looked surprised, but I had thought he would have probably lifted the game if I didn't let him have it – and who would miss fifty cents, anyway?

I started to think about other things. I read manuals, yes, games manuals, and even the manual of operation for the shop's only luxury: the newly purchased microwave oven. I know it seems like a strange thing to do, but I could lose myself in them. It was like being instructed and took my thoughts off other things. That said, I quickly read everything available and never found it helpful to read things a second time. That only reminded me of what I was trying to hide from.

At midday, I closed the door and locked up to go and grab a sandwich from the store at the end of the shopping strip. Then I purchased a newspaper that I could dive into and lose myself.

On arriving back at the shop, I found a visitor waiting for me. It was Detective Marsh. If I could, I would have turned around and disappeared, but he had seen me and made eye contact. He nodded.

I fumbled with the keys and opened the shop, turning my back on him. Soon, though, he followed me in and waited for me to assume my position behind the counter.

'So, you are the famous James Fitzpatrick?' he asked.

'What do you mean?' I fired back, knowing that he almost certainly knew what he was talking about.

'You discovered the body at your school when you were only young?' he continued. I could think of nothing smart to say so I just waited for his inevitable follow-up.

'And that body you said you saw in a dream?' He waited, his eyes burning into me.

'I did not see the body. I had a feeling that there was something wrong in that old bus shelter,' I answered, dreading the path this was taking.

'Let me understand this. You feel things that are wrong?' he said, not blinking; it was eerie how he could look as though he never blinked when he was questioning me. I felt sick.

'Look, I have left that world behind me through years of counselling, and I'm not going back there,' I answered, losing my cool and speaking far too loudly.

'No need to become all defensive. My grandmother was a clairvoyant, or at least she said she was. She always knew when something happened to a member of the family. She would be on the phone to the hospital before the injured person even arrived. Strange things are not always bad and not always that strange, you know what I mean?' he asked, tilting his head to one side. I had always hated that. So bloody condescending.

'You have no idea the circus that surrounded me after that incident. I was the "seer", the one everyone turned to for advice, I was only a primary school student, for god's sake, and for years they still came wanting everything.' I was angry now and as usual, my mouth wanted to flow with the injustice I had suffered for the greater part of my life since I found that body.

'I didn't come here to upset you. I just wanted you to know that the body we found'—he waved a hand backwards and forwards, indicating that he meant the two of us—'er, was, well, was a murder victim.' He looked at me to see if the information had sunk in and then continued.

'Yes, he and his dog were run down, but he was finished off with a blunt object. His skull was so badly fractured that slivers of bone had penetrated the brain.'

I felt sick, and the feeling was getting worse. I wanted to throw up and I knew that I needed a receptacle to use. I rushed behind the small modesty screen to the sink and was sick. I felt dizzy and had to sit down in the office chair, which was also situated in this only private part of the shop.

Marsh knew what was happening but followed me and stood looking at me when I regained my composure enough to look up at him.

'Christ, I didn't expect that. Sorry,' he said, and I could see that he was surprised. He waited for a few moments and then added, 'And you see all of this?'

'You are not bloody listening. I don't see anything – I just feel what happened,' I said in a slightly raised, disgruntled voice.

'Yes, so you said, but you saw the finger in the hole?' he fired back accusingly, though I sensed that he wanted an answer.

'Usually, I see nothing. Sometimes I say what I think I see. There, are you bloody happy? This will take months to get over – the sleepless nights, the looks from complete strangers when I pass in the street. It's a bloody nightmare,' I babbled an incoherent answer.

He stepped forward and placed a hand on my shoulder. 'I didn't mean to make it hard for you, but really, I need your help.'

I was not surprised. This was how it always started – *just help me with this, just tell me that,'* with me left a basket case.

'You have seen the cases of the missing children along the coastal strip? I have nothing. I have only one body and no clues,' he explained then paused, waiting for some feedback. I really had none to offer and so I just sat looking at him. I could see him thinking *give me something,* but I still said nothing.

'Um, well, I can't see another family destroyed by this bastard. I'm willing to try anything, that's why I am here.'

His voice was weak. He spoke in a very basic way; I believed that he was sincere.

'I don't see how I can help?' I questioned, shrugging my shoulders.

'But if you could help, you would?' he asked.

I thought for a moment and then said, 'Not if anyone else knows I'm helping, and I don't promise that I even can help. It's not something I really have control of. I have spent years trying to suppress it.'

'So, you will help?' he asked eagerly.

'I don't know how. Have you something in mind?' I answered slowly and deliberately. I wanted him to understand that the chance that I may be able to assist was very low in my own opinion.

'Do you sense things from people's belongings?' He found another seat in the little alcove.

'No, I never have,' I answered honestly.

'What about location from a map?' he pushed.

'Never tried,' I answered honestly again.

'Well, should we try that?' he asked.

'I would have to be in a very isolated place to read from a map, I think, away from all the clutter,' I explained, though I hoped he would understand that I really had never tried the method.

'We could go to the police station,' he suggested quickly.

'Not bloody likely. Someone was killed in that room I was in last night,' I continued as he readied himself to speak. 'Yes, I said killed. It was not a suicide – he was strangled.'

Marsh sat dumbfounded. His mouth gaped open, and he had no words, so I continued, 'You know what I am saying is true then?' I asked.

'Yes,' he answered but gave no more information.

'I take it that someone was charged then?' I continued.

'No, it's a legend in our station ... um, the officer who killed him went too far, and he couldn't live with it. He committed suicide. It was not possible to charge anyone. The family were given a settlement. This is over thirty years ago though?' he answered with every word sounding like a question.

'Yes, I could have read about this in the papers,' I said, seeing the doubt in his eyes.

'No, you couldn't, that's the point. It never got to the public.' A furtive glance then he quickly looked away.

'I know, you still can't believe me. Why are you really here then?' I asked in a harsher tone than I even meant. I was scared. The years of counselling I had gone through were very painful. Not knowing what was real and what would be accepted as real were very different things. I knew that I would suffer terribly if I helped him.

'I understand. I read your record and know about the asylum, but this bastard is killing children, and I haven't got a single clue,' he pleaded his case.

'So, what do you expect me to do about it?' I asked and loathed the expected answer, which came on cue.

'I want you to have a look at the file, go over local maps.'

'And what if that doesn't work?' I pushed him, though I didn't have any doubt what he was going to suggest next.

'Well, we could just travel around the town and see if you pick anything up?' His part-question part-answer was just what I expected, but these were children.

I had never had much to do with children. Even when I was a child, most mothers wouldn't let their precious ones be seen with me. I was a freak, but like Marsh, they came calling when they thought I could help.

Like any normal man, I would like to think that an hour with this animal would be enough to stop his rampage. This was, of course, bravado.

I don't know why I thought I would have the strength or capacity to do what it would take. I was no fighter. I had taken Judo in my teens just for self-protection, and I became proficient at a green belt level, but I didn't think throwing someone on the floor would help me here. Like most things, I had to give the art away when people started to find out who I was. Once again, ostracised.

They were children, I kept reminding myself.

'I think I would be wasting your time, but it is your time,' I said quietly and wondered if he had even heard what I said as he continued where he had left off.

'I have nothing. We have not been able to find a single clue.' His eyes were boring into me, and I had to look away.

I nodded. I really didn't think there was much hope. I was always surprised when I picked up on something that was proven to be true later. In short, I didn't really believe in my abilities myself.

'Great, can you start tomorrow?' he cajoled.

'I might be able to if I can get someone else to man the store,' I answered. I knew full well that I wasn't rostered on in the morning, though I would normally have fronted up to see if things were all in order. I prized my job; it was the only thing that gave me freedom and the security to get out of home.

'Shall we say eight o'clock then?' he said in an upbeat voice, like a young man getting a date. I nodded.

He offered a few pleasantries and then put his hand out and shook heartily.

'No one else can know about this,' I demanded.

He placed a finger up to his lips and then said, 'It would be bad for me too if anyone knew what I was willing to do to catch this maniac.'

With that, he turned and quickly left, possibly thinking I might change my mind, and how I wish I would have.

Chapter 3

True to his word, Marsh was waiting for me the next morning in my driveway.

I felt uncomfortable not having anything in my hands, so I retrieved an umbrella and a bottle of water.

When I reached the car and opened the door, he looked quizzically at the umbrella. There wasn't a cloud in the sky.

'Know something I don't?' he asked.

'Perhaps. I saw the weather forecast on the news,' I answered curtly. I still wasn't sure I liked this man, and I certainly didn't see any humour in him.

He handed me a folder with masses of paper in it. I understood what he expected of me and began to peruse. There were statements from members of the public and the victims' family statements. There were some photographs, but I wasn't about to look at them; they would just cloud my judgment.

The last of the statements I read was one of a mother whose son was still missing. We must have been driving for half an hour, but I still had not looked up when Marsh stopped the car, and we just sat there for a few minutes.

'Why have we stopped here?' I asked, looking around.

When he didn't answer, I added, 'Oh, I see, some kind of test?'

He shrugged his shoulders.

'No, he wasn't killed here. This is just where he was dumped,' I said then thought how callous I sounded.

'The red envelope,' he said, and I obeyed, opening it against my better judgment. Inside was a photo of a sporting field in which a body was covered with a sheet.

Lifting my eyes, I saw I was looking directly at that site in the picture, minus the body.

'So, you are testing me?' I asked, a little annoyed.

'Yes. To be honest, I still find it hard to comprehend,' he said. I appreciated his candour.

'Well?' I questioned.

'You are right. The body was found here; he had bled out but there was no blood here. In other words, he was killed elsewhere and dumped here,' he confirmed my statement, then added, 'That information was not given out to the public.'

We both waited for the other to speak. Eventually, I decided to break the silence and explain my process – if it could be called that.

'I have sensed the body here, but that doesn't help us in the least. He was killed elsewhere.' I knew being here would solicit no further psychic response from me, and I really didn't feel good about looking at photos of dead people.

'Ok, I won't take you to any more drop sites. What about where we think one of them was abducted from?' he asked tentatively. I could see that he was trying to keep me on his side, and I was starting to feel that he was no longer a threat to me.

'That might work. I would certainly pick things up at a murder site. I don't know about an abduction site. I've never tried,' I answered honestly.

'What if I drive you along the route we know one of the children was taking home?' he asked, shrugging.

'I sometimes sense things on the road so it may work,' I answered.

I was now thinking that this may be a man I could trust.

We drove through the main part of the town and headed slightly inland on a rough dirt road. There were houses equidistant on blocks of around five acres. We passed around seven or eight property gates, though due to bushland, the house was not always visible from the road.

About another fifty or sixty meters down a slight hill, I had a feeling of revulsion. Something was here. 'Stop, I need to get out,' I said with more urgency than I intended.

'What is it?' Marsh asked as I rushed to get out of the car.

I promptly lost my breakfast on the side of the road. I was doubled over retching when Marsh sidled up to within three or four meters.

'Well, that was quite a reaction. What did you sense?' he asked quietly.

'Something happened just over there,' I said, pointing toward a large corner post of the two properties.

'Well, this one is a bust. His route home to his house was two properties back, so he wasn't passing here,' he explained.

'Not bloody likely,' I said and pointed again. I was still doubled over, and I felt that I couldn't get things that wrong.

Marsh looked incredulously at me and began to walk toward the post. I righted myself and followed. The feeling that I could soon vomit again was terrible and got only worse as we neared the site.

I couldn't keep approaching the area, so I walked back to the car, regained my seat and sipped on the water I had brought with me.

A few minutes passed, which seemed like hours. I didn't want to be in this place, this awful, broken place.

When Marsh re-joined me in the car, he was carrying a plastic evidence bag. I couldn't see the contents, but I could feel its power as it passed me when he placed it on the back seat.

'What is it?' I asked.

'It's the reflector of a bike. His bike was found miles away from here, on the other side of the town. It was all smashed up and I think the reflector was missing,' he explained in a self-doubting voice.

'That has to be it. It is so strong, I don't even like being in the car with it.'

'I left a pointer at the post, and I will get the crime scene guys out here straight away. There may be other clues, but I doubt it. It's been over two months,' he said, starting the car. 'I will drop this off at the station, straight away.'

I could do little more than nod. I just wanted out of the area.

Arriving at the police station, Marsh drove down the long public driveway and around the back of the building, which was a staff parking area. He got out, retrieved the bag from the back seat and went quickly into the station.

After a short while, he returned with a uniformed officer. They both got into the car, and we returned to the site where Marsh had found the reflector.

The car passed the home of the murdered boy and as it did so, the young officer said questioningly, 'That was the home back there?'

Marsh turned his head and answered in a rather annoyed voice, 'I bloody know that. Who knows why he would be out this way? That's something to work on later!' He had a second thought and then added, 'Who knows if it is even his reflector, but we have no other clues.'

I caught the young man nodding and could tell that he thought he might be on a wild goose chase. Marsh also noticed his expression and said forcefully, 'You are to stay where I drop you until the investigation team arrive, and don't bloody touch anything. Understand?'

'Yes, Sir,' the officer quickly answered.

On our arrival back at the roadside where we had found the reflector, Marsh parked at least one hundred meters away from the actual site, and I knew that he was doing so for my benefit.

He walked briskly with the young officer and pointed to the place where he was expected to stand. He returned to the car, and we started on another quest.

I felt that I had assisted in a small way; it was a good feeling, and I was pleased that Marsh had in no way implicated me in the discovery to his underling.

We drove now to another site of interest to Marsh's investigation, the site where the bike had been discovered. I walked around the clearing, which was used by truckers to take breaks on long-haul trips up and down the coast. We were able to hear the ocean but not to see it as the area was thickly bushed with coastal plants, and there were some sand dunes.

Here, I got no feelings of an unsettling kind. We spent only a few minutes there and then headed further along the coast to the south. After only fifteen minutes or so, I was overcome with terrible dread as we drove past another roadside clearing. I indicated for Marsh to stop but as he had overshot the area where it was safe to pull off the road, he travelled around the next corner, looking for somewhere to make a U-turn safely.

Where we prepared to turn, I had another feeling of the bile rising to my stomach.

'Oh god, here too,' I said as I began to retch. I had to quickly exit my side door while covering my mouth with my hand. I felt the little bit of content left in my stomach was about to find its way out.

I was actually not sick, but I had to sit down with my back against the side of the car. Marsh came around to my side of the vehicle and gestured, with a shrug of his shoulders, meaning, 'Where?'

I pointed to the back of the area near the biggest of the shrubs. I didn't know what had happened there, but it was there that something awful had happened, of that I was certain.

There was a depression that ran down the left side of the clearing, and Marsh walked along it until, nearing the area I had pointed out, he went out of view. Several minutes had passed when a dishevelled Marsh walked back to the car.

'Anything?' I asked, dreading what he might say.

'Yes, bones. There were bones.' He looked at me with what looked to be fear in his eyes. 'I didn't think this through. I won't be able to just pass this off as coincidence, finding two sites within a couple of hours that we have been searching for, for more than two years,' he said, looking down, not engaging my eyes as he usually did when he was talking.

I had a real feeling of dread; he was going to have to throw me to the wolves. Like many people I had dealt with over the years, I could see that he had believed what I was telling him, only when it was easy. Now that things were real, his mind told him that I had to be involved.

'You made a promise, and now you want to renege,' I said quietly. I was getting angry, and I wanted to try to keep my composure.

'No, not that. I, um, I just can't think how I can present this to my superiors without dropping you in the shit,' he answered rather ineloquently.

Chapter 4

Now I sat in another question room, waiting. Two days had passed, and I had suffered, unmolested by the police or the press, who had covered the finding of the second boy's body.

I had stayed at home and ordered Chinese food to last several days, so I would not have to go out and face the world.

To his credit, Marsh had come to take me in for questioning himself. He was apologetic but said that I had to answer some questions about how I was able to locate the two places of interest, without some sort of insider knowledge.

I swore at him several times, something I was sorry about, really. I should have known that my involvement would destroy me all over again. I sat with my knees drawn up to my chest and my feet on the rung of my chair.

The door opened. Marsh and another officer in what looked to be a very expensive suit entered. The second detective introduced himself as Senior Detective Wilson from the Sydney Homicide Squad, and I detested him immediately.

Wilson immediately quizzed me over places and times, and after about ten or so questions, he came to the crux of the matter – well, at least in his eyes.

'Where were you on the eighth of June 2018?' he grilled.

'I have no real idea,' I answered truthfully, but he was not to be denied.

'Look, you have information about several murders, so if you want to spend time in gaol, just keep stonewalling,' he growled.

'I have no real idea. I was living in Melbourne at the time but more than that, I can't say,' I answered in as surly a tone as he had asked the question.

'I don't think you have a real grip on how much trouble you're in.' He started to sound much more threatening, and I'm sure that that was his intent.

'Well, I might have some paperwork of some sort at home, but I doubt it and as for being in trouble, I was just helping Marsh, and I don't know anything about any murders.' I started to get more annoyed, though I was trying to keep my temper. This man was an ass.

'Oh, yes, and how exactly were you helping Marsh?' Wilson queried in a sarcastic voice.

'I was trying to help him find the sites of the murders and disappearances,' I said and was quite confident I knew what his next question would be – oh, not through some ESP or something. No, through experience. The experience of being questioned every time I came up with some important piece of information.

'No, the ghosts didn't tell me!' I said curtly, and his reaction was one of surprise.

He leaned in toward me but before he spoke, I continued, 'No, I'm not being a smart arse. Your face is like an open book,' I said tauntingly.

His eyebrows rose, and I thought, *Another bullseye.* I didn't continue as he looked even angrier than I expected.

'Throw him in a cell,' he ordered.

'However he does it, he gets the information we need.'

'Alright then, how do you "get the information" then?' Wilson said sneeringly.

'I can read places. Not people, not names, not even the events, really, just the place,' I answered, knowing that his plodding mind would take a moment to take that in, so I paused and waited for him to catch up, then added, 'Yes, I do know you don't understand me.'

'Enough of the parlour games. You won't throw me off with your sleight of hand,' he blurted.

'You know nothing, you narrow-minded fool,' I fired back, beginning to really lose my temper.

There it is. The real *psychic* comes out.' He continued to blunder through the interview. 'Well, I know enough to keep you behind bars.' He sneered at me across the table.

'Good, that will give me time to get a lawyer and have him ready the case for wrongful arrest. I should have lawyered up as soon as I was brought in here, and I have to say, you didn't read me my rights nor offer me counsel.'

The immediate look that came across his face was one of petulance. He wanted to rant and rave but he was knowledgeable enough to know that I was not bluffing and that he and Marsh would be in deep shit if it came to the knowledge of their superiors, or a judge for that matter, that they had not read me my rights required by law.

I could see him trying to backpedal in his attitude, slowly thinking about what he should do next.

'Yes, I want a solicitor, now,' I said, trying to sound strong but not obnoxious.

'Naturally, that is your right, but you haven't been charged with anything yet,' he said in a quieter and less confrontational voice.

'Yet, yet! Have you ever been successful in an interview?' This, I admit, was obnoxious.

'Get him a duty solicitor,' he said to Marsh, getting up from his chair.

'Not bloody likely. I will have the representative of my choice, not yours,' I said, and I saw Marsh give a wry smile as the other departed the room.

'That wasn't the wisest thing to do,' he said, rolling his eyes.

'Why not? The man's a bloody fool,' I said, still not delighted by Marsh's part in this charade.

'The bloody fool who could make your life very unpleasant,' he answered.

'What, as opposed to now?' I said, and he got the sarcasm.

'Well, who do you want as a solicitor?' he asked, still smiling.

'How the hell would I know? I've never met one,' I admitted.

He gave a little scoffed laugh and then said, 'I'll get you a phone book.' He rose and left the room to find said book.

Two hours later, a short man who introduced himself as Alan Donne entered the room, and the door was closed behind him.

I wasn't sure where to start, so I sat waiting for him to take the lead. He went through some preliminary statements, warnings and his credentials. Though he babbled on a bit, I felt that it would be better to just let him go. That would probably end this all faster.

'Now, I don't know anything about the case. Can you tell me what it is alleged that you have done?' he asked, and his bifocal glasses dropped down so he could look at me over the rims.

'They haven't charged me with anything, and all I did was help Marsh with his enquiries. At his request, I might add,' I answered, trying not to say anything about how I was to help.

'Why did he ask for your help? Are you an investigator?' I could feel my eyes darting backwards and forwards, searching for something to answer.

'Well, I have come to people's attention as I sometimes, um, feel things,' I mumbled.

'What do you mean exactly?' he said with his glare seeming to bore into me.

'I have been heralded as a medium,' I answered, regaining my composure somewhat.

'So, are you saying you are a medium?' he asked quickly, not even blinking.

'No, others say so,' I answered awkwardly.

'So, you are not a medium then?' he continued. He was good at this. I felt like I was under cross-examination.

'No, that is... not exactly,' I answered and seeing that he didn't understand, I continued, 'I feel things. I can sometimes feel if something bad has happened in a place.'

'So, Marsh had heard about you and approached you?' he continued relentlessly.

'Yes, well, no. He arrested me when I discovered a body and reported it. He looked into my past. I had been involved in several cases as a teenager and helped solve them. I needed to go into care for nearly six months, being counselled, trying to get my life back together. It was a bloody circus. I have hidden myself away for years,' I explained in the rambling way I did when I was flustered.

'I see, and did you implicate yourself in some way?' he questioned bluntly.

'I can't implicate myself. I wasn't even here when the murders were committed,' I answered.

'I see. The murders of the children then?' he asked, crossing his legs.

'Yes, Marsh took me to the site where one of the boys was dumped, and I found where he had been hit by a car. The first body I had found had been hit by a car, and so I think he started to suspect me,' I answered as honestly as I could.

'You had no knowledge of these events prior to the first time you were interviewed?' he continued, nodding as though he understood.

'None at all. I think Marsh was convinced when I told him that a man had been killed in the other interview room, and he knew about that.' I was trying to convince him of my truthfulness but could see some seeds of doubt written across his face. I paused for a moment and then said, 'I think Marsh got rattled when I found one of the missing bodies.

'You found one of the bodies?' He raised his eyebrows and his voice questioningly.

'Yes, with Marsh. He took me to the area, and I was so overwhelmed that I was sick, then he discovered the remains where I had pointed,' I explained, becoming a little emotional.

'So, you did what the detective asked of you, and you were in no way involved in the murders.' He seemed to be making a statement rather than asking a question.

'That is the truth, and I didn't want to help as I knew how awful all of this fanfare could be,' I answered.

'Well, there are more things in heaven and earth,' he quipped. Then when he knew I was settled a bit, he added, 'Don't speak. I will do all the talking – that is, when they come in to continue on their enquiry.'

I nodded. This man was good at what he did, and I felt I could trust him. He didn't seem to believe that I was... well, what I was, but he did seem to be in my corner.

'Oh, one thing. I was not under caution at any time, and they didn't offer me a legal representative,' I said suddenly, remembering my best defence.

'Oh good, we will be out of here in just a few minutes then,' he said, smiling.

Soon, Wilson and Marsh were allowed back into the room and almost as quickly as they sat down, my defender started quite a tirade.

'Who the hell are you?' he demanded of Wilson, and Wilson, caught off guard somewhat, gave his rank and officer number.

'I don't think I have ever seen so many rules broken in such a short time. Where did you get your qualifications?' he continued. It appeared Wilson was going to answer, but Donne raised his hand to show that the question was rhetorical. 'You don't need to speak. Something you should have told my client.' He raised his voice.

'And how long has he been your client?' Wilson asked to change the subject.

'That would be covered under client-solicitor privilege, don't you think?' was Donne's curt reply. It seemed that he was so experienced that Wilson couldn't lay a hand on him. Wilson said little more and allowed Marsh to work out the rest of the encounter.

'We just need to know where you got the information you had about the deaths?' Marsh questioned.

'How dare you. You ask my client to assist you and when he is successful, you try to charge him with something. Very amateurish policing, I say,' Donne answered quickly and confidently.

'Yes, I am sorry about that, but everything pointed to an involvement,' Marsh answered, looking down at his papers and not making eye contact with either of us.

'Involvement? How dare you insinuate that my client was involved without any evidence.' He paused, and when no answer came, he added, 'Well, have you any evidence?'

'No,' answered Marsh, still looking down.

'Well, I think you have wasted enough of my client's precious time, don't you?' he said with a strong hint of sarcasm in his tone.

'We just wanted to give you the opportunity to assist us in finding the missing children, for their families,' Marsh answered and this time he did make eye contact with me.

'And did he do that?' Donne asked.

'Yes, that he did,' Marsh answered honestly.

Wilson looked as though he would explode. 'That help came from somewhere, and we'll find you out yet,' he growled.

'Well then, we are leaving, and you will hear from us about our ongoing suit,' Donne answered, and then, having a second thought, he added, 'I will make great efforts to single you out in this witch hunt.' He glared at Wilson and got to his feet. Taking my arm, he prompted me to rise.

Wilson was so enraged that he tried to have the last word. 'We will be watching you, *Mr Fitzpatrick.*'

'Very good, the threat to continue the harassment, that speaks volumes in a courthouse.' And then when he had ushered me out the door and made sure I was clear, he slammed it quite forcefully, with intent, one might say.

We left after I received my belongings and signed for them. The young officer behind the counter made a crack about revolving doors and was soundly rebuked by Donne. 'This is not some damned joke.'

Once clear of the station, Donne suggested, 'I think you should come to my office tomorrow and bring any evidence as to your movements over the last few years. Shall we say eleven a.m.?'

'Yes, thank you, but I may not have much evidence. I mean, I'm not in the habit of keeping evidence. I never thought I had to,' I answered.

'You will be surprised what you find when you look. Look at bank statements and things like that,' he suggested then he turned to leave. I suddenly thought of his retainer.

'Oh, um, I'm not sure I will be immediately able to pay your fees,' I said.

'We don't need to worry about that now, and I'm pretty sure the police will be paying your costs anyway,' he answered in his usual confident way.

'How do you know I am not guilty?' I asked inquisitively.

'Well, I am a good judge of people, and I believed you. But really, it doesn't matter if I think you are guilty or not, my job is to give you the best defence I can,' he answered bluntly.

'Thank you,' I said and thought how insufficient that sounded.

'Not at all, not at all,' he answered and then he got into his own car and left.

I fumbled for my keys and found that I was shaking. I hadn't even realised. I sat for a few minutes in the car, just getting myself together.

As I eventually pulled out of the carpark, I noticed Marsh on the front steps of the building, and he nodded. For some reason, I nodded back and then thought what a fool I was. This man had just put me through hell and for what?

Chapter 5

The next morning, I arrived at Donne's office at ten a.m. I wanted to get this all over, and I had to let Bob know that I would be opening the shop much later than usual, at some time after midday.

I introduced myself to the prim-looking but elderly secretary sitting at the enquiry desk.

'Hello, I think you are early,' she said, looking at her appointment book.

'Yes, I always come early. Sorry,' I answered. From the open door at the end of the room came Donne's voice.

'Show him in,' he said.

The secretary stood, walked me to the door and indicated the entrance with a quite formal gesture.

'Morning. Keen then?' Donne asked without looking up from the piles of paperwork strewn across his desk. It looked like complete chaos.

'Yes, I have some proof. I was in New Zealand when the boy we found was killed,' I blurted.

'Well, that will put the cat amongst the pigeons with your friend Wilson,' he said, smiling.

I stepped closer to the desk and passed the small bundle of papers to him. At the same time, we heard the receptionist saying, 'I'm sorry, you can't go in there...'

But even with her continued and loudening protestations, Marsh appeared at the entrance to the office. He stepped into the room and slammed the door in the woman's face.

'What the hell do you think you are doing, Marsh?' Donne said, getting up from his seat.

'I'm sorry but I have to talk to you both,' he said in an almost pleading voice and though Donne began to protest, he continued, 'There's been another one.'

'Another one what?' Donne asked, then the penny dropped. 'Another abduction?' he added.

Marsh nodded and looked at me desperately.

'Oh, I suppose I am to be blamed for this one too,' I said and immediately thought how callous I sounded, worrying about myself.

'No, no, we won't be having any of this ...' Donne said, heading toward the door as if to show Marsh out.

'But wait, please,' Marsh pleaded desperately. 'He was abducted while you were at the station yesterday.'

It took a moment for that information to sink in. *I'm cleared then,* I thought.

'Well, that is fine news. It will only help us with our case,' Donne said calmly.

'Oh, I don't care about your bloody case. I care about the boy,' Marsh growled back at him.

'And what exactly do you want from my client then?' Donne continued calmly under fire. He seemed like one of those actors at the head of some impossible battle, against all odds. If it were not so serious, it would have been laughable.

'I don't know. I need your help. I can't lose another one,' he almost cried as he spoke, and I felt sorry for him.

'And what does your fine Detective Wilson think of that?' Donne continued.

'He's run back to Sydney after he got a rebuke about yesterday.' There were a lot of assumptions in his statement, but we both understood him immediately.

'Well, what do you want of me?' I asked, thinking that this was all too much, but I knew that if I didn't help him, I could never live with myself.

'We think he was taken from near the skate park,' he answered bluntly.

'You want me to go there?' I asked redundantly. He nodded.

'Don't think you have gotten my client in enough trouble?' Donne asked, and then turning, he said to me, 'I have to advise you against doing this.'

'I know, but if I could help...'

'What exactly do you want of him?

'You need to come with me now to the park,' Marsh pleaded, looking directly at me and disregarding Donne.

'I don't see how that will help but I could try?' I said, more questioning myself than anyone else.

'If you are taking my client, you are taking me as a witness,' Donne demanded, and I'm sure he was surprised when Marsh immediately agreed.

As we hurried out of the office past the distraught secretary, Donne said in a surprisingly harsh voice, 'You need to cancel everything.' The woman looked stunned but did not argue.

Once in Marsh's police car, a far newer model than his own, Donne asked me, 'What are you hoping to do?' We had both taken back seats, and I saw Marsh looking at me in the rear-vision mirror.

'I, that is, I sometimes feel things. I could feel something.' I knew that I was sounding quite mad, but Donne didn't give me that condescending look that I had seen from so many people throughout my life. He just nodded and I could tell he was interested in what would happen.

Once we reached the park that surrounded the skate ramps, I noticed two young officers securing the entrance gates with police tape. The blue and white was very stark against the surrounding grass and cement. I felt sick.

As I walked toward the gates, the feeling left me. Whatever happened, it didn't happen in the fenced area. Marsh lifted the tape, and we walked the perimeter. I felt nothing at first, but then, near a rear corner of the area, I began to feel sick again.

'Here,' I said, pointing. As I turned, I could see the area was covered, somewhat, from the road by a rather dense Cootamundra wattle. Though it grew outside the fence, it encroached on the area several meters, both through and above the wire mesh fence.

Marsh got down on his haunches near where I had pointed. He felt the grass and then smelt his fingers. 'Oh, god. It smells like urine,' he said.

I nodded. This would have been the perfect place to relieve oneself if in a hurry to get back to the ramps.

The fence was only about a metre and a half high, and I decided to climb over it. I immediately wished I hadn't. 'Something happened here,' I said, pointing to the base of the tree.

Marsh again got low to see if he could detect something not visible to those standing. 'There are a few scuff marks but nothing very noticeable,' he said, looking up into my eyes pleadingly.

I walked a few steps further from the tree. I was not feeling much, I just didn't think the 'end' came here. I continued to walk. I walked for some minutes back and forward with Marsh and Donne mirroring my every move. At about one hundred and fifty metres from the fence, I noticed a toilet block. It had been hidden until that point by more trees. I pointed to it.

'It has already been searched,' Marsh said, but we continued in that general direction.

Reaching the fence that surrounded the area, we found a uniformed officer manning the gate. 'Let us through,' Marsh instructed. The young man lifted the tape, and the three of us walked underneath.

I pointed again to the toilet block, and Marsh nodded. We entered the men's toilets and though I felt uncomfortable, I had no sense of fear or loathing about what might be found. Next, we came around the back of the building and to the women's toilets.

Marsh marched straight into the area that had several cubicles. He searched each and found nothing.

'Do you feel anything?' he asked.

'No, not really, but there is something not right here. I don't know what it is,' I answered.

We walked toward the gate again, and then I was prompted to turn. At the front of the toilet block, there was a cleaner's room. It was covered from view by bushes when approaching the building.

I walked back, realising this was what I had sensed. Marsh, who was a few paces behind me, said, 'What is it?'

I pointed to the almost obscured door.

'Has the maintenance room been checked?' Marsh asked the younger officer who was still standing at the gate, some five or six metres away.

'I don't think so. I think it was locked,' he answered.

Marsh shook his head and quickly moved back to the building. The door was secured with a large secure padlock.

He looked desperately around the immediate area as Donne and I came to stand nearby. After fumbling through some bushes in the neat, heavily mulched garden, he found a large rock and proceeded to hit the lock. The rock broke into small pieces and Marsh was off again, soon pulling up one of the pavers that had been used as a border edge to the garden.

He returned with the brick and struck the lock several more times until it gave way.

The door now opened and inside on the floor, we could see the feet of a body. I could not move closer, and Donne also stepped back in fear of what he may see.

Marsh moved into the room slowly and I heard him say, 'You are alright. I am a police officer.' Then he followed up by saying loudly, 'Give me some help.'

I didn't want to enter, though I did. I could see a boy of no more than eleven or twelve cringing in the corner among the buckets and mops. He was naked. His hands and feet were secured by gaffer tape, and a large strip was wrapped around his head, covering his mouth and ears. The child was covering his modesty with his hands. Marsh realised, peeled his jacket off and covered the child.

Tears flowed from the youngster's eyes, and as Marsh removed the tape from his feet, he drew his legs toward his chest. He was the most terrified person I had ever seen. I moved toward him, saying, 'You are safe now.' I removed the tape from around his face carefully, and he cringed at my touch.

Marsh was also saying quiet soothing things. He removed the tape from the boy's hands. He recoiled into a protective ball, Marsh's coat covering him.

Donne had braved the entrance and now saw the bundle.

'Get the officer to get an ambulance here immediately,' Marsh ordered, and Donne withdrew as quickly as he had entered.

After just a few minutes, which must have seemed like hours to the boy, two ambulance officers entered, and we left the room.

Re-joining Donne near the gate, I could see that he was as emotional as I was.

'I would never have believed it if I hadn't been here,' he said in what was almost a whimper. I just nodded. I had shed a few tears, but I had become even more emotional as Marsh's humanity helped the child cope. It was a beautiful thing to witness in the terribleness of the event.

'Oh my god, you have a wonderful gift,' he said, patting me on the back.

I didn't feel that it was a gift at all. I hated feeling this violence. I wished it were someone else, but I was at least happy that the child had been saved.

Chapter 6

Marsh drove us back to Donne's office and on the way, very little was said. There was a feeling that we had achieved something and that was enough for now.

When we stopped outside the far too grand-looking building that housed Donne's rooms, Marsh turned and put out his hand. We shook.

'You've done a great thing today. I think we know what would have happened to the child if we hadn't intervened,' he said earnestly.

I felt his warmth. This, I decided, was a good man. I nodded and got out of the car. Marsh shook Donne's hand and thanked him for his assistance. As we turned to watch him drive off, Donne commented, 'I don't think we have seen the last of him.'

'Yes, and I was just getting used to this town,' I said, knowing that I would have to move on when the publicity of finding the body was released.

'If I may advise you, if he calls again, ring me. I will stop whatever I am doing and come. That way, an officer of the court can be present as your witness,' Donne said. We shook hands as I nodded, and then he entered his building, saying to no one, 'Darndest thing I ever saw.'

I walked slowly to my car. I didn't want to go to work; I knew I had to go but I felt like I could just curl up on the couch and sleep for a week.

On my arrival at the shop, I found that Bob had opened it himself. He greeted me positively, and I could tell that he was sympathetic. I had been totally reliable before that day.

'I'm sorry I couldn't get in earlier, but I had to meet with the police.' I saw the look of surprise on his face. 'No, I'm not in any trouble. They just needed my help to close a case.' I knew I sounded unconvincing and waited for a moment, then said, 'Look, I suppose I need to explain.'

Bob looked at me quizzically, and then said, 'No need unless you feel you have to.'

'Oh, you are probably going to hear it anyway,' I answered and then, taking a chair and sitting down, I added slowly, 'I have a talent of sorts, and I helped the cops find a missing child this morning.'

His eyes widened in disbelief.

'Yeah, I know. Most people think I am mad or some sort of charlatan, but I can tell if something has happened in a place. I, arr... don't see things. I just get these feelings, and they overcome me, and I know something violent has happened.'

His look of incredulity was impossible to miss, and I felt I needed to explain more, but what more could I really say? He would just think me completely mad.

To my surprise, his glare softened, and he said, 'That's not what I expected to hear, but you have been very good to me, and I feel that I need to support you through this.' He put his hand out.

I took it and said simply, 'Thanks.'

'Now, what do you need? Do you need some time off?' he asked kindly, and I could tell he thought I was having some kind of mental health problem. I shook my head in answer. There really was nothing more to say.

I started to work on some labelling I had been doing the previous day, and after a few minutes, Bob asked if I would like a coffee. He left to go to the nearby coffee shop we usually frequented.

On his return, he commented that the shop was abuzz with the news of the boy being saved. 'I didn't mention you, but they were all talking about how the child was found. Whatever you did, it seems to be almost a miracle or something?'

'Some bloody miracle,' I answered. 'I have no real control over it at all.'

'Look, I don't pretend to understand this sort of thing, but it is wonderful that the kid was found, however you got there,' he reassured me. I nodded again.

I stood on the wrong side of the counter, drinking the coffee – a great drop – and placing some of the labelled items on the shelves.

Bob continued the paperwork he had been doing, and we both went into our own little worlds.

About an hour later, the shop door opened, and Marsh entered. Bob came to the counter to serve him. I sort of froze to the spot and said nothing. Marsh produced his credentials and said, 'Your employee here'—he pointed to me—'helped to save a young boy's life this morning, and I wanted to come and tell you how invaluable he was to the case. You've got a good one here.'

I dropped my eyes, a little embarrassed.

'Yes, I know. I...' Bob started to answer but was interrupted by Marsh's phone ringing.

'Oh, sorry. I better take this,' Marsh apologised and moved to a corner to take the call, somewhat in private. Even so, I could hear the urgency in his voice as he was informed of events by the caller.

'Shit, what's the address?' he asked, and I looked up to see him writing in his notebook. Ending the call, he moved quickly back to the counter. 'Well, as I was saying, thank you for giving up Fitzpatrick's time. I must go. They think they have a suspect.' He turned to me. 'Do you want to come and finish this?'

I looked at Bob. He nodded and as I turned to Marsh, I said, 'We will need to pick up Donne. He demanded I call if you reconnected with me.'

I was frightened of this whole event and what would lead from it, but if I could see this bastard behind bars, it would be worth it.

'Good. Ring him and we can get him on the way,' Marsh answered, and as I followed him out the front door, I turned and thanked Bob. He just gave me a nod and continued as if nothing had happened.

Donne took up his seat in the back of the car. This time, I sat in the front seat with Marsh. I felt no animosity toward him now and wanted him to know that.

We drove for about twenty minutes, and as we neared the little settlement to the south of the town, Marsh explained that the house would be raided by trained officers who would secure the site and anyone inside. We were to wait and join when this part of the operations was complete.

A small clearing at the entrance to the nearest property was the meeting place of all of the officers and Donne and I were left in the car while Marsh arranged his troops.

Three cars were left with us, and another was waiting behind, the other car being forensic investigators.

We waited, glued to the radio, which was transmitting messages from those breaching the property. Soon, the team notified that they were in place, and Marsh gave the signal, 'Go, go, go!' and we listened as several calls of 'down on the ground' were yelled. There was a lot of yelling and then a shot, then two more.

'The next few calls were obviously operational instructions, and I have to say, I didn't understand until the last words, 'Suspect down!' Then there was silence.

Marsh quickly started the car and, with lights flashing but without sirens, we rushed to the scene.

'Stay in the car until the site is declared secure, and I will come and get you,' instructed Marsh.

We sat without comment, wondering what the call of 'suspect down!' meant. I presumed that the meaning was that the man was on the ground. The radio calls became less urgent and the forensic team were called in to take control of the site. The radio was silent until Marsh's voice rang out. 'All tactical groups, stand down.' Then after a few more minutes, a second order came. 'All tactical officers, return to base. Site secure.'

Another period of silence was followed by Marsh coming back to the car and telling us we were safe to get out now. We followed him to the main rear entrance of what was a very strange house. There were three rear doors and two side entrances, which I could see. Though I didn't ever go near the front of the house, there would have been at least one front door, and later, when we had walked to the outbuildings, I could see a large set of double patio-type glass doors. They, like all of the windows in the building, were covered with black plastic. Marsh led us into the rear hall, which ran right along the building. At our end of the hall, there were white goods and a sink. It was obviously being used as a laundry, and indeed, the washing machine was running.

At the far end of the hall, we could see two men working on a body. The man was dead. It hadn't occurred to me that that was what 'suspect down!' really meant. Marsh saw both of us looking in that direction and quickly led us to another room.

'He came at the officers with a handgun, so they had to shoot him. I wanted to take him alive so we could get further information on the other missing boys,' he explained without taking a breath. He pointed to another room, and we followed him in. The walls were lined with shelves on which were hundreds of DVDs and VHS tapes; it was obvious that they were pornographic. Some bore pictures of minors.

Donne let out a cry of 'oh, my god!' and I must admit that what I saw made me less certain that a god could even exist.

I wanted out of that room and turned to go, but Marsh took my arm and led me into the next room, which had to be walked through to get to another room. This was a loungeroom and very similar to most loungerooms, other than for the fact that it had three large-screen televisions on three walls.

The layout of the house was why the man had been able to get a weapon before the officers were able to gain entrance.

Marsh led us to the centre of the room, and we stopped and waited for a few seconds before he turned and said, 'What do you sense? Anything?'

I shook my head; I didn't feel that this was right. I was certain I would be feeling unwell at least if this was a site where he had tortured or killed anyone.

Marsh gave me another few seconds, then added, 'You don't get a sense of the other missing boys then?'

'No, nothing like that,' I answered honestly.

'Well, at least he is off the street. Kids will be safer,' Donne put in.

'No, I don't think so. This man is not the killer,' I answered and both of them turned to me quickly.

'What?' Marsh asked incredulously.

'No, there is no death here. I certainly don't think he held or hurt anyone here. In fact, I am sure of that,' I answered.

'Oh, shit. Are you certain?' Donne asked.

Marsh followed up with, 'What do you mean exactly?'

'I don't feel the presence here of the man who did the killings – at least, not of the bodies, I, um, I helped find,' I answered, and I was convinced I was right.

'But this has to be the guy, just look around you,' Marsh answered.

'Sorry. This was one sick bastard, but he was weak. The videos are on display, but all of the windows are blackened. I bet this place hasn't seen another person for years,' I answered, knowing that he did not believe me.

'So, you think we killed the wrong man?' he asked.

'No, this guy was the one who took the boy at the skate park, and who knows what he was going to do, so no, he is better off the street,' I answered, trying to settle Marsh, who I could tell was getting a bit worked up.

'This is not the killer?' he asked bluntly.

'No, I don't think he is the killer,' I answered honestly.

'You don't think?' he said with a little sarcasm in his voice.

'What he thinks has been good enough until now,' Donne put in indignantly. He could see that I was getting a little annoyed.

'Oh, yes, but could you be wrong?' Marsh asked. He had put so much into catching the killer that this would have been a great relief to him – getting his man, so to speak.

'I don't think so, but I have been wrong before. It's not always perfect, but I can't even drive past a prison – where there are murderers and the like – without feeling sick, and I feel nothing like that here,' I answered, trying to stay calm.

'What if he didn't do the murders here?' Marsh fired back. He wanted me to be wrong, and so did I.

'Yes, that would make a difference, but he is here, and I don't think he is the killer. God knows I hope I'm wrong, but I don't think so,' I answered, trying to placate him.

'Those higher up will want to do press releases to say this is the killer,' he mused, looking worried.

'Well, what do you think this sick bastard will do if this man is not the real guy?' I said, and then realised what I said was almost unintelligible. 'What I mean is...'

He cut me off, raising his hand. 'I understand.' He paused for a moment, thinking. 'I may have no control over that.'

I didn't have anything helpful to say. I could understand his predicament, but I could also see that this was not the murderer.

Marsh got up and started going through drawers and cupboards and lifting things on the table as though he were going to find proof of the crimes.

'I think we should go,' I said to Donne. I just wanted this all to end.

Donne nodded and then, turning to Marsh, asked, 'I hope we won't be receiving another visit from our friend, Wilson?'

'No, he was given the wearing of the green over the last debacle, and he left for Sydney. I don't think he will ever come back our way willingly,' Marsh answered, giving a little smile, though it disappeared almost immediately.

'I would appreciate it if you contact me again before involving my client in any more of this,' he instructed. Marsh just nodded. I'm sure he would have gladly never seen me again, but that was not to be.

Chapter 7

The very next day, the world press descended on our little town. They walked past the shop, trying to get some angle on the story. The press release from the police was short and to the point: they had stopped an abduction, and a man was killed while resisting police with a deadly weapon. Marsh had tried to play down the 'Bicycle Murderer' angle. He had watched the papers over the next few days but they were plastered with such headlines as 'Killer Killed!' and 'End to Reign of Terror!'

Marsh had been on screen while a more senior officer, once again from Sydney, told of the saving of the young boy. He had been pushed about the possible connection of the two cases, and his answer was simply that 'the investigation is ongoing'.

This did nothing to temper the media. Even radio reports were heading the story with the 'Bicycle Murder' tag.

Luckily, I was not approached by anyone for comment. All that the spokesperson said was that the police thanked members of the public for their assistance and support for the continuing enquiry.

I kept my head down. I didn't want anything to come out of this that in any way implicated me as a member of the public.

The weekend came and went, and I spent as much time at home as I could.

Early Monday morning, I opened the shop as I always did, earlier than the official opening time of eight a.m. There were still visiting press in the town, and a network van had been parked in a very prominent position near the local Coast Motel. I had to pass it every day with its bigger-than-necessary number emblazoned on the side. I wished they would just leave.

Bob came in around midday and relieved me for lunch. I could tell he wanted to talk about the investigation, but he resisted until I returned with some food and two coffees.

'So, are you alright, you know, with the cops?' he asked as I sat down at the table next to him.

'Yes, it was just that, that guy they killed was a customer,' I lied.

'One of our customers?' he said, sounding surprised.

'Yes, they wanted times and things,' I answered.

'What, the times you saw him here?' he asked, suspecting I was not really telling him everything.

'Yes, here and around,' I answered.

'Really?' he asked in an incredulous tone. When things like this happened, I always thought I could just lie. I even practised the lie sometimes. Obviously, I wasn't a very good liar. People saw right through me, especially those who knew me the best.

I just struggled with the whole 'explain yourself' world in which we now live.

To my surprise, he dropped the subject, though I could see the doubt in his eyes.

Two more days passed, and though the story persisted in the press, the throngs of outsiders had gone on to their next crusade. I had started to settle in my mind. The wrong man had been killed, but he really was a terrible man. Perhaps the world was a better place with him not in it. But who was I to decide that?

As I hoped, the press did not come looking for me. Nobody came looking for me. I was keenly aware of a car that followed me to work one morning. It was a small car with roof racks, and I thought that it certainly wouldn't be a police car – it wouldn't go quick enough to chase anyone. But then this was not trying to chase anyone down.

As I parked, the car came and went on the main road. Inwardly, I laughed at the possibility of me being followed by the police.

I didn't see the car again until the second afternoon. Again, it was behind me, and when I took a random turn, it carried straight on. Still, I was jumpy and wondered if I would need to move on.

The car was, it turns out, being driven by a woman, and she seemed not to even notice me as she passed.

On the Wednesday following the killing, I was awakened by a loud knocking on the front door. When I opened it, I found Marsh. He looked like shit.

'Looks like you were right. Another kid went missing last night, right out of his own bed.' He waited for me to fully comprehend what he was telling me, then asked, 'Will you come and have a look?'

I felt sick; it had not all gone away as I had wished. Marsh was eagerly waiting for an answer. I didn't want to say yes, and yet I heard myself do just that. Then I said, 'We will need to get Donne.'

'Yes, I thought you would say that. He won't be at the office yet, but I know where he lives.'

As Marsh knocked on the door of a particularly beautiful Georgian double-storey house, I took note of the extensive grounds and even the tennis court. The law was obviously a good profession to be part of – well, at least, it seemed, for Donne.

After knocking several more times, Marsh began to move off the front step and return to the car. The door opened and Donne's secretary appeared, not betraying the fact that she had just risen. She took instruction from Marsh and somewhat reluctantly re-entered the house, closing the door.

Marsh came back to the car and got in, saying, 'He'll be out soon.'

'Oh, so the secretary and the boss?' I said half-jokingly and Marsh, getting my meaning, explained, 'That's the wife. I think she is the brains of the operation.'

I got his meaning, and we both smiled.

Soon, a somewhat bedraggled-looking Donne exited. He was straightening his suit and adjusting his tie, then as he sat next to me, he took a comb from his pocket and ran it blindly through his receding thatch of black hair. Amazingly, he looked like he had been ready for hours. He was one of those men who could straighten themselves up to face court in but a few moments.

'Where are you taking us?' he asked.

'There has been another abduction. From the boy's house this time. It seemed that he went to bed, and when the father got home after his night shift at the hospital, he was gone. The front door was open, and the boy was gone,' he explained.

'Oh Christ. Will this bastard never get caught?' Donne said. 'Oh, that is, um, I don't blame anyone. He just seems too clever.'

'No, you are right. We have no idea about him – who he is, where he is, what he is doing this for. Can there be a reason? We have nothing,' Marsh answered, and I immediately felt sorry for him. Yes, this was on his watch, so to speak. I wondered for the first time if the 'seal of friendship' was possible. I did, kind of, respect him. He was trying to do the right thing, and he had kept his word and not allowed the press to know anything about me.

I will find a way not to trust him, I thought, *and then the way I process things will make me resent him and the possibility of friendship, like so many before, will be lost.*

I promised myself that I would try to trust these two men. Neither seemed to distrust me, so I must try to return the compliment. I must learn to trust someone. Life is simply too hard not to have anyone to believe in.

'What do you want me to do?' I asked.

'We will go to the house, see what you can pick up there?' he answered in a questioning tone as if he were asking for permission. I nodded.

'You might have to put Mr Fitzpatrick here on salary,' Donne said mockingly.

'That would make it impossible to keep him a secret, wouldn't it?' Marsh answered, and both men smiled. I wanted to say, 'I'm right here,' but I knew that, even though it was at my expense, they were joking.

We arrived at the house of the missing boy. I had no feelings of connection along the way.

On the veranda, we were met by a distraught couple of parents. The mother of the boy was sobbing into her husband's chest.

'Well, what is the news? Have you found him?' the man asked in a broken and emotional voice.

'Nothing yet, but everyone we have is out searching for the boy,' Marsh answered. He was somewhat clumsy when talking to grieving families.

'He has a name; his name is Thomas.' The mother sobbed.

'Oh, yes, sorry. I have literally just become involved. What can you tell me about last night?' Marsh said. 'Can my colleagues see the bedroom?'

The man nodded and pointed toward the second door on the right side of the hall, which we could see from where we stood in the entrance foyer.

Seeing the couch in the lounge room, Marsh almost led the couple to it and got them to sit down so he could continue asking questions while Donne and I went to the room. Now I began to feel disturbed; this was going to be terrible.

Donne opened the door and stepped out of my way, gesturing for me to enter. I didn't take the bait; I was being drawn further down the hall. I ended up standing in front of a family bathroom, which was far more lavishly decorated than seemed necessary. As I stepped through the doorway, I suddenly became unconscious and fell.

I had no idea what happened when I woke with Marsh and the two parents of the missing boy standing behind a crouching Donne. He was trying to revive me. It took me around thirty seconds to be fully aware of what had happened, and then I said, 'He was taken from here,' and put my head back on the floor. I had never had this happen before; it felt like I was the boy, and I was feeling the effects of some drug or something.

'No, his bedroom window was open, and who the fuck are you, anyway?' the father asked. His wife stood by his side and was now just glaring at me.

'He is just a colleague. He is helping with the case. He has been unwell; sometimes, he has a reaction to chemicals. Do you keep chemicals anywhere near?' Marsh explained, turning his answer into a question as he often did when grasping at straws.

'That's bullshit,' the father said, getting louder.

'I am sorry,' I said, still on the floor, feeling disoriented.

'I want you out of my house, now!' he shouted.

'Oh, shut up!' the mother blurted. 'I don't care how they find him – I just want them to find him.' She was crying, and her husband re-embraced her. She again wept into his chest. Freeing one hand, he gestured to me twice and I took it to mean I should continue.

I began to struggle to my feet, and Donne and Marsh both helped me. I felt almost as if I were drunk. I moved out of the door and headed further down the hall, stopping when I came to a laundry. Looking inside, I could see that there was a door out onto the backyard, obviously so there was access to outdoor clotheslines.

I moved into the room and immediately felt as if I would fall again. I touched the washing machine to steady myself, then recoiled. He had touched the washing machine. I pointed to the machine and Marsh quickly approached it. Taking a small torch from his inner jacket pocket, he switched it on and lit the darker side of the machine. There was blood. Not a lot of blood, but blood, nevertheless.

'Oh, god!' the mother squealed as she realised what Marsh had found.

She began to fall, and her husband caught her. Between him and Donne, they moved her to the hall, where the husband sat down against the wall with her head in his lap.

It was destroying both, and I could give them nothing but heartache as I again thought I was going to pass out. Marsh noticed and, getting under my left arm, helped me through the rear door, being careful that neither of us touched the machine or the handles. He paused a moment and then asked, 'What the hell was that?' as he sat me down on the second of four steps that led to a lawned area.

'I don't know. I have never had it happen before,' I answered. I was telling the truth, but I could see doubt in his eyes, even though he was not looking directly at me.

'I haven't,' I added, trying to convince him, and he gave just one nod. 'It feels like I was drugged. I was the boy… I think I was being carried? I know, I sound mad. This is new. I can't explain it, but I think I can follow–'

I stopped suddenly. I had a terrible pain in my head, and I needed to lay down.

Marsh sat down on the grass next to me. I put my head down on my knees. I thought I might pass out, and he put his hand supportively on my shoulder.

We sat for perhaps two minutes, and then I felt well enough to get up and move again. As I did, I noticed the missing boy's parents standing at the large glass doors of their dining room, watching our every move. It seemed strange; the emotion in their eyes was still evident, but a feeling of distrust was also reflected.

The feeling of dread and the pain in my head took over again, and I began to stagger down the long-fenced backyard. As we neared the back gate, I again felt sick and pointed toward the small woodpile to our right. Marsh knelt and, without touching anything, scanned the pile. There was a small amount of blood on only one of the logs. He took his phone from his pocket and photographed the spots.

Moments later, the father of the missing boy appeared right behind us. I looked up to see him glaring at me and behind him, I could see his wife being comforted at the back doors by Donne.

'Who the hell is this?' he demanded.

'Sometimes we use behaviouralists at a scene,' Marsh said calmly.

'Bullshit. I saw him stumbling around. He knows something.'

'I need to understand what happened, and I often act out what might have been the escape. I think he left through this gate,' I answered, trying to avoid the ugly scene.

'So, you're some kind of bloody medium?' he demanded.

'Sir, sorry, but you are making our search for your son more difficult.' Marsh raised his voice in what was an obvious warning.

The man readied himself and then thought better of his interference as his wife put her hand on his arm, trying to draw him away. He turned to her, and they embraced – the embrace of terror – and he remained silent.

I moved to the gate, and just beyond it, we found another small amount of blood on the grass. This area was a kind of lane behind houses, but it had, over years of disuse, become overgrown and the grass in places was several feet high. One set of car tyre impressions were very visible, and I began to follow them.

Marsh took my arm and stopped me. 'Forensics must look at this first. There may be clues in the wheel impressions or the wheelbase or something,' he instructed.

I hadn't even given that a thought, so I stopped and as Donne led the distraught couple back inside the gate, I retraced my steps and waited for Marsh to give his next instruction. None really came as he quickly phoned the forensic investigations branch and gave instructions as to the area he wanted tested and for what. 'There was a car of some sort at the rear of the property, and there is blood on the washing machine, on the grass near the laundry door and on the grass just outside the back gate,' I heard him say.

Marsh stood for a short time and then came to meet me inside the gate. 'We will try to trace the car from the other end of the lane,' he instructed.

I nodded and then turned to follow him as he moved back toward the house. Donne had led the couple back to the doors we had seen them exit from. A uniformed officer rounded the corner and neared us.

'Any luck?' he asked Marsh.

His superior came close and said quietly, 'Forensics will be here in just a few minutes. You need to keep the family inside and away from the laundry and the backyard at all costs, do you understand?'

Marsh led me around the other end of the building and Donne followed. As we disappeared, I heard the man say loudly, 'Where the hell are they going?'

Marsh didn't waste time giving an answer. He quickly led us back to the car and started it and drove out of the driveway, only just allowing us to get in as he hurried off along the street, south to where the lane and street joined. He quickly got out, and before I had really seen what his intention was, he had opened my door and was helping me to my feet.

Donne also got out and questioned, 'What are you looking for exactly?'

'Anything. Anything I can get, or Fitzpatrick can get,' Marsh answered, pointing at me though he was looking elsewhere.

After a few minutes, I said somewhat urgently, 'I think the car left here,' and I pointed toward the east. Soon we were in the car again, heading after the diminishing shadowy hint of a memory.

After around two or three minutes, we approached a crossroads and Marsh asked, 'Which way?'

I had lost the feeling of being the boy and of his presence. 'I need to get out,' I answered.

We stopped, and after a few minutes of walking around, I had to admit that I now had no sense of the boy. The three of us looked despairingly at each other and Marsh motioned to us to get back into the vehicle. He headed across the intersection, and we drove around for almost half an hour before admitting defeat.

The boy Aaron Wills was gone. I felt nothing, and I thought that he must have died before crossing the intersection as I had no feelings of him, of his fear, since driving down that road.

Chapter 8

Several weeks passed, and there seemed to be no action on the case. No one else disappeared and I had no feelings of impending doom. I went back to work in the shop and though I had one awkward incident when Aaron's mother came in and asked me if I knew anything, I settled into the mundane life that I craved.

On the morning of the twelfth, I arrived to open the shop at the usual time – around half an hour earlier than required – and to my disgust, I was confronted by a woman reporter and her cameraman.

'Mr Fitzpatrick?' she questioned.

'How can I help you?' I answered, fearing I knew what she was about.

'Sir, I believe you have been assisting police in the local boys' disappearances?' she asked bluntly.

'No, I'm not assisting anyone with anything,' I answered honestly. I hadn't seen Marsh, or Donne for that matter, in more than a week.

'But you were the psychic they were using?' She pushed not only with her words but also at the door as I tried to shut and lock it in her path.

'I am not a psychic,' I answered, but I knew that the genie was out of the bottle. I got the door closed and turned the lock, but they were going nowhere. She just stood there tapping at the door and repeating, 'We know you are the psychic they were using,' and 'Why won't you talk to us?'

By opening time, the gaggle grew by two more film crews, and I knew there was nowhere I could hide. The rabid dogs had smelt blood. I hid behind the partition, took the phone off the wall, lifted the receiver and hung it up again to stop the ringing. I was starting to feel that this was already out of my control.

I lifted the receiver again and dialled Marsh's mobile number. After three rings, he answered, 'Marsh?'

'What the hell have you done? The bloody shop's surrounded by reporters.'

'I expected that. They are here as well, dozens of them. Someone fed them the story of "a psychic assisting police". It is in the news this morning. I didn't tell anyone what you were doing, and the three officers who working with me all swear they haven't said anything.'

'Well, can you get them out of here or not?' I demanded.

'It's a free country. I can't do anything really unless they enter your property,' he said apologetically.

'I can't live like this. How the hell can I even get out of here?' I asked frantically.

'Is there a back door to the shop?' he asked.

'Yes, but it only backs onto the railway,' I answered bluntly.

'Could you get across the line there, to the other side I mean?' he continued.

'I think so, but I have never tried,' I answered honestly.

'Ring Donne and get him to pick you up on the other side in half an hour,' he ordered.

I could see what his idea was, but knew also that it was only a momentary fix.

'Get him to take you to his place, and I will meet you there this afternoon. In the meantime, I will come to the front of the shop and cause a distraction, you know, so you can get out,' he instructed, then added, 'Ring me back if he can't get you and I will try to do something else. Ring me if you do get out, ok?'

'Yes, I'll try,' I answered and hung up to hear a commotion at the front door. I looked around the partition and saw Bob trying to get through the throng, now six or seven reporters deep.

'I can't tell you anything, now get out of the fucking way,' I heard him say. He got the door open and, after turning to push the nearest man out of the way, he entered and re-locked the door. He had more sense than I did and turned the vertical blind cord that covered the door, then in turn, he did the same for both windows.

'What the bloody hell have you got yourself into?' he asked me as he rounded the partition and thrust a Sydney newspaper into my face. The headline read 'Psychic for King Hill Killer!' It was a complete nightmare.

'I have been helping the police. But it's not that way. I, um, I do sense things, and it has been a help in their enquiries.'

'What do you mean, sense things?

'It is hard to explain, and I know you will think I'm mad, but when something violent happens, the place where it happens seems, ah, broken, scarred or something, and I can feel that, sometimes for years after.' This answer was rambling and hard to follow, as was the answer I gave every time I tried to explain to someone I wanted to stay friends with.

'Ok?' he said slowly, obviously meaning that he didn't really get what I was offering.

'Oh, for god's sake, this has been happening all my life. I become friends with people and when they find out, they don't want anything to do with me,' I answered honestly, thinking this would be the last conversation I would have with him.

'Now hang on a minute. I'm not saying I understand, but I would never want our friendship to be destroyed. You picked me up off the floor when I was at my lowest, and I will always be grateful to you,' he said earnestly and put a hand on my shoulder, then continued, 'How can I help to get you out of this?'

'Detective Marsh has arranged a distraction at the front doors in about twenty-five minutes. Donne will pick me up on the other side of the railway line,' I answered, looking at my watch.

'You do what you need to do. I will look after the shop until you can come back sometime, if you can,' he said, being far more understanding than any other boss I had ever had.

'I just have to ring Donne to get him to come,' I answered as he shook my hand.

I dialled Donne's mobile and soon had organised for him to pick me up.

In just a few minutes, we heard raised voices at the front of the building, and I could tell Marsh was at work, so to the parting 'good luck' from Bob, I returned a 'thanks, mate.'

I quickly slipped out the rear door, clambered over the wooden paling fence and found myself in chest-high grass and weeds of all kinds. The bank was very steep, and I tripped several times, skipping sideways down to the railway drain.

Crossing the lines was of little consequence, but climbing up the opposite bank was much more difficult. I had to scarper for about fifty yards to my left to find a place that I could ascend.

I was covered with grass seed and must have looked a sight as I clambered over the fence into the civilised world again. Luckily there was no one there to see what a mess I was, not even Donne.

I was beginning to panic ten minutes later when he finally pulled up in a rickety old Ute with some landscaper's advertisement on its now open door.

'Get in quick,' Donne barked, and I obeyed, though I was a little bemused at his choice of vehicle. 'They have been camping out at my front gate since early this morning, so I had to get the gardener to come around and lend me his Ute.'

'This is all such a fuck up,' I said, beginning to lose my cool.

'Well, yes, but we will get through it. I have a granny flat in the grounds at home – my mother-in-law spent her last couple of years there. It's, well, frankly, it's decorated for her. You know, lots of flowery wallpaper et cetera, but you're welcome to stay as long as this goes on,' he offered.

I thought what a good man he was and thanked him, suggesting that I would pay for his help.

'Not likely. The place is just sitting there, and I know you are upset by all of this but, frankly, I haven't had so much fun in years. Going around the scenes and meeting the families, getting out where I always wanted to be. I never wanted to be a lawyer. I would have given anything to have been a cop like Marsh. It's a much more honest profession. All I do normally is deal with dishonest people trying to stay out of jail,' he said, and seeing the surprised look on my face, he added, 'Yes, looking a gift horse in the mouth, I know. The money is good, but it can get very boring.' He glanced at me again. 'I suppose that is pretty callous to you, sorry.'

'It's just that this mad fervour has caught me up before. I couldn't have a normal life in my teenage years with people always wanting something from the "great seer". I couldn't go anywhere or do anything without some bastard sticking a microphone in my face and asking stupid bloody questions,' I explained.

'Well, have a few days with us. They might leave you alone if they can't find you. I came out the rear gate at home so I wouldn't be noticed, you know, driving this,' he said, patting the steering wheel. 'I think you may need to get under the cover in the back so we can get back into the house, unseen.'

I nodded. I knew he was enjoying all this cloak-and-dagger stuff, but I would have given practically anything not to be in this position.

Soon, he pulled over, helped me into the rear of the Ute and refastened the cover. He had done this on a quiet street so that no one would notice, and it seemed to work.

We soon approached the rear gate of his property, which was on a magnificently gardened five-acre block. Indeed, the 'garden of the year award' had been bestowed three of the last five years by the local council.

We were seen by reporters entering the lane, but none showed the slightest interest as far as I could tell. I could see a little through the corner of the old vehicle's tray. When we had entered the grounds, Donne got out, closed and locked the six-foot-tall gates and then, when he thought no one was watching, he undid the cover over me and helped me to my feet. He then quickly walked me to the small but well-formed granny flat. He opened the door and signalled for me to go in. I obeyed and was confronted by his wife.

'Welcome, Mr Fitzpatrick. I will change the sheets later in the day – they are not appropriate for a man,' she said in a brash, dismissive way.

'Oh, thank you so much. The sheets don't matter to me at all,' I said.

'I dare say, but they matter to me,' she said, giving what could have been a smile.

'I'll need to go into work, to keep the wolves from the door, so to speak,' Donne said and continued with, 'My girls will get you some lunch and I will let you know our situation when I get home around four.'

They both left me, and I slumped into an aged but very comfortable reclining chair. I did feel safe here, but I felt sure that the safe harbour wouldn't last.

I was bored almost immediately but took refuge in sleep. I must have been there hardly moving for at least an hour before being awakened by a knock at the door. I quickly jumped up, not knowing if I should answer it or not. Soon, the handle turned, and Mrs Donne entered with another younger lady. Each was carrying a tray.

'Mr Fitzpatrick, this is my daughter, Sylvia, and your luncheon is served,' she said, placing her tray, full of an assortment of sandwiches, in the middle of the table.

Sylvia deposited her tray, which contained a pot of tea, a small milk jug and a large display of cakes of several different kinds. It looked as though they were providing a high tea for three or four people.

'Oh, thank you so much. What a fine spread,' I said in a somewhat clumsy way.

Mrs Donne turned, rolling her eyes and said, 'Just leftovers, I'm afraid,' then as she reached the door, she added, 'Come along, Sylvia, and stop gawking.'

The girl blushed; she had been sizing me up and down. She was dressed in a perhaps cream skirt and a bright floral blouse. I smiled and thought how much like an English aristocrat the older woman seemed. Sylvia smiled back but quickly followed her mother out dutifully. Now I understood the comment Donne made about his girls looking after me.

I sat to eat and to break the monotony, I turned on the radio on the sideboard, found a station I liked and began to eat. The food was excellent. Some sandwiches were filled with what seemed to be a home-made corned beef, some with pickles and others with a fruit chutney. I was not delighted to be here, and I thought I wasn't hungry, but I ate and, in fact, I overate.

The music playing on the radio was some quiet classical piece, and I decided to move back to the couch. The mood was set for some more sleep but before I could drift off, another knock sounded at the door.

I got up and went to answer it. I found that it was Sylvia. She had come with sheets to change the bedding.

'Oh, thank you. Just put them over there, or I could take them,' I said, unsure of the correct etiquette. I waited a moment while she decided what to do.

'Mother said to make the bed, and it's always best to obey,' she said, smiling broadly. She was quite a pretty girl. I thought she would be around twenty to twenty-five, just a couple of years younger than me. She had long flowing red hair, which was tied back from her face with a blue ribbon.

I helped her to remove the existing bedding and spread the appropriately black and white fitted sheet.

'Thank you, I can do the rest,' she said, obviously not delighted with my efforts.

I stepped back and let her go at it until it came to the bedspread, where I attempted to place it with the accuracy and neatness she achieved. I was not very successful, and she fixed my fumblings.

'How on earth do you cope normally?' she said teasingly.

'I use a doona, much easier,' I answered, and we both smiled.

She turned to go, and I added, 'Thank you for your kindness.'

She looked over her shoulder and blushed again, saying, 'You're welcome,' and she left me.

A little piece of kindness can make such a difference. I lay on the bed and was soon sound asleep.

I was awakened after what seemed like a long time by a more rambunctious movement playing on the radio. It was some piece of Tchaikovsky's, I think, and it was far too loud to sleep through.

I got up quickly and moved to turn it down. As I did, there was another knock on the door and Donne entered. His red face and receding hairline made him look older than usual. He was clutching a small parcel tied with brown string.

'This is from Marsh,' he said and handed it to me.

I quickly pulled the string off and ripped the paper away. A small box inside contained some folded note paper and a USB stick.

I unfolded the paper and began to read out loud. All of this was as much Donne's business as mine.

'We have not found the boy.' This existed as a paragraph unto itself. The next words were typed. 'There are no clues. We are bringing in everyone who has a record of violence in the area, though there are only a few that we know of and no known paedophiles. Yes, I know there are no indications that this killer is a paedophile, but we are trying everything. If you could, I would like to show you some photos this afternoon, from around 5 pm. I hope that is alright with Donne?' The letter was signed with his illegible scrawl. Then, he must have had a second thought and added, 'P.S. the USB stick contains some pictures of the people we have brought in so far.'

Naturally, as I hadn't come to stay with all my bells and trappings, I had no device to look at the pictures on. Donne must have been thinking about that as he said, 'You may use my laptop. I will send my old one down for you to use while you are here.' He passed me his computer and I immediately started it and then realised he had to sign on and handed it back to him. Once it had booted, I inserted the stick and found a file, which I opened. There were seven mug shots on the first page. I ran my fingers across the screen, trying to feel something. Eventually, I realised that the seven were also loaded individually as a full-page picture, and I continued with Donne watching from behind me, where he had moved to be able to see the shots.

There were no names and no information, only the pictures. As I went from screen to screen, I felt nothing until I reached the second last man. None of them were particularly fine upstanding-looking characters, but this one was particularly scruffy. He had dark bags under his eyes and his hair was dishevelled. He looked like hell, and I sensed something.

I kept the screen open for much longer than I had with the others as I pondered his possible involvement in our case. I didn't feel that he was our man, but there was something dark and unpleasant about him. I moved to the last of the pictures. Quickly dismissing the man, I moved back to the one I had found an interest in the first time through.

'Do you have something?' Donne asked quietly.

'Not exactly. I think the last one may be a cop, and I think all have violence about them in their past, but this one,' I said, pointing at number six. 'This one has killed. I'm sure of that.' I was certain of my opinion. I don't know why; I was never totally certain about anything I sensed.

'That's bloody amazing,' Donne said, and I felt he was about to say more but he held himself back.

'Oh, by the way, none of these sad bastards are our man,' I continued.

'I don't know all of them, just the two you singled out. The last one is a cop, that's true. The other was one of my clients. He killed his wife and is at Her Majesty's Pleasure for life.'

This annoyed me a little. Was Marsh still putting me through tests? *Bloody arrogant thing to do,* I thought.

I closed the laptop and handed it back after taking out the memory stick. 'Thank you,' I said bluntly.

'You are angry?' he asked in a quiet voice.

'Yes, well, I hate all of this. Running away from the press and hiding, and then to get this as some sort of test. Naturally, I'm annoyed,' I answered, trying not to sound too ungrateful to him. He had only been kind to me and kinder than he needed to be. After all, he had invited me into his home and given me shelter. I was just another client to him – not a friend, just an acquaintance.

'Sorry, I am most grateful to you. Thank you for everything,' I said and stuck my hand out to shake. It was a clumsy attempt to step back from what I had just said, but he shook and answered, 'I have enjoyed being involved. Watching the way your mind works is enthralling. It re-invigorates one to see some real investigation work. Usually, I am on the other side, seeing the evidence on paper, trying to see the crime scene in my mind or in photographs.' He added his left hand to the shake. I knew that he was genuine, and I trusted him from the moment I met him.

'I'll bring the other laptop down at dinner time with the meal. I have this building covered so you can use the internet.' He paused and then asked, 'Is there anything else you need?'

'Well, yes, I would like to see the daily papers if that is possible. I want to see what people are saying about me,' I answered honestly.

'I get them all so that won't be a problem,' he answered and left, quietly closing the door.

Duly, the meal was delivered at about six-thirty, and I was pleased to see that the deliverer was Sylvia.

'Settling in then?' she asked as she deposited the covered tray onto the table.

'Yes, very comfortable, thank you,' I answered and thought how formal I sounded.

She had brought the meal on a small wooden trolley; the second level had the laptop and one newspaper.

'Father says he will bring the other papers down when he has finished them,' she said and quickly moved to the door. Turning, she asked, 'Oh, do you need anything else?'

'No, thank you. You are all too kind,' I answered, and she was gone, gone before I could engage her further. I wanted to engage her further; she was a stunning-looking girl and had shown me nothing but kindness, unlike her mother whose all-knowing looks made me feel like a criminal.

I sat, eating the beautifully prepared feast: steak, baked vegetables and a very tart lemon pudding of some kind served with a sweet custard, which turned the senses from sweet to almost sour and back again in that way the taste buds were at their most titillated.

I prepared a pot of tea and finished one cup. I started on a second before a knock came at the door, and I rose to answer it somewhat slowly. A second, more impatient knock came as I turned the handle. It was Marsh, with Donne. I stepped aside and allowed them to enter. Marsh looked like hell. He had obviously had a bad day and looked as though he hadn't slept for days.

'Sorry for being so late. I couldn't get away. There are members of the professional standards up from Sydney, and they are checking on everything I am doing,' he explained.

Donne handed me another paper. I placed it on the table and sat at one of the four chairs. They both joined me.

I finished my tea, and before I could offer, Donne was up emptying the pot and refilling it with water at the sink. 'Tea?' he asked, turning to Marsh.

'I'd really like something a lot stronger,' Marsh answered, probably joking, but Donne soon produced a bottle of expensive-looking scotch. This was obviously where he spent his time away from the boss of the house, his wife, stealing a few moments having a stiff scotch and a cigar. Marsh nodded gratefully but I declined. I had always hated the taste of the vile nectar, not to mention most other spirits. I did have a bit of a liking for white rum in milk, but I rarely partook of that, as I knew the milk would quickly put on the pounds that I always had to fight.

'Don't drink then?' Donne asked as he filled two coffee mugs with the scotch.

'Not much. I never really developed a taste for it,' I answered and then seeing the look both gave me, I added, 'I'm not a teetotaller or anything. I don't hate a glass of red wine with a meal, but it does loosen my tongue, so I keep it at arm's length. I can get myself into too much trouble. Most people don't want to hear what I have to say, if you know what I mean?'

They both nodded at me. So many times, I spoiled friendships by saying too much.

We all sat quietly for a few awkward moments until Marsh produced some paperwork from an inside jacket pocket and placed it unfolded on the centre of the table.

'What did you find out through the photos I sent you?' he asked.

'Well, I didn't appreciate the test, actually,' I said, sounding even snider than I intended.

'What do you mean?' he asked, though I was certain he knew exactly what I had inferred.

'Police officers and bums, give me a break,' I answered, still sounding far surlier than I really needed to.

'Oh, that is just what we must do in line-ups. We must present at least six alternatives, including the one we suspect. It wasn't a test – I just quickly added the line up to the USB when I wasn't being watched,' he explained, and I immediately felt stupid for not understanding.

'Alright, I'm sorry. I'm just a bit jumpy. This being hounded by the press isn't my thing,' I babbled.

'Quite right, none of their bloody business,' Donne put in, pouring Marsh a second.

'They will probably leave us alone, at least a bit. The only good use the boffins from Sydney have is a professional media spokesman. He gave the press a rollicking about saying we were using a "medium" in our enquiries. But he also ordered me not to have anything more to do with you,' he explained in an exasperated voice.

'Oh, so they don't want me involved. Well, good for them,' I said indignantly. I was the one being chased down and bothered by the press.

'Fuck that, I'll use anything I can to catch this bastard. I don't have anything, nothing at all. No leads, no forensics, nothing I can catch him up on,' he answered, trying to assure me of my importance to his investigation. As usual, I kind of felt sorry for him. He was between a rock and a hard place, and there was not any real way out until he caught his prey.

'Ok, what do you want me to do now?' I asked, hoping to let him off the hook.

'Well, these are the things I have on paper. I haven't found anything I can use in them, and the rest of the information is on this,' he explained, producing a second storage stick.

I took the stick. 'I'll give them a look, but I can't think I would make anything out of them if you haven't,' I answered.

Donne looked at me and then at Marsh and said, 'You do realise I have to advise my client not to take this any further?'

Marsh nodded but didn't answer. Donne turned back to me and continued, 'What do you want to do?'

'I can't let this animal just run around killing people. I'll try,' I answered uncertainly.

He turned back to Marsh and said, 'Let's get this perfectly clear. You are risking your job, and my client has no risk?'

'That's right. I know what I am doing, and I will keep your involvement away from the force and from the press. That is, if I can. The press are already running with your name and an old story from your childhood.'

I grabbed up the paper Donne had just brought in. The page three headline read, 'Child Psychic Assists Police.'

'It reads like I am a child,' I said and read further.

A psychic accredited with solving a murder in his youth is now said to be helping police with the child abduction and murder case. The man, now in his mid-twenties, James Fitzpatrick, is said to be helping police with the four disappearances and two murders of young boys on the central coast.

Fitzpatrick was responsible for discovering a body in his teens and leading police to the killer. Our source informs us that Fitzpatrick has already been involved in the discovery of a hit-and-run victim in the region in recent weeks.

Police have denied that they use psychics in the course of their investigations, but our source has confirmed that the man continues to be involved.

'Who the fuck is their "source"?' I asked, feeling betrayed.

'I don't know that, but I will find out, if I can,' Marsh promised.

'This is really going to stuff up my life,' I said. My stomach churned, and I felt the doubts swallowing me.

'I don't know what to tell you. I'll come here to see you for information, and not take you to any of the sites, but I know that's not really any help. I'll keep denying that you're involved, but no one wants to believe me,' Marsh answered, and I believed he was genuine. He hadn't meant to put me in this position, but here I was.

'As you would understand, I must recommend to my client that he not be involved in the case any further,' Donne said, then after a few glances between the three of us, he added, smiling, 'Of course, my client is wont to disregard my instructions.' They both looked at me expectantly.

I shook my head. 'Well, as I'm fucked anyway ...' I said, and they both smiled.

'So, you're in then?' Marsh asked, and I nodded, looking to Donne for his response.

He shrugged and said, 'I thought that would be your answer.' He continued to smile. I could see that he was pleased. Though I knew he was enjoying his involvement, I certainly was not.

With me not really responding, they both left me. The next day was Saturday. Marsh promised a visit the next morning, and Donne suggested that he might come down and have breakfast with me.

I appreciated their support. I could have fallen apart, like I had some years before. I know it sounds a little pathetic, but I wasn't that strong – mentally, I mean. I had ended up in care a couple of times, and those places are so dark. Terrifying, really.

I made another pot of tea and sat pondering the folder Marsh had left for me. I didn't open it. I moved it a few times and tried to do the crossword in the paper. I was just fooling myself; I knew I was going to give in and look at the work, so after another half an hour or so, I gave in and sat with my head in my hands. And then I began.

Chapter 9

I woke to a scream; not a very loud scream, more a startled noise than that of a person terrified. Still, I jumped to my feet and ran to the door. Sylvia had dropped the tray of food she had been bringing. She just stood looking toward the back gate.

I rushed over to her and knelt to pick up the pieces of food and broken crockery.

'What happened? I asked, looking up at her.

'There was a man there looking in your window.' She pointed. I got up and quickly walked to the rear gate. There was no one to be seen in either direction down the lane.

'There's no one there now,' I reassured her, then added, 'Are you sure about what you saw?'

'He just stood and stared at me, I felt that I might know him but his face was covered. Oh god, it gave me a hell of a fright,' she answered, and I could see she was shaking. I thought to comfort her, but before I could get back to where she stood, Mrs Donne had appeared and was quickly by her side.

'What on Earth is going on?' she asked, glaring at me.

'There was a man standing looking in the window,' the shaken girl said and still did not move. Her mother placed an arm around her, and as she did, Donne appeared behind them.

'What's all the shouting about?' he demanded, coming right to me, passing the two women. I think he thought I had done something.

'There was a man, just standing there, looking in the window,' Sylvia said from where she had knelt to assist in picking up the broken crockery.

'What did he look like – what did he do?' Donne fired the question at his daughter as he quickly moved to the rear gate. I followed him.

'I didn't see anyone; the lane was empty,' I informed him.

He looked in one direction and then the other, almost as though he didn't believe me. Once satisfied, he turned and said quietly, 'I don't think it can be the press. They wouldn't run.'

I nodded. 'Well, who then?' I asked and as he raised his eyebrows, I realised what he was thinking. I nodded, and he put a finger to his lips. We stood looking at each other for a short time, then Sylvia appeared between us.

'What was he doing, do you think?' she asked.

'Probably the bloody press,' Donne answered her. He didn't sound as if he believed what he was saying.

He was right to doubt. I had a different idea; I was certain he was not one of the press.

Donne moved a little closer to me and put a hand on my shoulder. 'You had better come and have breakfast inside, and I'll ring Marsh.' He directed me to the path, and I moved, though I had quite a deal of doubt. Was I putting Donne's family in danger by being here?

The women quickly prepared a second meal, and though I was very uncertain if I should stay, I ate everything placed in front of me.

Donne soon came into the room and announced that Marsh was on his way.

I nodded in answer, and for several minutes, we all sat. There was nothing to say; this was difficult enough. It was obvious that Mrs Donne was not delighted to have the likes of me in her kitchen.

Sylvia eventually broke the silence, though awkwardly. 'I'm, err, I'm sorry for making such a fuss,' she stammered.

'Nothing of the sort, you got quite a shock,' Donne said and placed his arm supportively around her shoulders. She smiled awkwardly, though her affection for her father was obvious.

'Look, he can't stay here. I'm sorry, but it's not safe,' Mrs Donne said without looking up from the plates she was washing in the sink.

I understood her feelings, but I still resented her saying it. She was right; it wasn't safe for her and her daughter if I stayed there.

Donne, looking to placate his better half, turned and patted her on the shoulder sympathetically. 'I know, I will arrange another place for him to stay,' he reassured her.

The woman turned her face to me for just a moment and said, 'Sorry,' then she dropped her eyes guiltily.

'There is no need to apologise. You have been very generous,' I reassured her.

I understood, but I felt that this was almost like an earlier time, a time when it was all too much for my own parents. Mother had argued in my corner for as long as she could. My father was much less easily assuaged.

I really didn't resent his attitude, but our meetings since had been very awkward. The one I felt most sorry for, really, was my mother. She kept the peace as well as she could, but there was no doubt that it had affected their relationship. I felt lost, I felt guilt, and most of all, I felt unwanted anywhere.

'I will get my things together and go now,' I said and stood.

'Nonsense, you will sit down and finish the food we prepared for you,' Mrs Donne ordered. Donne placed his hand on my shoulder, and I took his lead and sat back down.

Sylvia sat, looking at me furtively every few moments. Eventually, she got a few words out. 'I'm sorry. I feel terrible that you have to go because of me.'

'It certainly isn't anything to do with you. It's just these press people don't have boundaries,' I reassured her. I don't know how believable I sounded. I was certain that the man she had caught looking in the window was not a member of the press.

I ate, and the feeling in the room was very tense. I resolved to get out of there as soon as I could.

Donne gave me about twenty minutes to get my things together; I was ready in half that time.

We left by the front entrance in his work car, and this time we tried to hide nothing, and there was no one waiting. That confirmed for me that there was no way I had been visited by a reporter; they would have been at the front gate in droves if they had any idea where I had been hiding.

I feel stupid to say hiding, but that was exactly what it was; I was hiding from the world. Hiding like I had done most of my life.

Donne had contacted Marsh and arranged to meet him at my home; this would allow us to see if I was still the flavour of the moment and to allow me to get anything I needed to take with me.

No one seemed to be watching the house, and I slipped inside and quickly closed the door behind Donne.

I invited him to sit in the lounge room, and though he said nothing, I thought that he must be judging me. He looked around with interest.

My little unit was not as big as his granny flat. Actually, most of it would have fitted into the bathroom.

I rushed around, gathering anything I thought I might need in the next few days, bills I knew were about due, more clothes and the small amount of mail that had piled up just inside the front door.

When I entered the kitchen and opened the fridge, I was greeted by that tell-tale smell only emitted by sour milk. I removed the carton, opened the rear door and placed it into the garbage. As I did, I noticed many cigarette butts that had been dropped and ground into the first step. They caught my attention as I didn't smoke and never had visitors who smoked. I paused for a moment and looked around the small yard. It was about thirty by ten feet, and I noticed the gate was open.

This was one of my peculiarities; I would never leave a gate open, much less leave a mess on the steps. If I saw it, I would have to clear it up and I set about that now. I quickly shut the gate.

I had a terrible feeling come over me and felt that this was not what I would have expected from a reporter, even if he had been waiting for hours for my return. The feeling grew much worse as I grasped the screen door handle to re-enter the house. He had been here, and he had touched that very handle. A chill went down from the hackles on my neck to my hand, and I almost let it go. Oh shit, he had been here. But this wasn't rational; these were not the feelings I usually had. This was not the place where something had happened. Oh god, I was a mess.

Donne met me in the kitchen and, noticing my appearance, he said, 'What is wrong with you? You look like you've seen a ghost.'

'Someone has been here, there were–' I began but was interrupted by a very loud knock on the front door. We both jumped and then looked at each other. The knock came again, and Donne took it upon himself to open it. I followed him. I was thinking that we shouldn't open it but before I could say so, Donne had done the deed and we both stood looking at Marsh. We knew he was coming and yet his knock had startled us. Bloody stupid.

'Well, what is going on?' Marsh asked, sounding more than a little disgruntled.

'Someone found me, at Donne's, and they have been here too,' I blurted, hoping to get through this and get the hell out of there.

'What do you mean someone?' Marsh asked.

'I didn't see him, but he scared the hell out of Sylvia and then took off. Here, there were heaps of cigarette butts on the back steps and the gate was open,' I continued to babble, but I wanted out of here, out of the whole thing.

'Reporters?' Marsh asked in a more urgent voice.

'I don't think so. My daughter said he was just standing there at the window, just looking in and then when he saw her, the guy took off,' Donne answered.

'What do you think?' Marsh asked with that glare that meant *'you need to tell me the truth'*. I didn't know if you got that from training or if you just had it, but I remembered it in my grandmother. She seemed to look right through you.

'I think it was him. I think he thinks I may be able to identify him,' I said honestly.

'Nonsense, why would he come looking for you?' Donne asked in a voice that I'm sure he hoped would give me some sort of comfort. It didn't.

'Well, either way, we have to get you out of here and somewhere safe,' Marsh said.

'Yes, I've been thinking about that. I have a small country place, just fifty acres, I hope to retire on one day. It's only about forty miles inland – used to be a dairy, you know. The only thing is, it's on poor roads and takes about an hour to get to, and you need to have a four-wheel drive,' Donne explained.

'Well, we can get a four-wheel drive, and I suppose we would need to get some food together and anything else you think you need?' Marsh said in a 'what do you think' sort of voice.

'Yes, anything to get out of here,' I answered.

'Good. I'll borrow a four-wheel drive from a mate, and I can have groceries delivered to the station. Um, what will you do till I can get things arranged?' As usual, Marsh's statement ran into another question.

'I think he better spend the day with me at the office,' Donne suggested, then, having second thoughts, he added, 'We have a parking bay at the practice. You can drive around the back. We can get you in on the floor of the vehicle, covered with a blanket or something?'

'I like that, and if you go home and bring some blankets to your office, anyone watching will think he's staying at the office overnight. That way, I can stake out the place overnight and see who tries to get in if anyone does,' Marsh suggested. I was amazed at his speed in thinking up a plan almost out of nothing.

They both turned to me to see what I was thinking. To be honest, I was not really thinking about much, other than getting out of the house, so I nodded.

Chapter 10

Everything went as planned and I waited in the solicitor's office while he headed home to gather blankets and bedding, making sure that anyone watching him would see what he was bringing.

While he was gone, Mrs Donne had secreted me away in a second waiting room normally kept for the families of bereavements who needed privacy and not to be in a public waiting room.

She locked me in and left without saying anything. It must have got on her conscience though, because within ten minutes she returned and placed a cup of coffee and a nice arrangement of assorted cream biscuits on the table. She then left, and as I thanked her, she muttered, 'Well, you're not an animal,' and as she had done the first time, she locked the door.

I smiled as I thought to myself that her passing comment was more to convince herself than to show me any humanity. Really, they were a rather eccentric but kind family.

After around an hour and a half, Donne arrived back with arms loaded full of blankets and at least one pillow.

It was Sylvia who first attended to me, unlocking the door and knocking then bringing a couple of blankets in. She deposited them on the table next to the empty coffee cup. She also deposited the computer I had forgotten to bring from the house.

'I hope you are alright. I'm so sorry Mother kicked you out,' she said, looking sheepishly into my eyes.

'Oh, no, she was quite right, and your father has given up more than anyone who has ever helped me,' I answered, knowing that Donne *was* the most helpful man I had ever burdened with my problems.

I smiled widely, trying to convince her, and thought to myself that in another place and time, I could easily have fallen for her.

She was soon followed in by Donne himself, and he deposited a few extra blankets. 'That was no trouble. Now we just have to wait for Marsh to return this afternoon,' he said and then added, 'Sylvia insisted on coming back with me.' The girl blushed but found no words, just turned and took charge of the coffee cup and left the room.

'Do you need anything else?' Donne asked.

'No thanks,' I answered and then thought I should say some words to show my appreciation.

'Good, well, I better go and make a living,' he said and turned to leave.

'Thank you for everything, Sir,' I said quietly and rose to shake his hand.

'No need for thanks. Wait till you get my bill,' he joked and left smiling.

Soon, Sylvia returned with another cup of coffee and placed it on the table. I thanked her but she only blushed again and locked the door behind her.

It was one of the longest days I have ever spent. There was nothing to do and I was not able to go anywhere. I soon made up for the sleep I had missed over the last few days. I was startled when a loud knock woke me; it was Mrs Donne, who had brought sandwiches and more coffee. I lifted my head off the table, thanked her and asked if I might use the bathroom.

On arriving back at my room, I secured the door with the affixed chain and returned to my nap. There was nothing else to do and I knew that I would not sleep that night in a new place, in unfamiliar surroundings.

At four o'clock, another knock roused me, and Marsh and Donne entered. I rose and started to get my things together but was halted by the detective.

'There's another one,' he said as Donne closed the door. 'There is another missing child. This time it's a girl,' he said bluntly, and looked for any expression I was about to make, trying to read me, the way he always did.

'I don't think sex is his thing. It's the suffering he wants, or needs,' I answered and sat back down.

'What makes you think that?' he questioned, sitting opposite me.

'Well, he hasn't interfered with any of the others.' I knew he wasn't going to leave it there, and pre-emptively, I answered, 'And I think it is all wrapped up in the first body I found, the man that was run down.'

'But that was years ago, and it was an adult. What makes you think–'

I interrupted him. 'What makes me think anything?'

They looked at each other and nodded knowingly. I think both realised that they had no idea how I ticked.

'I keep seeing the man dying, like I'm with him when he dies.' I looked at Marsh, and the expression he gave was one of total ignorance; I'm sure he found me harder to understand every time we spoke.

For what seemed like an eternity, no one spoke.

'Can this be used to help in this case?' Donne asked.

'I don't see how?' Marsh answered bluntly.

'What if you get the old case file and give it to… to go through? It might not help, but it sure can't hurt?' Donne questioned/answered in his usual style.

'That would be against the law, but if I were to save the notes and any evidence on the disappearance to a place on the internet, perhaps someone could access it without me knowing,' Marsh answered, thinking on his feet. He took out a pen and wrote down an email and password that he used infrequently and handed it to me. I took my wallet out and filed it away.

'Naturally, that won't be added to the file until tomorrow. Is there internet coverage at your farm?' he asked Donne.

'We aren't in the outback, you know. We even have electricity,' Donne answered, feigning insult.

'Then if a person were to access that file from your farm, no one would ever know?' Marsh said, nodding at me.

I nodded back. At least this would give me something to do while I was isolated.

'What about the girl though? Can I get you to look for her, you know, on a map?' Marsh asked tentatively.

I nodded consent and soon, Donne had found a large map, which he spread out on the table.

This remote viewing was not my thing, but as if I knew what I was doing, I ran my hand from left to right, trying to feel something, anything. I didn't, and I could see the disappointment in the expectant faces looking at me.

'I'm sorry, but it was a long shot at best. This is not how I usually see things,' I apologised, and seeing them both look at the map and then back to me, I decided to pick the map up and hand it back to Donne.

Bloody maps are always much harder to fold than to unfold, and my first attempt was feeble. On my second attempt, I got a hit, a feeling, and realised that the more detailed map on the back of the main map was where I was getting the feeling from. I stopped dead and lifted the smaller map closer to get a better look. When I got it close enough, I realised that I was pointing to the same street where the last boy had been taken from, where we had visited his home.

'Oh, it's just the last case,' I said, handing it back to Donne. It was intercepted by Marsh.

'No, that same street is where the girl lived; they don't think that is where she was taken from, though,' he said, handing the map back to me.

This was weird and something I had never done before, but I had the urge to sit back down and, placing the map on the table, I put my forehead down on top of it. I have no explanation, I just felt it was the right thing to do. I felt sick.

'What is it? What are you, um, seeing?' Marsh asked urgently.

'She was taken from this street, but much closer to the main part of town. There doesn't seem to be a bike involved,' I answered, though I didn't feel at all confident.

'That's right,' Marsh interrupted, but I silenced him by raising my hand. I didn't want to be influenced by anything he said.

'Was she taken from a car?' I asked, then added, 'No, don't tell me,' as I felt that Marsh was going to answer.

'She was taken from the shopping centre. Oh god, from her mother's car. Oh shit, there's blood everywhere.' I lifted my head. I knew that I was going to be sick and the only receptacle I could see was the wastepaper bin, which I quickly grabbed and heaved into. This was so unbelievably terrible.

'Oh god, sorry,' I blurted between retches.

They both stood there just looking at me, their shock written large on their faces.

It took me a few moments to regain my composure; I sat again and pushed the map away from me, then put my head down on the table again. I needed to stop seeing the blood.

Both stood and for quite some time said nothing, but eventually, Marsh decided to break the silence. 'You are right, but you knew that. I'm sorry but the girl is still missing,' he said, putting one hand on my shoulder.

I could read him, and what I saw was a broken man. He blamed the killings on himself. That was simply not rational; he was doing more than anyone else to stop this bastard and I felt I needed to tell him so. Before I could say anything, though, I saw something else. A darker side; a desire to kill this monster. It was there for just a moment, but I saw it.

'You can't just kill him,' I blurted, and he pulled his hand away, startled.

Donne now surpassed the feelings I had for him. 'Anyone in your position would be thinking of taking him out. But you need to let me do that with the law when you catch him,' he said with great gravitas; he loved the law, and I knew Marsh did too.

Marsh nodded then looked to me. 'We need to catch him first. Know that I would like to end him, but I would never do that. The families need him in the dock.'

I nodded, though I was not sure that everything he said had conviction. I knew him to be a good man, so I put these feelings out of my mind. Only time would tell.

'So, you found where she was taken from. Can you tell where she was taken to?' he asked calmly, not wanting to upset me.

I looked across the table at the map; I didn't want to touch it again, but I knew that that was exactly what he was asking me to do.

I put my head down and reached for the terrifying piece of paper. I unfolded it without looking at it and ran my open palms over the whole surface. I felt sick again. Twice. This must have been where the two children had been taken from on this side of the city. I felt nothing else other than a slight sense of moving north. I pushed the paper away again; I had still not opened my eyes.

'Anything?' Donne asked impatiently.

'Nothing, but I think she was taken north. I don't know that. I only think that,' I answered, only lifting my head off the table enough to be able to speak. I felt sick again.

'Is she alive?' Marsh asked in the quietest voice I had ever heard him use. It was calm and in a monotone.

'No... I don't think so,' I answered and put my hands over my eyes. Oh, how I wished I was not seeing this dreadful evildoing.

I began to really lose myself and started sobbing uncontrollably. Marsh placed a hand on my shoulder again. As I looked up, the door opened, and Sylvia entered with a tray of coffee for the three of us.

'Oh, what have you done to him?' she blurted, seeing my distressed condition. No one answered, and she prompted in a harder voice, 'Well?'

'There is another child missing,' her father answered, almost whispering.

'Oh no,' she said, putting the tray of drinks on the table. I noticed a tear run down her cheek and was surprised at the immediacy of her reaction. She stood and stared at the map.

'Were you able to help?' she asked, raising her eyes to meet mine.

I now broke the gaze, and looked down and ashamedly answered, 'No, I don't think so.'

'But you tried?' she coaxed.

'Yes, I tried,' I answered.

She placed the three cups on the table, and taking the tray, left the room.

'Well, I think it's time we got you out of here,' Donne said as he took his cup and swallowed about half the contents in one gulp.

Both of us followed suit and then I asked, 'How is this going to work? I mean, how are we going to get out of here without me being seen?'

'Donne is going to lock up here and drive his family home and leave the upstairs light on, so it looks like you are still here. I'm going to leave first in the Ute. It's only a two-seater, and the area behind the seats is usually full of tools. This time it will be full of you. It is a tight fit, but you will be alright. Then I'll drive to the police station and Donne will come and meet us there.

'The back cover is off the Ute, and it will be empty. Your gear and food are on the Ute floor and will stay there. Donne and I will then take you to his farm. You will be uncomfortable on the way, so we'll put the pillows and blankets in for you.

'If anyone followed us, they would see you were not with us and anyway, we would see them if they followed us along the dirt out near the farm,' Marsh answered in what seemed to be a practised diatribe of which he was so fond.

I just nodded; there was no need to argue. These people were my only hope, my only help.

Marsh and I hurried down the stairs and exited, after he had checked that no one was watching. He prepared the seat and then bustled me into the small birth that I was going to inhabit. As he said, it was a very tight fit, but it was possible if I turned my face to the rear wall and squashed one pillow under me and the other at my feet.

Marsh moved the car and soon stopped and met Donne at the front of the driveway. He deliberately left his door open, so anyone watching could see inside. They both stood talking for a longer time than necessary; I could hear Marsh thanking Donne and the two ladies and then he got back into the car and drove off without acknowledging my existence.

As we slowed to turn into the police station, after what I considered a very uncomfortable ten minutes, Marsh whispered, 'I will leave the window down a bit.'

Next came a wait of about half an hour. Luckily, it was not a very hot day, and Marsh had parked in the shade of a row of golden cypress trees that ran down the side of the police station car park. Even so, I felt I would have passed out if the wait was any longer.

Marsh's door opened first. I felt someone sit down then I could feel him leaning to his left and unlocking the passenger's door. Another person began to get in with difficulty.

'Got enough room there?' Marsh said.

Donne replied, 'I'll fit. It's a bit of a squeeze, but I'll fit.'

I was relieved to hear both and even more relieved that both rolled their windows down.

I could feel us move off, and after we left the car park and joined the road, Donne asked, 'Are you alright back there?'

'I'm alright but it got bloody hot,' I answered quietly.

'It will be a bit more pleasant when the air conditioner kicks in for real,' Marsh said, and I heard him turn the fan up.

In a short time, it was much cooler and they both rolled their windows up. The area was still very uncomfortable, and I tried to stretch. There was little point, and I gave it up for a bad joke.

Soon, we were travelling quite quickly, and I felt a bit more relaxed about things. I was out of the office and out of the town and no one knew where I was. I felt safer.

About half an hour into the trip, things took a turn for the worse as we joined the dirt road, and Donne's comment about it being a slow and rough trip soon became real as I was buffeted all over the place. The car seemingly found every corrugation and hole in the road.

It was a great relief when we finally pulled up outside the first of two gates that were on the main entrance road to the property. This showed Donne's affluence as the last hundred yards to the gate and the driveway were beautifully covered with bitumen.

'Oh, god, can I get out?' I complained and Marsh, who had stayed in the car while Donne opened the gate, said shortly, 'No, not yet.'

Donne re-joined us after shutting the gate behind the car, and then he repeated the task at the second gate. We had arrived. As soon as I could, I exited the car and began to stretch like I had never stretched before. I had never felt so stiff, even after a hard game of football or a ten-kilometre run, which I must admit I hadn't done since moving to the new town. I had simply gone soft, not feeling I needed to bother with the fitness regime that had meant so much to me in my late teens.

Really, there was no one I was trying to impress, and I could never impress myself.

I turned to look at the house; it was a bloody mansion, even bigger, it seemed, than the Donne residence in the town. It had obviously been a large farmhouse of beautiful traditional design, made in large sandstone blocks. Donne had made his mark by adding a rather vulgar 'cape cod' extension clad to look like it was weatherboard.

I found out that the four bedrooms on the first floor had replaced the two downstairs when they were opened into an open plan living/dining room and kitchen. The only other ground-floor room was a large library.

'Well, let's get you settled in,' Donne said as he retrieved several bags of groceries from the car. He indicated with his head that Marsh and I should gather the rest of the bedding and my own small bag.

We did as instructed, and followed him to the veranda where he put everything down. After taking out his keys, he opened the building. As we entered, the distinctive smell of mothballs or something similar greeted us.

'I'll open things up and the smell will go.' Donne made himself busy doing exactly that, opening the front sliding windows and the kitchen door in order then the rear double sliding doors, which opened onto the rear veranda.

Surprisingly, an immediate breeze sprang up from the rear to the front of the building.

'Follow me and I will show you around,' he continued. We both followed him on a direct course to the library. The room contained two desks, one grand and obviously that of the tour guide and the other with the feeling of a lesser being, Mrs Donne.

The furniture was all grand and like something that would have seemed more at home in a grand English mansion. The leather-studded chairs and matching chaise lounge looked very inviting, though the latter proved to be much harder than expected as we seated ourselves. He continued to the shelves at the back of his desk where a well-stocked bar displayed many well-labelled bottles.

'Whisky, I think?' he said, drawing a bottle of a very expensive brand and began to fill three beautiful crystal glasses, which looked as though they would have cost a month's wage to plebs like Marsh and me.

Marsh began to protest, and I would have followed suit had the host not said, 'Nonsense, nonsense,' and handed us the glasses.

With the first little sip, I could taste the decadence. To be honest, I don't really like spirits, and it caught my breath.

Marsh seemed to have no difficulty, however, savouring the tipple.

Returning the bottle to the tantalus, Donne moved to the end of the room furthest from where we sat and opened a large wooden cabinet displaying an amazing collection of guns. Many were obviously collector's pieces. A splendid-looking pair of dress duelling pistols, perhaps as many as ten rifles and almost as many pistols were all on display behind what looked to be a locked laminated door. Taking a set of keys from his pocket, he fumbled through them for a few seconds and then used one to open the arsenal. He removed one plain-looking rifle, which I thought I recognised as a twenty-two land a pistol.

He walked over to me and thrust it in my direction. 'This should make you feel a little safer when we are gone,' he said, and before I could protest, he was beside me, showing me where the safety was located. 'It is the only gun I keep loaded.' Looking at Marsh, he added, 'Well, I've worked with all kinds of people in my career. You just never know.'

Marsh rolled his eyes, obviously knowing that giving Donne a lecture on the safe handling of guns and giving one to an unlicensed shooter was probably a waste of time, so he shook his head disapprovingly.

'We do need him to feel safe,' Donne said, smiling widely and Marsh shrugged in tacit approval.

I had no intention of shooting anyone; indeed, I didn't think I could even pull the trigger, but I took it and stood staring down at it, awkward in my hand.

'Have you never held a gun before?' Donne questioned.

I shook my head and answered, 'I have held a rifle but never a pistol.'

'Well, it won't bite you, man.' He took the gun back, pointed to the side and said, 'This is the safety. You just move it like this, and the gun is ready to fire.' He paused for a moment. 'Don't point it at anyone unless you intend to kill them.'

The comment shocked me a little and I stepped backwards. 'I don't think so,' I said in a weak voice.

'Well, it's your funeral, but I will put it here in the second drawer where you can get it if you need it, alright?' he instructed opening the long draw below the glass case and bent forward a little, expecting an affirmative answer.

'Yes, well, thank you,' I answered, sounding quite feeble.

We all stood for a few moments and then Marsh said, 'We ought to be leaving. I will give you a couple of days to settle in and then I'll bring some more of the case notes and photos out so you can have a good look at them.'

I couldn't think of anything that needed saying so I just nodded. Donne gave me a light slap on the back. 'You'll be alright,' he said, and they both moved toward the front door.

I wanted to be alone and yet I was a little afraid to see them go somehow. I stood holding the front door half open until their taillights disappeared down the rough driveway.

I returned to the kitchen and began to prepare a pot of tea. I didn't really feel like a drink, and I think I was just compensating for not having anything to do, nothing to push me.

Retiring to the living room, I sat sipping tea and bemoaning my fate to an audience of one.

Within minutes, I was sick of my own company and reached for the TV remote. The mid-evening shows were on and as usual, they were a collection of mindless so-called reality shows, someone jumping off cliffs or cooking something within an inch of its life. I was bored already. I couldn't see how I could stay here for any length of time. The surroundings were salubrious, far more impressive than I was used to, and yet I was bored. I knew that I needed to get to work on the case notes, evidence and pictures left for me by Marsh. However, no sooner was the first of the folders open than I was asleep.

Chapter 11

I had slept on the couch in the living room, though I didn't remember moving there, and I only woke because I was cold. A morning frost had settled, and it couldn't have been much above zero degrees.

I moved to the most impressive and ornate marble fireplace and, seeing that there was a fire prepared and ready to light, I helped myself to the matches on the shelf and lit the paper. Soon, a more than adequate fire was lighting the room, and I felt no need to put a light on. I could see the paperwork well by the firelight.

I scanned everything, turning photos of the last disappearance area to look at it from different directions as if that was going to make a difference. It didn't. Likewise, the map was turned backwards and forwards in the hope that something would jump out at me. Nothing did.

Eventually, I became bored and decided to have a good look around the house. The main rooms were, I thought, very grand and somewhat pretentious. The service areas, like the kitchen and bathrooms – there were three – were much more normal. Indeed, the main bathroom seemed a little out of place with a very modest bath and shower, tiled in a plain cream with blue accents. It was the room I liked most in the whole house, much more what I was used to, I thought.

I decided to run a bath and relaxed in it, almost going to sleep again until I heard a loud noise on the rear veranda. It was a noise like something being dragged. I froze, listening, as a chill ran down my back. I waited for some time but only heard some minor scratches and an occasional bump. It didn't sound like anything particularly threatening, but it still got the best of my curiosity and, after quickly throwing a pair of pants on, I took the gun from the desk and cautiously made my way, as quietly as possible, out the rear kitchen door.

Once outside, I stood still and waited and watched for any movement or noise. After a short pause, the sound of something being lightly dragged along the wooden decking on the side of the building seemed to be coming in my direction.

A slide-clunk progression got slightly louder as it neared the corner. A chill again ran down my back as the slide-clunk halted for a moment and then came again, ever nearer. I found myself backing away and I tried to speak but nothing came out. *Slide-clunk!*

After a few seconds, I regained what composure I had and demanded, 'Come out, I have a gun.' And with the words sticking in my throat, a sudden roaring noise came and then the head of an equally scared cow emerged. As it neared, I could see that there was the remnant of a piece of fencing wrapped around one of its front legs and up over its head, dragging along the animal's side.

There was blood. The great beast looked to me for help; it was obviously domesticated but what did I know about cattle? Nothing, nothing at all. I realised I would have to do something, so I neared the head and reached out to try to disentangle the suffering face where the barbed wire was biting into the flesh around its right eye, down across the cheek and wrapped around the poor thing's throat.

Surprisingly, the animal allowed me to near, not even reacting as I tried to find the end of the wire with the intent of just pulling it off.

The great beast was compliant and still, as I fumbled and traced the wire. I couldn't really see where the ends or beginnings of the wire were, so clumsily I tried to remove the most painful-looking piece that was running across the front of her face.

The pain was evident as she shuddered and pulled away. It was only then that I realised that I had bitten off more than I could chew. The loop of barbed wire tightened as she backed away and wrapped around my fingers and wrist. This must have made it tighter, and as it bit into her eye and around her face, she lurched backwards, which made things all the worse.

Now we were both trapped, and as she tried to move away from me, she simply tightened the snare. I didn't know what I was doing, and with no gloves, not to mention no shirt or shoes, I was now a captive of the bovine. The pain was intense. I could feel three of my fingers being crushed and blood running down my arm, though I could not really tell if it was my blood or that of my host.

Simply, I was trapped and every time I tried to move, she would make a countermove, which seemed to ensnare me more tightly. I forced my right leg in between her front legs and anchored it with my left foot. This, at least, made it difficult for her to move away. I was now becoming used to the dim light and could see where the rusted star picket fence post was attached.

As I tried to reach it, the cow moved and became even more entangled, tripped and fell forward. I was propelled like a rag doll up and over her body. I heard bones breaking and knew that they were my fingers. Only when I landed could I see the bloodied mass of my hand and how it was mashed.

This had all happened so quickly that I felt that my shoulder had been pulled out of place. The pain was excruciating; I knew that I had to get out of this quickly. I struggled to my knees, and the cow tried to get up too. I again wrapped my legs around hers in a move to keep her down. After a moment's struggle, she seemed to understand and stilled. I could see two pieces of the wire had crossed over and wound deeply into my right arm and this was, like a lever, holding my hand tight in the crux. Whatever I did, it was going to hurt so I calmed myself and reassessed my real position.

After a few seconds, my brain clicked into gear. I needed to either swivel around the two wires or prise them apart somehow. Using my free hand directly on the wire would only make things worse so I resisted the urge. I would have to lift the picket and throw it right over the top of us to free my arm, but this still wouldn't loosen the clamping wire wrapped around my hand.

I glanced around us but could see no sticks or anything that I could use to reach the post. I lay across the cow for a moment, trying to think of some way of freeing us both. She had almost stopped struggling. It was as if she understood that I was trying to help. I suddenly thought of my belt; I could get my belt around the loop in the wire.

If I could lift the top piece of wire away from my hand, I may then be able to move the post to lever it off me altogether. My first movements were clumsy as I fumbled for my belt with my free hand; eventually, I could feel it unbuckle, and I began to unthread it, though it was quite difficult. Once I was able to wrap the leather around the wire and lift, my hand was freed.

I stayed on top of the animal for a short while to gain my composure. I was almost sick when I saw the condition of my hand. I had virtually de-gloved my last three fingers, and my small finger was at a terrible angle.

Getting up, I realised that I was going to be of little assistance to the poor stricken beast and so I staggered my way back to the house. I had no idea as to the treatment that I would need but could not resist the urge to place my hand under the cold-water tap in the kitchen. The increase in the pain made me sick again, this time with a result.

I tried to clean the sink and area around it but began to feel pain and staggered to the bathroom, taking two towels and wrapping them around my still freely bleeding hand.

The pain increased but I knew I had to stem the bleeding. Again, I felt faint, though I am sure that was from shock, not the blood loss. On entering the lounge area, I sat on the small chair, which was next to the quaint little 1970s phone table. I knew I had to get help and thought for a moment.

Who could I ring? I didn't have a number in my head for Donne or Marsh. Really, I had nothing in my head. I just needed help.

As I began to lift the phone with my left hand, I noticed the towels had stopped being a barrier to the blood and it flowed freely onto the carpet and began to pool. I put the phone back down for a moment and tried to wrap the cloths tighter. This was terribly painful and practically of no use.

I lifted the phone again and placed the receiver under my chin, holding it there until I could dial 000. Almost immediately, the operator's voice asked, 'Which service, please?'

I responded, 'Police, please,' and almost immediately, another voice asked, 'What is the nature of your call?'

I must admit that I was a little slow to start my answer as I was thinking about how to tell her what I wanted without her transferring me to the ambulance line. She repeated, 'What is the nature of your call?'

'I need to be put through to the local police station,' I babbled.

'Is this an emergency?' she asked.

'Yes, please don't hang up. I need to speak to Detective Marsh.'

'Is this an emergency?' she asked again. I told her the town I wanted to be put in contact with and added that it was a matter of life or death.

'I will try the station for you, but you should ring directly,' she said, sounding very sceptical.

'I would if I could. I am under police protection, and I am badly hurt,' I blurted indignantly.

'Do you need an ambulance?' she fired back.

'No, I don't know where I am and need Marsh,' I answered, becoming a little frantic. The line went silent and then there were three rings before a trained voice stated the police area and station and asked if he may be of assistance.

'I need Detective Marsh. This is urgent!' I answered.

'I think the detective has left for the day. Can I assist you?' he answered calmly.

'Bloody hell, I am under the protection of Marsh and have been badly hurt. Only he knows where I am,' I ranted.

'Ok, I will see if he is still here,' he said, sounding at least a little more interested.

After a short time, which seemed like an eternity, he came back on the line and said, 'Detective Marsh has left. I will try to put you through to his mobile.'

Another long pause came and then the ringing of a line, three, four times. 'Marsh.'

'Oh god. I'm hurt. I can't...' I babbled and found the emotion welling up in me so much that I couldn't continue.

'Fitzpatrick, is that you?' he interjected quickly.

'Yes, I need help. I am hurt badly and will need an ambulance or doctor or something,' I ranted and again started to blubber. I was embarrassed but the emotion was getting the better of me.

'What has happened?' he asked.

'I have smashed my hand and am bleeding. God, bleeding a lot,' I answered.

'I understand. I will get to the ambulance station and come with them. You better not hang up this line as I don't have the number,' he instructed.

'Hurry,' was the only word I could get out. I felt faint again and slid to the floor, dragging the phone down with me. Marsh must have heard the sound of the old phone hitting the floor as he shouted, 'Are you still there?'

'Yes, I'm on the floor,' I answered and then must have blacked out as I don't remember anything for some time.

When I did wake, I was not sure immediately what had happened, then it came back to me and I held the phone to my ear again and asked, 'Are you there?'

I could hear noises, loud noises, driving noises, then Marsh's distant voice came on.

'We are nearly there,' he reassured me then added, 'Hold on.'

Strangely, I nodded to the phone and was just affected enough to think how stupid that was as I again lapsed from conscience.

In what seemed only a few seconds, I came around again with someone holding my injured arm up in the air. Someone was tapping my cheeks and then I heard the voice of Marsh.

'Are you back with us?' he stammered uncertainly.

I suddenly had the feeling I was going to be sick again and though I started the involuntary action, I held back the little that must have been left in my stomach.

One of the two ambulance men attending me produced a vomit bag and asked Marsh to hold it in case I needed to use it, and though I thought that was likely, it never happened.

I was now painfully wide awake and felt every movement as one of the men began to unwrap the towels from my hand. I looked up and saw fresh blood start to flow from the wound where the base of my little finger should have been. I could see the three fingers lying across the back of my hand and looked away, too frightened to see what they were going to do next.

In turn, they treated the bleeding and then secured the fingers before re-wrapping the mess in sterile bandages, but the blood flowed through them, and the decision was made to double wrap the hand with triangular bandages, which were thicker and larger. This action stemmed the bleeding as far as I could tell, and the officer then turned to my wellbeing.

'You must be in quite a bit of pain. On a scale of one to ten, where would you say your pain sits?' he asked.

It was quite an ask. Here I was with half my bloody hand missing, and he was asking me to do some sort of equation.

'Twenty,' I answered in as sarcastic a tone as I could muster.

'Are you allergic to anything?' he asked and as I had little to say, I just shook my head.

'I'm sorry but you will have to answer me verbally,' he instructed.

I knew that he was doing the right thing, so I mumbled, 'No,' and he placed a small tube into my mouth and told me to take some deep breaths. I complied and though it seemed like some type of joke, I soon felt the effects of its contents. I felt faint again and moved my head toward the vomit bag being held by Marsh. Again, nothing resulted, and Marsh looked relieved.

The pain level was, however, too high for this green whistle to control and soon one of the men decided I was to have an injection. I heard him tell his partner what he was about to inject, and then I was in the back of the ambulance travelling at speed over the very rough ground. I remember nothing until waking the next morning in a strange bed in a strange room. A hospital room.

My right arm was in what seemed to be an over-engineered supporting calliper of some kind and was suspended above me. It was so heavily bandaged that I was unable to see any definition, and immediately the thought came to me that they had removed my hand.

Startled, I turned to see who was in the room. Next to me sat Donne and on the other side, my left, was Sylvia.

'Oh, good. You have come around,' she said, sounding relieved.

'What have they done?' I asked her, looking toward my dangling arm.

She went to answer but was cut off by Donne. 'You were quite a mess, but they say you will recover quite quickly. They said that a degloving wound can be one of the most painful injuries but that if the nerve damage settles, you should be fine,' he said in his usually slightly pompous way.

'Get me a doctor,' I said, and my voice was affected again by the drugs.

'Sure, sure,' he answered and began to walk out of the room.

Sylvia took my uninjured hand and gave it a slight squeeze. 'We were quite worried about you,' she said supportively.

I couldn't access words without tears so I just nodded, hoping she would understand.

Soon, a white-coated man entered and asked how I was feeling. Donne followed him with his mobile phone up to his ear and said, 'Marsh, he's awake.'

The doctor wheeled around and said in a surly voice, 'There are no mobiles in here.'

Donne nodded his understanding and placed his phone back into his pocket. It is strange how drugs of the morphia family affect one's sense of right and wrong, important and unimportant. I thought to say that there was a mobile in here, taking his meaning literally, but I began to feel sick again and just lay silently.

'You had quite a close call,' the doctor continued, looking over the glasses he wasn't wearing. He went on when there was no response from me. I remember thinking, *Close call? Half my bloody arm is missing.*

'Your little finger was severed,' he said, holding his own hand up to model what a little finger looked like, then continued, 'The other fingers were crushed and badly broken but they will recover. The little finger could not be saved.' He again modelled by grasping his little finger to give me the sense of it being gone. 'Your collarbone was also broken. It has been reset.'

After a few moments to let me take in what he had told me, he added, 'You were very lucky, really.'

I didn't feel lucky. I didn't feel much of anything.

'What about the cow?' I questioned Donne.

'Yes, a bit of a mess that. We were able to get the wire off it, but its eye was badly damaged, and we had to put it to sleep, I'm afraid,' he answered.

I felt so terrible, the thought of that poor animal. All of this was in vain. I shook my head; I found it hard not to think of myself in its position. Would Donne have put me down?

'What the hell did you think you were doing, going out without shoes or half your clothes in the middle of the night wrestling with cattle?' Donne demanded in his usual blustering way.

'Well, I heard a loud noise at the side of the house and then I found the poor thing tangled in the fencing wire,' I explained.

'Dangerous things when injured,' he said, paying little attention to what I had answered.

'Well, I couldn't just let it suffer,' I answered indignantly.

'You were trying to help, so kind,' Sylvia put in, seeing that I was getting a little annoyed with her father. She smiled at me, and I must admit, I felt a bit stupid. She wouldn't have been inexperienced enough to try to untangle the beast bare-handed as I did. Probably only I would have been that stupid.

'I suppose the old joke about never being able to play the piano again would be out of order,' Donne said, trying to bring a lighter feel to the conversation.

I didn't see the funny side to it at all, but I played my role, answering, 'I know, I couldn't play before the accident, anyway.' I knew that he was just being himself, but I really was not in the mood.

These ramblings continued for a while and the pain came back with a vengeance. Sylvia was tuned in to what my face was saying and told her father that they should leave.

'He will need lots of rest in the next few days. I will be back tomorrow,' she instructed him and reassured me.

I could only raise a 'thank you' and close my eyes. They left, Sylvia virtually pushing her father out the door. I could hear her berating him as they walked away from the room.

I had a look around the room. It was a neat four-bed ward, but I was the only patient. I looked at the bedside table and noticed the assistance buzzer hanging at the side. I took it up and pressed the little red button. After a few seconds, a nurse, her long hair tied in a top knot to be proud of, entered.

'Can I help you, er, Mr Fitzpatrick?' she asked, looking at the name label at the head of my bed over her glasses.

'Yes, sorry, but I have a fair amount of pain,' I answered truthfully.

Taking up my patient chart, she answered, 'Yes, the doctor has listed you to have some pain relief as needed. I will go and arrange it.' She bustled away.

I must admit, I thought what a large lady she was as she left. I felt guilty. After all, I was no Rembrandt myself. As she re-entered, she said in a loud voice, 'You can have a second dose after an hour, but if you are still struggling after that we will have to contact the doctor to get instructions.'

I nodded consentingly. What could I do but what she said? I wasn't one who used a lot of painkillers anyway. Usually, they made me feel sick and didn't stop the real pain, so I would be sore and feel sick.

Dutifully, I sat up a little and swallowed the two capsules she handed me in a little disposable cup. Though I was worried about everything, I found that the pills did their job and soon I was sound asleep, asleep and dreaming.

I dreamed about the incident that had put me here, but the real dream came as I saw a young girl playing, then unthinkingly, she wandered out from the safe position she had been in and directly into the path of an oncoming car. The car stopped in time, and I breathed again. The girl started to move off the road. Then, as if it had a mind of its own, the car quickly accelerated and ran her down. I knew the sound was a figment of my imagination, as I had never heard someone run down before. Then I saw blood – nothing but blood.

Chapter 12

I stayed in the hospital for three days recuperating, and on the last day, I sat next to my bed waiting to be collected by Sylvia. She had been at my side each day in the morning and afternoons. She had also been with me when the doctor had given me the all-clear to go home the next morning.

I sat thinking about what my life had become. Why me? How would I cope with this hand all messed up, and would it ever work properly again? I think I would have spiralled into a deep depression if she had not come to bring some piece of fruit or a homemade confectionery or cake that she had prepared herself. We joked that I would soon be the size of an elephant.

To be honest, Sylvia was the only thing that kept me sane, and I couldn't help having feelings for her.

While I waited, a modestly built doctor entered my room. He was wearing a mask and looked a bit strangely at me, then, saying nothing, he took my chart up and looked at it. He made me feel uncomfortable. I don't know why. He seemed to be looking over the chart straight into my eyes. I thought he may be reading me somehow. I took a moment to pluck up the courage to say, 'You're not one of my doctors?'

He shook his head but did not break eye contact. I felt even more uncomfortable as he continued to stare.

I noticed things. He was not wearing a name tag, something all the staff did religiously. He had rough shoes on – they were leather uppers, but they were not very clean – and his pants appeared to be denim. I had never seen one of the staff members so casually dressed. I began to be frightened; I didn't trust this person, and my skin was crawling.

He advanced one step toward me and then, looking as though he had re-thought his plan of action, he turned and exited the room. Almost in the same second, Sylvia appeared at the door. She was beaming and pushing a silver wheelchair.

'Ready to leave. Your chariot awaits,' she said, gesturing toward the chair.

'Did you see a doctor leaving as you came in?' I questioned her.

'Yes, he was walking away as I came to the door. Why?' she asked quizzically, turning her head on one side as she often did when she was asking a question.

I reached for the buzzer button and pressed it. Soon, a different nurse appeared at the door. 'Ready to leave then?' she asked.

'Nurse, who was that doctor who was just in here?' I asked.

'What doctor?' she returned.

'He was just here. He had a white coat, but no name tag and he looked unclean – um, I mean, his clothes were not clean-looking?' I said, realising that I sounded as though I had lost my mind.

'Sorry, you must have been having a dream. There are no doctors on the floor at present,' she answered in a condescending tone.

'He wasn't sleeping. I saw him as I came in,' Sylvia said, packing me up.

'Oh, well it doesn't sound like any doctor I know?' she said, still obviously not believing me.

'I think he went into the first door on the left,' Sylvia added.

'What door?' the nurse asked, still seeming to doubt us.

'Come and I will show you then,' Sylvia answered, not accepting the attitude. She walked toward the hall and though I was supposed to be in the wheelchair, I waited for the nurse to follow her before I got up and walked to my room door.

Sylvia had reached the first door and opened it.

'You see, these are only staff stairs, you know, for staff to get up and down quickly when needed,' the nurse pressed her point.

Sylvia, not to be thwarted, stepped through the door and soon returned with a white doctor's coat draped over her arm. 'See,' she said, thrusting the coat toward the disbelieving nurse. 'Call the police,

Detective Marsh, now,' she insisted. Now, looking decidedly unsettled, the older woman turned and bustled off to make the call.

About half an hour later, Marsh arrived with a subordinate, looking all business. 'Fitzpatrick, Miss Donne,' he said, touching his non-existent cap in her direction and he shook my left hand.

'What the hell is going on?' he asked in a brusque manner. I thought he was trying to impress his young offsider.

'I think he was here,' I answered quietly.

'Who?' he asked and then a strange look of realisation came across his face. 'You don't mean the killer?'

I nodded uncertainly.

'What makes you think it was him?' he responded with some urgency.

'There was a man in a white coat with a mask on. He came in and looked at my chart and then looked at me and his eyes were the eyes I have seen,' I answered slowly, hoping he would understand without me going into deeper detail.

'Did anyone else see this man?' Marsh said loudly.

'I saw him leaving. He went down the staff stairs,' Sylvia answered.

Marsh turned to the nurse and said, 'Well?'

'No, I saw no one and there were no doctors on the floor at the time,' she answered.

'You are certain?' Marsh continued.

'Quite,' she answered curtly.

'Oh, there was certainly a man here, and he was wearing this coat,' Sylvia put in, holding out the white coat.

'How do you know?' Marsh questioned.

'When the nurse came in, we followed the man to the stairs and found the coat, just inside the door,' she answered, and I thought how concise she was with her answers. A product, no doubt, of being raised by a legally minded father.

Marsh looked to the nurse for confirmation.

'Yes, we did find the coat, but that doesn't mean someone unauthorised was there,' she said. It seemed that she was trying to protect the hospital.

'Oh, so your doctors are in the habit of just dropping their coats, are they?' Marsh demanded sarcastically.

'Of course not,' the woman answered indignantly.

'Then it follows that someone else was there,' Marsh added.

'If you say so,' she answered and turned to leave.

'I haven't said you could leave,' Marsh added loudly and the woman, somewhat startled, turned and looked at him with an almost belligerent air.

'This is connected to a murder case,' he added.

She faced him fully and clasped her hands in front of her. The attitude continued.

'Are there any security cameras set up on this wing?' Marsh questioned in a slow, deliberate tone; it was as if he was going to keep her there as long as he could.

'No, there are no cameras on this ward. Only at the front doors,' she answered and then added, 'Now, may I get on? I have a ward to run.'

'Yes, now you may go,' Marsh said a little sarcastically.

The woman turned and harrumphed out the door.

'Let's get you out of here,' Marsh said and then, having second thoughts, he added, 'No, perhaps that isn't the best idea.' He pondered for a moment then said, 'Press that call button and get that bloody woman back here.'

I raised my eyebrows inquiringly and he nodded. I didn't understand why I was bringing back the surly woman, but I pressed the button anyway.

After a few seconds, the stormy face arrived at the door followed by the agitated owner. 'What now?' she asked in the very unpleasant tone she had established earlier.

'I want the hospital's manager here right away, and find me a doctor,' ordered Marsh loudly, forcefully.

Her haughty countenance seemed to drop away as she thought her boss was being called for.

'Are you sure that is necessary?' she said with an attempt at a smile, which I thought only made her look pathetic.

'Stop questioning everything I say, and do as you are told,' Marsh said in a slightly less loud but still commanding voice.

The woman turned, looking much less a leviathan than she had. *The beast tamed,* I thought.

Soon, we were joined by a man in a business suit. He introduced himself as 'Jamison, Hospital Administrator,' offering his hand to Marsh. 'Is there a problem?'

'Detective Inspector Marsh, and yes, there is a problem,' Marsh said, playing the seniority game that obviously pervaded the establishment.

'How may I help?' the much slighter man asked compliantly.

'You are sworn to secrecy, and you will need to readmit Fitzpatrick here for another night,' Marsh ordered.

'Oh, well, that is not up to me. A doctor must order admissions and discharges, but I'm sure that can be arranged,' he answered and then added quietly, as if he didn't want anyone to hear, 'Has he been mistreated?'

'No, and don't ask questions,' Marsh answered. The little man raised his eyebrows but remained silent.

'I asked that bloody woman to get me a doctor. Please sort her out,' Marsh instructed, and he also brought his volume down. Jamison hurried away toward the nurse's station.

'What are you thinking?' I asked Marsh.

'I will make a big fuss about leaving and then I'll come back through the rear of the casualty department, then I will spend the night,' he answered. It almost seemed that he had been working on the plan for days.

I must admit I didn't like the idea of being bait, but I could see things from his point of view. This would give him the best chance to ambush his prey. I nodded a tacit approval.

Sylvia was not delighted by the idea. 'You must be joking. Lay there and wait for someone to come and do who knows what to you?' she said, looking at me and disregarding Marsh completely.

'Where else would I be safer?' I asked and I am sure it sounded more like I was questioning myself rather than her.

'I don't like it. It's not safe,' she continued and then turned her scorn on Marsh. 'You expect too much.'

Marsh squirmed a little, which was a first in my eyes, then he answered, 'He will be quite as safe as I can promise. Anyway, the man may have been just a reporter, trying to get a story.'

'Rubbish. Why did he not ask any questions then, or take any photos?' Sylvia demanded.

'Look, I don't have all the answers, but we have no way of knowing who came to visit. Best case scenario, he comes back, and I catch him, and the killings of the children stop and Fitzpatrick here'—he gestured at me—'can go about his life.'

'I still don't like it. What if he has a gun or something?' she continued to protest, on my behalf no less. Oh god, she was fantastic.

I felt I had to say something, but I wasn't sure what that something was. I ummed and ahhed for a few seconds then said, 'I think I must do it. The children are too important to let this chance get away.'

Sylvia shook her head. 'What if the police were here? One could be dressed up as you, and have a gun, and they could be waiting for him without him being able to hurt you at all.'

'No, that would be too hard to set up in the time we have, and Fitzpatrick might be seen when leaving,' Marsh answered in a quieter voice.

A few more minutes passed, and I began to see real impatience in Marsh, then a short middle-aged man entered the room. He was not yet wearing his work coat but was carrying his stethoscope.

'Doctor Andrews,' he said and stuck out a hand to meet Marsh's.

'Detective Marsh,' Marsh said. 'I need this man to stay in for another night.'

'Why? He will recover much better at home,' Andrews asked.

'No, I need him to be here where he can be protected. He is at threat, and he had a visitor today who may be a problem,' Marsh answered, trying to keep the story as simple as he could.

'What do you mean, a problem?' the littler man asked inquisitively.

'I don't want to say more. The less you and the staff know, the better. Everyone will be safe. I will be here as well,' Marsh instructed.

Andrews picked up my discharge papers, which had been prepared by the nurse and signed off by another doctor. Reading for a moment, he paused and looked at me over the top of the papers. 'Is this what you want?'

I nodded. He wrote something and then looked at the sheets again and said simply, 'Done.'

Moving to the bottom of the bed, he replaced the papers on the clipboard where they had been prior to the planned discharge and turned to walk out of the room. As he neared the doorway, Marsh instructed, 'You are to keep this to yourself, Doctor.'

'Naturally, patient confidentiality,' Andrews said, turning his head and smiling as he thought he was in the know.

Marsh soon followed the doctor out of the room with a parting, 'I'll be back,' and I was left, to my delight, with Sylvia.

She clucked and cooed about the state I was in and the extra worries about the man coming back and how she didn't like leaving; eventually, though, we ran out of small talk, and she said her goodbyes and left me on my own.

I was tired. I felt like I must fall asleep, but I didn't want to be unprepared if the masked visitor came back. I got off the bed and onto the chair next to the bed that was provided for visitors. I sat there, trying not to drop off until about twenty minutes later, Marsh re-entered.

'Everything alright?' he asked, and I reassured him that I hadn't seen anyone since Sylvia left.

'Quite a girl that one, and she certainly has your back,' he said, giving me a knowing grin.

'Give me a break. She has only known me for a couple of days,' I answered, shaking my head as if faking disgust.

He continued to smirk to himself and took up residence in the visitor's chair. We talked for a short time quietly, and he filled me in as to the progress or lack of progress in the murder case. The police had dedicated another two officers to the case, but yet, nothing had come to light.

Marsh pulled the curtain around our area to darken it. He then went back to the position. I hadn't seen a nurse for hours; it seemed that no one wanted to be caught up in the subterfuge.

After about half an hour, I had drained the rest of the water I had in a small plastic bottle and was certainly going to need more through the night. Marsh decided to see if he could arrange cups of tea. He walked out through the curtains and headed to see the nurse. I knew there would be another nurse on shift and thought how funny it would have been if Marsh was confronted by his sparring partner from earlier in the day.

Almost immediately, the curtains were dragged back, and Donne was standing next to the bed.

'Oh, you startled me!' I exclaimed. He was the last person I had expected; it must have been 9 p.m.

'You didn't think I was going to let you capture the killer without me being present, do you?' he said quickly.

'Ah, well, so much for the effort being secret,' I answered.

'Don't blame Sylvia. She was worried about you.' He paused a moment and then added, 'She has taken quite a shine to you, young man.'

I didn't have anything to say, and I could feel myself blushing.

Soon, Marsh re-entered and greeted Donne with the same surprise I had shown.

'Wasn't about to let you two have all the fun,' he quipped.

'It was supposed to be secret,' Marsh answered, feigning indignance.

'There are no secrets between Solicitor and Client,' Donne said, smiling widely then added, 'I have told her not to tell anyone else.'

We all knew the 'her' he referred to was Sylvia.

'I'll get another chair,' Marsh concluded.

Soon, I had one of them on each side of me. We sat in silence.

I'm not exactly sure how long it took the tea lady to come but it seemed like another half an hour. She doled out weak teas to each of us.

Once my two protectors took the opportunity to catch up on the case progress, there seemed to be an impasse. We really didn't know a thing about each other, and it was obvious. Small talk can be the hardest thing to do in a confined space.

I suppose it was rude of me, but I soon fell asleep and was only reawakened when the curtain was flung open in the middle of the night when my temperature was taken.

The nurse raised her eyebrows when she saw my two visitors. She had known Marsh was with me but not Donne.

Sticking the thermometer under my tongue, she said, 'You must be important then?' in what was an almost perfect Scottish accent, if there is such a thing.

'Not really,' I answered, not knowing what that really meant. I suppose I was important in Marsh's case.

The night came and went, and though I slept well, the same could not be said for my two fearless protectors.

Donne looked dishevelled, for him, and Marsh, though he always had a somewhat 'lived-in' appearance, looked a wreck. Both were rubbing their necks and knees and just about every other joint. I couldn't help thinking that if an assailant had suddenly appeared, they would have been of little or no assistance.

Chapter 13

The night ambush at the hospital had been a complete waste of time. As Marsh had said, the man with the eyes was probably a reporter trying to get an inside story.

Donne had taken me back to his home, and we had eaten a spectacular breakfast prepared by Sylvia. I thanked her and her parents for their hospitality and left to visit the bathroom.

On my return, I was halfway down the hall when I heard the discussion between the family.

Donne said, 'I think he would be ok out there again.'

'No, not on his own,' argued Mrs Donne.

'He could stay here,' said Sylvia.

'Certainly not,' said Mrs Donne. I had always felt she didn't like me, but I was a bit surprised at the comment.

'If he stays out at the farm, I can go and stay during the nights,' Donne said, sounding like a teenager trying to get permission for a sleepover.

'Certainly not. You have the Percival trial starting tomorrow, and anyway, you need to be here protecting your family!' the woman snarled at him.

'I could go and stay at the farm, to look after him,' suggested Sylvia.

'That is the worst suggestion yet,' scolded her mother.

'Well, I will see Marsh and get him to stay there at night,' Donne suggested.

'If that is the only option.' The old woman gave a little ground.

'That's settled then,' said Donne, and I cleared my throat to let them know I was coming down the hallway.

I entered and Donne said, 'I will arrange for you to get back to the farm during the day, and I'm sure Marsh will want to stay with you tonight.'

'Thank you so much. It is very kind of you,' I answered, seeing Sylvia looking decidedly put out.

'See that you don't go wrestling any more of my cows,' Donne quipped, smirking.

'You're not funny!' Sylvia said in quite a serious voice. The humour of the thing got me and I laughed. That seemed to break the tense mood, and everyone smiled.

Midday came and went, and Sylvia popped into the library where Donne had set me up, every fifteen minutes it seemed, to make sure I was alright. It was quite pleasant to have such a beautiful young lady obviously caring for me. I was not used to the attention, and after the fourth or fifth visit, I pretended to be sleeping on the expensive-looking chaise lounge.

At around 1 p.m., Donne arrived home and parked his car near the front entrance to the house in the large turning circle. I heard him enter the large double front doors and call out to Sylvia.

After a short time, he entered the room and asked if I was alright. I nodded and thanked him.

'I don't know if anyone is watching the house or not, but I have a plan to get you back to the farm without anyone knowing.' He paused then added, 'Sylvia,' and Sylvia walked in, wearing a set of men's clothing. She also wore a man's hat, which was pulled down over her eyes. She carried a casual sports bag. I just gazed in amazement. What was he thinking, putting his own daughter at risk?

'No, I don't think so,' I said pointedly.

'Well, it is only for a moment as we exit the house and drive to my office where she will be able to change into her usual clothes. It must only fool him for a second as we go from the house to the car. I will open the door, Sylvia can crouch low and run out to the car and get in the back seat, trying not to be seen. But really, she will make sure she can be seen,' Donne explained long-windedly as he usually did.

'No, it is too risky,' I said uncertainly.

'I don't think so. No one will be looking for me – they will just see some man trying not to be seen,' Sylvia explained.

'Then when we get well away, my brother, Adam, will come and take you to the farm,' Donne continued.

I shook my head, still uncertain that it was in any way fair to put Sylvia at risk.

'That is settled then,' she concluded and went to leave the room.

'No, I don't like it. You would not be safe,' I argued, looking into her eyes as she swung around to face me again.

'I will be perfectly safe. I will spend the day in the office and keep out of sight until four or five o'clock then come out in my own clothes and return home with Father,' she instructed, and I instinctively knew that this plan had been her doing.

I had little or no feeling that this was going to put her in danger, though I had protested, so I reluctantly agreed, nodding in tacit approval.

Just a few minutes later, they departed, and within ten minutes, the rear doorbell rang. I could hear Mrs Donne answer it and talk to someone, though I couldn't hear the words.

I was wondering if I was supposed to go to the kitchen when she came into the library and behind her walked a shorter version of Donne.

'This is my brother-in-law, Adam Donne, Mr Fitzpatrick,' she said to both of us, gesturing with her hand face up as an introduction.

He advanced, and we shook hands. 'Glad to meet you,' he said in a husky, well-educated voice.

'Me too,' I answered, sounding as awkward as I always felt when meeting new people.

'I'm parked out the back,' he said and turned to leave via the kitchen door.

'Look after yourself,' Mrs Donne said, trying not to sound too interested.

'Thank you for your hospitality. You and your family have been very kind,' I said and stretched my hand out to shake hers. Again, this was an awkward gesture, but she took it and, giving a quick shake, she returned to her duties.

Adam Donne had been well instructed, and he motioned for me to stop near the rear gate. He exited, looking up and down the lane, then he gestured for me to quickly exit and enter the truck through the door he had opened. I obeyed and got onto the floor in the passenger well.

It was not comfortable, but it was more so than the Ute I had last been transported in. I was not jolted around very much as the ten-tonne truck, though slower, was very stable.

We trundled along for around fifteen minutes and then I could sense we had turned onto a dirt road.

'You can get up now,' Adam said, adding, 'There won't be anyone around on this road.'

I obeyed. It was a great pleasure to hit that somewhat comfortable bench seat.

'So, you are working with my brother on some secretive case? Who are you hiding from, the police?' he asked, obviously trying to initiate a conversation.

'Something like that,' I answered vaguely. If Donne hadn't given him any detail, then I certainly wasn't going to.

He probed a little further, but I was determined not to give anything away, so he changed the subject to what the farm produced, and he sounded particularly proud of the livestock.

'She was a beautiful cow, that one. You, um, er, met, and just as nice on the plate,' he boasted. I thought how callous he was, but then I had a second thought. He was a farmer; there was probably little room for niceties. Everything produced was produced for one reason: consumption.

'I see,' I said non-committedly.

'I reckon she would have brought around a thousand dollars if we had sold her,' he continued.

'Oh, yes. I will repay you when I can,' I answered obediently.

'Hell, no. My brother should be paying you. You tried to help the poor thing,' he insisted. I found his way of speaking was somehow like that of the southern states of America, and yet there was a little Canadian in there as well. Donne himself didn't have a country drawl, and I wondered how and where it had been acquired.

When we arrived at the farm, everything was 'lit up like a Christmas tree', as Adam commented.

It had still been dark when they had carted me out a few days before.

I was dropped at the front veranda and Adam went on to park the car, commenting that he would bring my bags in before he went back to town. I simply obeyed; there wasn't much in my bag, but I had no desire to carry anything. I felt sick again and soon found myself hunched over the toilet. After my dry retching, I got up and exited the bathroom. I decided to go into the lounge and felt sick again when I saw that my blood had pooled on the carpet where I had sat waiting for help to arrive. I couldn't face the clean-up job at that moment, so I walked over to the larger of the two lounge chair recliners. They were beautiful, black plush leather, and they looked and felt expensive.

I could have gone to sleep right there and then, but I had the feeling that was not a good idea. I didn't know why, but I was still feeling uncomfortable in the Donne house.

That feeling of something not being right troubled me, and I thought that it was probably my previous experience.

Soon, I heard the rear screen door squeak as it invariably did, and Adam came in. Seeing me, he walked over and handed me my bags.

'You going to be alright? You're as white as a ghost,' he said as he stood over me. I had often noticed that short men often did this; perhaps it was some deep-seated act of not feeling inferior.

'Yes, I will be fine,' I assured him.

'Well, I will leave my number just here next to the phone,' he said, placing a piece of paper on the phone table. I was a little surprised that he was that organised, then I thought that it was probably Mrs Donne's influence, with her self-interest to the fore. If I had her brother-in-law's number, perhaps I would bother him and not her immediate family.

'Thank you. You have all been very kind,' I said.

'T'wasn't anything. It's what we do in the bush, look after each other,' he answered, that drawl fit for an American Western of the 1960s coming to the fore again.

He paused for a moment, and I realised he had thought to shake hands but then, remembering my hand, he gave me an awkward wave and headed back out the rear door. I found that surprising in itself; he was a member of the family, but he had entered through the back door of both Donne houses. I guarantee he felt as uneasy around Mrs Donne as I did.

When I heard the truck start up and drive away, I had an uneasy feeling again. Now I was alone again and I remembered what had come of that the last time.

I fell asleep in the chair, and after an amount of time, of which I had no reckoning, I woke. It was dark. It took me a few moments for me to get my bearings. Oh yes, but where were the light switches? I couldn't see anything. I stood, remembering that the phone table had a standard lamp sitting on it, and searched backward and forward as I neared the area where I thought the table was. I bumped into the lounge and realised that it was another couple of steps to my left.

The light was welcome, though I had never been afraid of the dark. I was in someone else's house, and I was uneasy.

I wasn't wearing my watch as I hadn't remembered to get it out of my hospital bag. I glanced around, looking for a clock, but could only see the grand old armature on the mantle above the fireplace, which looked – though expensive – as if it hadn't worked for many years.

I remembered that there was a clock in the kitchen above the large stove. I walked over, put the lights on and could see that this clock also looked defunct. It appeared that the hour hand had fallen off, so I turned to the only other idea I had – and that was to turn on the computer at Donne's desk.

It started much faster than my laptop. *Best of everything,* I thought as it opened an identification page. Donne had left a small sheet of paper the first day I had come to the farm, on which there were instructions as to the operation of the computer and television. There were even directions pertaining to the microwave and the heaters. I couldn't think of anything other than the thought I was completely inept.

Once on the internet page, I could see that the time was 5.30 a.m. I had slept for at least twelve hours if that was correct, and I was surprised. I thought I'd had only a short nap.

I decided that it was time to try to make sense of some of the press releases of the last few days. I loathed the mention of my name; it only complicated things even more, but I needed to see how they were portraying my involvement. I had not rung my parents or contacted anyone else, family or friends. I knew that my mother would be worried and convinced myself to ring her later in the day.

In online media, I was no longer the flavour of the day. I was, however, mentioned once by name in the previous day's Telegraph. Bloody press, they didn't care who they hurt if they got their headline.

The statement, 'A medium has been brought in to consult,' was echoed among the other reports.

'Well,' I said to myself, 'that isn't too bad.' At least the photos of me as a 'child sleuth' had not been used again. Not that anyone would have recognised me from those pictures – I was young, had blond curly hair and none of the ravages of time. I know I'm only in my twenties, but teenage acne and my fullness of face gave me quite a different look.

Obscured by the detritus of musings by the reporters was the information I was looking for. They only used my name as an 'unsubstantiated consultant'. God, how I hate the press.

I made breakfast of a sort, some sachets of a less-than-satiating porridge. The milk was a long-life boxed supply, which I now placed into the fridge. This was all just a sugar delivery device, really.

I made a pot of tea, retired to the front veranda, and sat and watched the last of the pink sunrise fade. I could see the cattle in the next paddock and shuddered at the thought of my last encounter.

I was already healing. That is, I was mentally getting to grips with my situation. If nothing more positive could be said of me, at least I was resilient, once I got my head around a setback, whatever it was.

This beautiful start to the day was just the prelude to what I knew would be an extreme commitment to the paperwork and clues on the USB stick that Marsh had left with me.

I got off my butt and started.

Chapter 14

The handwritten notes in Marsh's notebook were the hardest thing to decipher. I almost needed a translator, but when I realised that his 'e's and 'l's' were almost identical, things went easier. I had always had the same difficulty reading my father's handwriting.

Though I read everything Marsh had written, and all of the case summaries and interviews of the few witnesses there were, only one thing hit me: though the method of each of the crimes seemed to be vehicular homicide, there were few other similarities.

Oh, yes. The first were all boys; they were usually riding bikes, but the last case was a girl, and she was in her mother's car in a carpark prior to being killed. Perhaps she was just a victim of convenience, a substitute for what it was that he really craved, whatever that was. I didn't kid myself; I couldn't understand the motive. Most sane people wouldn't, I suppose.

What other similarities were there? They were all children, young and helpless. No one came to their aid. No one saw anything happen. No witnesses other than those who had seen the child last and those who had discovered the bodies. What wasn't usual was the lack of disposal of some bodies while others were secreted away. Why? All seemed to be crimes of availability to some extent, but I couldn't put out of my mind the first case of the man and his dog, which I had discovered at the lookout. This older case was, to all intents and purposes, too long ago to be relevant. Plus, it was an adult. He and his dog had been scrupulously secreted under the new earthworks of the rest area's building.

It may seem ridiculous to others, but I was certain there was a link between the two events. I argued the case in my own way, in my own mind.

If the first case was related, the murderer would be at least middle-aged now, and why had there been such a long time between the cases?

Was the person in gaol or had he left the area and just recently returned?

Could I think of any other motivation? Well, no, frankly, but I wouldn't. No one sane would. There was not a sexual motive; well, at least it seemed that that was the case. There could be no financial gain.

Suddenly, I had a feeling that I understood. It was seeing the child suffer. Oh shit, who would want to see a child suffer? I felt sick, dirty, used, as I often did. It was almost as if I were taking on the persona of the murderer. I was the bloody maniac.

No, I just had to stop looking in case I was to see that which I couldn't forget.

I felt sick. I decided that I needed to leave this well alone, at least for now.

I pulled on a jacket and went for a walk. I needed to get my head straight. I was just going around in circles with the case anyway.

I thought I would be able to forget it all in the brisk morning, but nothing was further from the truth. I mused, I worried, and it just wouldn't go away. When I looked up, I had walked perhaps a kilometre and not even noticed.

I wandered to all four corners of the farm, but I knew I had to get back to the business at hand. My psyche was not going to let me rest until I had made sense of it all; perhaps never until the murderer was arrested.

At around 11 a.m., I returned and made more tea, then threw myself at it all again. I needed to find something, or I would go mad.

Immediately, when I picked the papers up this time, I had a feeling – that feeling you get when you are certain of something, but I wasn't certain of anything. All I could see were the children. Each flashed across my mind, and then they were gone.

Well, that makes sense. They are all gone now, I thought.

'There is something to do with paint. What is it about paint that I need to remember?' I said out loud, though I was alone. Who was I asking? Your guess is as good as mine, and no answer came.

I put my head down on the papers in front of me. I hoped this would help my perception of what had happened. It didn't, and I fell asleep again.

I dreamed.

I dreamed of a time when all this murder, hatred and violence was gone. I dreamed of being a normal person, of not seeing anything but that which everyone else could see. Then I dreamed there was a man. He was standing over me and I woke with a start as someone shook my shoulder. I almost jumped out of my skin, quickly getting to my feet, a chill running down my spine.

It was Donne. 'Are you alright?' he asked as I held my hand up to repel him.

'Oh, it is you?' I spluttered, feeling like I had lost time again. Hours had gone by, and I had just put my head down. It was dark again, and I felt cold.

'Where were you, lad?' Donne questioned, looking worried.

'I… um… I think I was with the murderer?' I answered, but it was in such a questioning tone that he seemed compelled to answer.

'Well, you are back with us now,' he said, smiling widely.

God, it felt creepy for him to smile. I certainly wasn't bloody smiling.

'What time is it?' I asked and he lifted his arm to look at his watch. I don't know why but I flinched.

He noticed and answered, 'Seven fifteen. Man, you are worked up. What can I do for you?' His answer became a question; it was one of his little idiosyncrasies.

'Oh, nothing. I was just dreaming,' I answered uncertainly.

'What about a meal? I brought Chinese. I hope you like Chinese. Oh, I'm here because Marsh can't come tonight. There is a bit of an upset at the station. It seems that the locals have been taken off the case and Sydney's homicide branch have taken over,' he questioned, answered and started putting food containers out of a bag on the table, all at the same time.

'Ah, well, yes, but I'm not sure I am feeling like food just yet. I better go and wash up,' I said, trying not to seem completely insincere.

I walked toward the bathroom and as I did, he added, 'Better hurry before it gets cold.'

When I got out of the room and closed the bathroom door, I took a deep breath and, looking in the mirror, I thought to myself, *You look like death warmed up.* Then my mind ran on. *I was laying with the murderer standing over me and then it was Donne standing over me. Oh, don't be bloody ridiculous. The man has done nothing but help you. It was just a coincidence. Now, pull yourself together.*

I was sweating like never before. I bent down to wash my face and then stood up, looking into the mirror again. I couldn't believe how old I looked. I feared I was cracking up, losing it. Then Donne's voice shouted near the door, 'Are you alright, man?'

It seemed to shake me out of my stupor, and I answered, 'Just coming,' as I dried my face on the hand towel and exited.

Donne had dished out two plates of food, and I had to admit that I suddenly felt hungry.

We ate in silence mostly. He made a few attempts to engage me in meaningless chit-chat, but I simply couldn't think of anything to say.

At the conclusion of the meal, I had emptied my plate, and though Donne had finished first, he had sat waiting for me. Picking up the plastic dishes the food had come in, he said, 'Don't worry. I will do the dishes,' and crammed them into the swing-lid garbage bin, which was positioned next to the back door for the convenience of emptying.

I smiled dutifully. It was slightly humorous at best, like his version of a 'Dad joke'.

He then took our two plates, rinsed them under the hot water tap and placed them in the drying rack.

'I have court tomorrow. The coroner has to hand down his findings in the case of the body you found on the mountain. The cause of death and that sort of thing, you know, tying it all up in a neat parcel, so to speak.'

'Oh, do I need to come?' I asked in what sounded like a worried tone.

'No, I will be there, and Marsh has your written statement, which I can attest to,' he assured me, and I took a deep breath and let it out to show I was relieved.

'Are you going to be alright? Should I get someone up to stay with you?' he asked.

'No, I will be ok. It's all just a bit too much now,' I assured him.

'Well, if you are sure. I could get the wife to come up?' he offered.

'No, thank you,' I answered a little too quickly.

He smiled widely and said, 'She's not that bad.'

'Oh, no. I didn't mean it that way. You have all been more than kind to me and I appreciate it, but I would rather be alone now,' I answered, trying not to sound too blunt.

'That's alright, man. I am just pulling your leg,' he commented and then, having a thought, he added, 'We are all just a phone call away. I have listed all our numbers, even Marsh's mobile, in the little blue book next to the phone.'

'Thank you so much. I am trying to concentrate on the case, but I don't think I'm getting anywhere,' I answered, uncertainly.

'You just keep at it when you can. No good driving yourself round the bend,' he insisted, and I nodded agreement.

Donne went to shake my hand and then remembered my injury and offered his left hand, which I took. As quietly as he had come, he was gone again. I heard his car driving away, though I didn't hear it start, which seemed strange.

How ridiculous was it to suspect Donne? I was losing my mind.

There was no good reason for him to have helped me, nor to take me into his home and now to put me up in the country. Nothing pointed to him as a suspect; he had just been there to wake me up, that's all.

I put the television on and began to tele-surf to avoid the news. It wasn't easy. Each station in turn seemed to be introducing their version of the exclusive news of the day.

I flicked finally on a true-life type of program and became engrossed in the world of finding or trying to find gold.

Most of the rest of the evening was spent similarly glued to, as my father used to call it, 'the idiot box'. I did a crossword on the computer and, as usual, was stuck with several words that I thought must have been made up to fill out the squares.

Eventually noticing that the clock on the screen had ticked past 11 p.m., I decided to stretch my legs. I walked out the front door and strolled along the veranda. Nothing was stirring, though I could see outlines the cattle were all at the far end of the front paddock. There was no sound of birds, just the faintest breeze moving through the leaves of the one tree in the yard.

I marched up and down dutifully. I was so bloody bored. I was thinking of my father quite a lot and remembered another of his sayings: 'It's easy to stand with the crowd. It takes courage to stand alone.' While it may not have been completely relevant, it served my purpose of thought. I spent most of my life alone, and now I couldn't stand my own company.

At about 1 a.m., I retired to the bedroom that I had so far avoided, and though I had spent far too much time asleep over the last couple of days, I almost immediately dropped off again.

Not even there in my sleep could I get the rest my mind craved. I dreamed. I tossed and turned, never quite sure that I was still asleep. Hell, the subconscious was a strange place to visit. One minute, I was reliving a game of cricket I played while at school; there was no reason to remember it. There was nothing special about that game; it just must have been the next thing on the replay list. Then I was in a dark place, and I couldn't get out. I couldn't find a door or window. I was cold, I was hot, I was running scared. What was I running from? I had no idea.

Then a shot was hit through the covers, and I was chasing it all the way to the fence. No, someone was chasing me to the fence, and I couldn't get out. I awoke, startled, and realised I had been snoring. My throat was sore, and again I thought of my father's use of pithy sayings. 'Laugh and the world laughs with you, snore and you sleep alone.'

There was nothing funny about my father, and there was nothing funny about my current situation. Perhaps that was why I was thinking about him. I knew I must ring my mother.

The next morning, I got out of bed, though I was exhausted from all the night's exploits. It was nearly the middle of the day, 11 a.m. I couldn't believe that I had slept for that long again. I resolved to ring my mother right away, knowing that my father would be at work.

The phone took a long time to be answered, and I was almost ready to put the receiver down when a curt, deep voice answered and said, 'Yes?'

It was my father, and I still almost replaced the handpiece. 'Um. Oh, hello,' I mumbled.

There was a slight pause then my father said, 'Christ!' and I heard a fumbling on the line as he passed me on to my mother.

'Where have you been?' she demanded. I felt a little confronted by her curtness. I usually expected that from my father but not from her.

'Well, actually, I've been in hospital,' I answered, knowing that this would bring her back to me from the dark side.

'What happened?' she asked and the sympathetic tone I expected in her voice was evident.

'Oh, I was hurt in a farm accident. My right hand is pretty messed up, but I will be ok,' I answered.

'You will need to come here then?' she said, and I heard my father in the background say, 'Like hell!'

I could hear my mother covering the receiver with her hand and saying, 'Oh, shut up, he's hurt,' then she returned to me, 'When will you come?'

'Thanks, but I don't need that. I am being looked after,' I answered, trying to take the pressure from my father off her shoulders.

'Oh, well, if you think that is the best.' There was a pause. I could tell she didn't know what to say, but then she continued, 'Do you need any money?'

'Like hell!' I heard from the background, and Mother was again trying to quiet him.

'No, nothing like that. I just wanted you to know I was alright. I didn't want any of this to happen, but, well, I found a body. What was I supposed to do?' My answer was rambling, but I resented my father's imputation that I was just looking for money. I had never borrowed money from either of them. How bloody dare he?

'He's just upset because the papers have been knocking the door down and ringing at all hours,' she explained.

'I'm sorry to be such a burden for him,' I said with no little amount of sarcasm in my tone.

She paused, not knowing what to say to help. I knew she would have been badgered by him for days since the use of my name in the papers, and I felt sorry for her. She had always been between us, trying to keep a peace that never really existed.

'I'm sorry, Mum. This will all go away when they catch this bastard,' I said and I could tell, even though there was no noise, that she was crying. I paused for a moment to let her get herself together then I added, 'I will call you at the end of the week?'

'Today's Saturday?' she said quietly.

'Oh, I thought it was Friday,' I said, thinking. 'That explains why Father is not at work. Well, I will ring next Saturday, ok?'

'Yes, well, look after yourself,' she said in a sad voice. I knew that she would have come to look after me if she could, but the tyrant who ruled the house was never going to cook his own meals, god forbid. I was glad of that. I hated to be 'mollycoddled'. I'd rather be alone when I'm sick.

I said, 'Love you,' and she reciprocated, and we both rang off.

Strangely, I wasn't angry with my father. This was not anything new; he had always treated me like some kind of leper – well, ever since the first investigation that brought the police to his door. I supposed that I knew where I stood with him. 'As far away as I could get.' I smiled at the thought and got back to work on the case.

Chapter 15

Now that I had Donne in my thoughts, I kept thinking things like, *What a good cover, a solicitor,* and, *He could leave work any time he liked. No one could prove that he wasn't at his office.*

This was bloody ridiculous. He couldn't be involved. Now, I needed to get to work to prove it to myself.

When I drew up a timeline, I cleared him almost immediately. He had been with me when the small girl had been killed. I felt like such a fool. How could I have suspected one of the only two people who had my back?

Right, now to the little girl's case notes. I read and reread Marsh's notes, making sure that what I was reading was what he wrote; his handwriting was so appalling.

But something wasn't right. It just was not the same M.O. It was a girl for a start, and in a well-lit, well-patronised public area. The body was just left. There was no bike involved. In my mind, it just didn't seem to be truly related to the other cases.

Well, I thought, *how many murderers of young people are there out there? No, it has to be related.*

I had read all the notes at least twice when I realised that I was not really getting anywhere. No one jumped out at me as a suspect. I couldn't see his face. In the girl's case, I couldn't even see him as involved. I kept seeing her distraught mother, and that was strange to me. I had never to my knowledge met or even seen her mother and I didn't just see strange people – that wasn't how things worked, well, not in my case, anyway.

No, there was something more to that case. I didn't believe our murderer was the guilty party.

So, where does that leave me? After hours of reading everything, I could not say anything for certain, except that is that all of them were dead.

Two of the murdered boys were from a state-run school, three were from a private school and one, the first victim, was home-schooled. No contact there then.

Two of them played tennis. The rest played other sports, from rugby league to soccer and basketball. None were in the same teams.

A couple took piano lessons from the same teacher, but the rest did not.

Each lived in different parts of the town; they didn't even go to the same church. In fact, all but one didn't go to church at all. They had not attended the same pre-schools. There was no real way they could be placed in any community group that overlapped – hell, they didn't even go to the same barber.

None of the parents worked together or were involved other than one mother and one father, who were on council committees, though not the same committee. In fact, it seemed that they were all unconnected, almost so unconnected as to believe that they had been selected because of how unconnected they were.

I was without a clue. Nothing was coming to me. The supposed 'gift' seemed to have dried up.

I turned the TV on and tried to get interested in some quiz show that had been made at least ten years earlier. I was bored again, so walking seemed to be the order of the day.

For the second time, I reached the outskirts of the farm. There were around fifty-five acres and though the soil looked good, rich and black, nothing was laid to crops. There were about twenty head of cattle, which I had seen, that is if I hadn't passed some of them more than once.

A true hobby farm. Even I knew you couldn't make a go of things as a farmer with only twenty head of cattle. We had suffered several drought years, and this one was not much better, with about half the expected rainfall to that point.

Donne would have to do a lot more if he ever wanted this place to be a going concern. He had, obviously, had professional work done on the two small dams, but this had not helped them fill. Indeed, the second was still as empty as the day it had been completed.

I just wandered aimlessly. After all, this was not my land. I found three outbuildings and two separate lots of cattle pens. There were also several machines for shearing and crutching and pizzling sheep, whatever that entailed. I had heard the term many times; my paternal grandfather owned a sheep station, which I spent some holidays visiting as a child. I had never seen it done but understood that the sheep ended up upside down, to be worked on.

On the way back to the house, I attempted to open one of the gates and forgot about my hand injury. I reached out and banged the back of the bandaged limb. It hurt like hell, and I thought what a fool I was, not just for the action but for getting the injury in the first place.

Arriving back at the house, I decided to take a bath. The hand was hurting, and I knew I was supposed to keep it as dry as possible, so I went to the trouble of wrapping it in two garbage bags that I found under the sink in the kitchen.

I lay in the beautiful hot water, refreshing it a couple of times so it retained its heat. It was a great luxury as I only had a shower in my flat. I could feel the heat on the injured hand and though it felt uncomfortable, I thought the warmth would do no harm. Naturally, though, the water found its way into the bag and before I realised it, the bandages were soaked.

Getting out of the water, I wrapped the bandaged hand in two towels and then worked to dry myself and redress, not realising how difficult that was with one hand. Eventually, I was able to put on a shirt, but I had to remove the wrapped towels to get my arm through the sleeve.

Now, I realised how drenched the bandages were. I knew I couldn't leave them like that, so I searched for a first aid kit and found enough bandages to redress the wound. I wasn't relishing the idea of removing and replacing the bandages on my own, but I knew it would need to be done so carefully, I began to unwrap the hand.

I felt faint when I saw how much damage there was. The flesh from above the wrist to the tips of my fingers was swollen to more than double their usual size. I remember thinking that I should have asked how many stitches it had taken to close me up again. Looking at the wound, I couldn't tell what constituted a stitch – all I knew was that there were a lot.

Starting to tie a bandage with one hand was very hard, and I ended up with quite a messy covering by the time I had finished. The hand throbbed, especially the knuckles and by the time I had regained my position in front of the TV, I was sorry I had bothered to take the bath in the first place.

Most of the wound had looked relatively alright, but the few stitches that were on my middle finger were very red and I immediately thought they must have been infected. I knew I couldn't leave them as they were so I decided to ring Marsh to ask if he could bring some antiseptic and fresh bandages when he came that night.

The phone took a long time to answer, and I had to try twice more before Marsh answered.

'Sorry to make you wait but I was in a meeting with the task force they have put on the case, and I had to make an excuse to get away so they wouldn't know who I was talking to. I have been ordered not to speak to you or Donne,' he said.

'Oh, sorry. What will you do then?' I asked, a bit bewildered by this ban. I had only tried to help and there were at least two bodies that may never have been found if it weren't for me.

'Fuck them. I am going to run my own race. I have asked for three day's leave to cope with family problems. I know that three days won't be enough but by the time I am back at work, they won't be thinking of me being involved,' was his well-practised answer.

'Well, sorry to put you through all of that. All I was ringing for was to see if you were coming out here tonight. I need some antiseptic powder and some more roller bandages. Could you get them?' I asked.

'I'll see what I can do. Might be a bit late before I get out of here though,' he answered, and I could hear the stress in his voice.

'That will be ok. Would you rather leave it till tomorrow then?' I asked, not wanting to be an extra burden.

'No, no. I want to get your insights into where you think things in the case are at,' he answered quickly.

'Ok, whenever you can get away,' I said, and his line went dead. He was not one for fake niceties.

I made an evening meal of toast and eggs. Though I usually liked meat and there was plenty of it in the fridge freezer, I thought I had seen enough blood for one day.

I went back to the computer and was finally interrupted by Marsh knocking at the back door. I welcomed him in, and I must admit that I felt much safer with him present.

He bore a large white paper bag, which contained six very large sausage rolls. He placed three on each of two plates and brought them to where I was sitting. I had already eaten but sausage rolls were one of my weaknesses and I tucked into them after thanking him. By the time I finished the second, I was full, and I offered the remaining one to Marsh. He declined.

Now both totally sated, we got to work on the papers.

'I don't think that the girl is our case,' I said and waited for his rebuke.

'What makes you say that?' he enquired and though this was not the response I expected, I knew I needed to make a strong case if I was to convince him.

'It feels wrong. There are so many differences, and I just can't connect our man's presence with her,' I explained. He raised an eyebrow and shrugged his shoulders.

'This is driving me around the bend. I even began to suspect Donne,' I admitted, and I felt guilty for saying it, but I had to put it right. 'I know he is not involved. He isn't the presence I felt, but every time we talk about the crimes, I feel that there is something he is not telling me, something that he knows,' I explained.

'Well, what the bloody hell do I do with that?' Marsh asked and though I knew it to be a rhetorical question, I answered.

'You need to establish an alibi for him for the time of one of the murders.'

'But he was with us when the last murder happened. That seems a pretty good alibi to me,' he answered.

'I know that, but I don't think that case is ours. I don't know why, but I don't think she was even murdered,' I explained.

'Bloody hell. You sure are worked up about all of this,' Marsh said.

He looked into my eyes as I cringed and then answered, 'Well, I don't have any reason to think this, but did you have their family car checked?'

He frowned and looked down at the floor. 'I think you're cracking, mate.'

'Yes, I may be, but I think the family car is involved, not the car they arrived in. Is there a second car? Oh god, I don't know what I'm talking about,' I babbled. I was emotional and frankly felt like a fool.

'I will have it checked out. I don't believe it for a moment. I saw the mother and how distraught she was – I can't believe that she had anything to do with all of this,' he answered.

I shrugged my shoulders. I had no other response left in me. If this was all wrong, I would never live it down.

Marsh walked into the kitchen and phoned someone. Though I couldn't hear most of the conversation, I heard his last few words.

'I know I am on leave but bloody check it anyway!'

'So, they have two cars and naturally, it was never checked – I mean the second car. There was blood on the door of the four-wheel drive that the mother took her to the shopping centre in, but we didn't check for anything else as we had a body and blood on the ground around her,' he answered, and it seemed that he was paying my sense of things due deference.

'Sorry about this. I didn't sense much other than the girl being killed and where the body was. I know something is wrong with all this, and I have been trying to make rhyme or reason of it,' I rambled.

I made tea and we sat drinking in relative silence. About half an hour passed and we both just sat quietly, though if my mind had been my voice, I would have had a sore throat. I knew Marsh was thinking as much as I was as his face gave that away.

'More tea?' I asked and he nodded. I returned to the kitchen, filled the electric jug and waited for the water to boil.

When I re-entered with the second tea pot, I saw that Marsh had disappeared, though I had not even heard him move. I waited for a while and then I heard his phone ring down the hall and realised that he must have been at the toilet.

I could not hear any of the discussion, but I could hear his muffled voice. There was quite a long pause after the conversation. It was Marsh trying to take in what he had learned.

He re-entered the room and sat down opposite me again then lifted his cup to his mouth and took a sip. 'It looks like you were right. My sergeant rang back. They went to the family's home and found blood evident in the second car. They have impounded both cars,' he explained, though he didn't look up from his cup.

'Oh, shit, I'm sorry,' I said and could feel his embarrassment. All the high-quality detective work and forensic methods and a thought from me puts it all to the sword.

'No, well, I suppose that makes Donne a suspect. Not that we have any proof or real reason to suspect him,' he answered but lifted his gaze to see what I thought of the idea. Well, it was my idea, but I didn't believe it.

'I'm sure I would have had more strong feelings about things. He can't be involved, can he?' I tried to reason, but still, I really couldn't make head nor tail of it.

'I think we had better investigate his past and see if we can find anything. I can use the computer here to get non-public information,' he answered and then got up and moved to the desk where my laptop sat next to the home computer of the Donne family.

I thought I might be able to help if I started my laptop up also and looked at one of the search engines for newspaper reports involving the family.

We sat together, and I continually looked over his shoulder, the other man's grass always being greener. Though, it was me who had the earliest results. The first story was about the graduation of Sylvia from the University of New South Wales. It didn't surprise me; she seemed very bright, but I had not thought of her as the university type.

Next, I hit a run of stories about Donne and his representation of many who had fallen foul of the law. It seemed that he had a very good rate of success; he was obviously better than his small-town status would imply.

I quickly scanned each story to see if anything had any bearing on the current case, but I could find nothing. Added to that, Donne and his wife were upstanding members of the local community, donating generously to each fundraiser going. Mrs Donne also belonged to several community charitable committees and often opened her home for fundraising, garden parties and dinner events for charity.

How the hell did I suspect this man? In local parlance, he could have been lorded, put forward for canonisation.

I had shown him respect from our first meeting; now I knew he had earned it and more.

I started feeling guilty. This was ridiculous. What a hide I had to be, looking through his metaphorical closet for skeletons.

'I'm not finding anything bad,' I told Marsh. I got up and went to the toilet, all the while believing that I was biting the hand that was feeding me. On my return, Marsh was still staring at the screen, his face lit by the light it emitted. The room was very dark, so I turned on a light.

'The only blot on this copybook seems to be the brother,' Marsh said, pointing to the screen, then he added, 'Donne has represented his brother in several legal cases, mostly due to damages sought by local residents with some sort of civil grievance, and each time they have been settled out of court.'

I sat back down and read some of the headlines: damages for a fence, non-payment of accounts, damages for an injured cat. Prosecution for lighting a fire in his own backyard, which got away and seemingly damaged a boundary-paling fence. Several cases of drunken disorderly conduct, and perhaps most telling, one case of driving under the influence of alcohol.

This didn't paint Adam Donne as a real criminal but did show him to be a liability, trouble that Donne could have done without.

'Of course, that doesn't prove anything bad about Donne himself,' I said. I got up and walked over to my usual sitting area on the couch. I had had enough of this; I could see it was a waste of time, and I wanted it all to go away. I wanted to stop thinking about Donne and his brother and the rest of the case.

I sat for perhaps half an hour and started to drop off to sleep. Every now and then I stirred as Marsh made an exclamation of some small interest in what he was reading. I couldn't have cared less, to be honest, and wished Marsh was going home.

Finally, he re-engaged with me, saying, 'Come and have a look at this.' I wasn't that interested but I felt committed to his efforts; at least enough to get me off the lounge.

I sat back down next to him and read, 'Death, Albert Donne. Today, the coroner announced that the hanging death of local farmer Albert Donne had been suffered at his own hand and that no further legal action need be taken. Donne was discovered by his two grandsons on Sunday morning in a shed on the family farm. The arrangements for the funeral of the late gentleman were in the hands of Undertaker J. & B. Haddon.'

'So, not the greatest start to life,' Marsh commented.

'It doesn't help us in any way though,' I answered.

'No, it is a textbook case of one of the two young people being affected in different ways after a traumatic experience as young people. One goes on to be a pillar of the community and the other, a tortured soul,' he mused in what I thought of as backyard psychology. Marsh had no more knowledge than I did when it came to psychologists and being analysed.

'There seems to be nothing bad to be said about Donne. Looks like your radar is off on this one,' Marsh said and stood and turned the screen off. 'More tea?' he asked and headed toward the kitchen.

'No, not for me. I think I'll go to bed. The hand is giving me a bit of pain so I may take a couple of pills,' I answered and headed for the bedroom.

'See you in the morning then,' he concluded, and I heard him filling the kettle as I headed to bed.

I slept. I'm not sure if it was the safety I felt because of Marsh's presence or if I had just had enough of the whole thing, but I slept.

I didn't dream, which was such a godsend for me. I hardly ever got real sleep, unfettered sleep.

When I finally rose, I felt so much better, though I was a bit embarrassed that it was nearly 10 a.m.

I found Marsh in front of the computer once more and the coffee table, which had been in the middle of the room, had moved. The centre of the floor had become a working case file. At the top, as I looked at it, there were the photos of the victims, and I have to say I almost burst into tears.

These were not the pictures of the bodies or remains; these were pictures of the six boys in the flush of youth. A couple of the shots were school photos, and I felt hollow as I looked at them. What a terrible thing this was. How sad, how cruel.

I halted in my progress, and Marsh looked up. 'You look a bit better.'

'Yes, no dreams last night,' I answered and then seeing how much work he had achieved, I added, 'You must have been at this all night?'

'No, a lot of it was already prepared for my case board at work,' he answered.

'What have you found, anything?' I asked.

He pondered for a minute then said quietly, 'Not much other than his desire to kill young boys.' He shook his head and then asked calmly, 'What about you?'

I shook my head to indicate the negative. He looked frustrated as he stared down at the evidence.

I got down on my knees and began to examine each face, lifting each picture. I could now not see anything other than blood and after the third photo, I wanted to stop, but I felt I owed it to Marsh to get it done.

'I don't see Donne in any of this, but I have the sense that these are not the only six,' I said, and I could see his face change. His frown deepened and he lifted his head, looking past me as if trying to understand.

He was becoming bitter at what he saw as his failure, a failure that he believed he owned.

'What do you see?' he asked without turning his head toward me directly. He stared at the faces, those young innocent faces.

'I see two more boys, but not here. Somewhere different, somewhere distant,' I recounted what it was I was seeing, and I knew that he believed me as his head gave a little nod.

'Is there anything more?' he asked.

'Well, yes. I am seeing them as a newspaper report,' I explained.

'Where does the paper come from? Can you tell?' he asked, finally facing me, his eyes set beseechingly.

'Ah, no, no, not the paper, but a name keeps coming to me. Cho,' I answered, closing my eyes as if that was going to help me see better. It never did.

'How do you spell the name? Is it a first name or a surname?' he pushed.

'C-H-O, and I don't know if it is a first or last name,' I answered, trying to see more. I strained, but instead of the name becoming clearer, it faded completely from my mind.

'I don't know. I think that is a Chinese name, but I think it may be Korean as well,' he mused out loud, not really talking to me. Getting up from where he had been kneeling, he walked over to the computers and started typing. I moved and sat next to him.

He had written 'Cho' and 'murder victim Australia'. The computer was slowly considering the request. After a few seconds, the words 'nothing found under Cho – murder victim Australia' came on the screen.

He shrugged his shoulders and slowly deleted the word 'Australia'.

The case of a murdered woman came up, but nothing seemed relevant as the woman had been murdered in the USA years earlier.

He read, as if I couldn't, out loud then he re-entered the word 'Cho' and added 'accidental death'. 14,500,000 results came up almost immediately. We started to scroll through the headings but nothing relevant came up.

'What if you add "child"?' I suggested.

He did the typing, and the numbers reduced to around five thousand hits.

Before I could suggest another move, he re-typed 'Australia'. The five thousand reduced to the 'nothing found under Cho – accidental death – Australia'.

'Well, that doesn't help much, five thousand and none in Australia,' he said, looking disconsolate.

'I suppose we will need to scan a few pages and see if anything fits?' I queried. I had a feeling he was not going to be that keen on the idea, and he soon put my thoughts into action as he got up and walked back to the evidence on the ground.

'Wild goose chase,' he exclaimed and went back to reading notes of evidence.

'I might keep looking. I know the name is right,' I said, and he grunted, shrugging his shoulders.

For the next few hours, I read the headings that had come up. There were five thousand headings and none really fitted, so I went back to the couch and tried to clear my mind. I sat for a while, just staring into nowhere, nothing, and nothing was what I got.

'I think I might go for a walk. Sometimes that makes me think,' I said and got up and exited via the back door. I left Marsh sitting on the floor, reading his own reports. He said nothing.

I wandered in a slightly different way to the farthest corner of the property. This time, I passed the sheds and the first of the property's three dams. These dams were of regular oval shape, around thirty yards across at the widest point and were filled with very dirty-looking water.

When I got to my destination, I stood for some time with my injured arm resting on the round corner post. Again, I looked out into nothingness. This was not helping. I needed some kind of inspiration, a flash of light or someone knocking on the metaphorical door. But nothing like that came and I began to despair. This misery I felt was all-consuming. Sometimes, I'm sure it tipped me over the edge, and I hated where that took me.

On the walk back, I started to think about goldmining. I don't know why but there it was, people all along a riverbank panning for their future. I tried to put it out of my mind but still, I could see the scene. There were perhaps twenty people on the water's edge, and all were busily employed. It was strange. It seemed to be a still scene – that is to say, though I could see what they were doing, they weren't moving. Was this a photograph or was it a painting? I stood still again, closed my eyes and again tried to make sense of what I was seeing. Then it hit me: they were all searching, searching along the river.

I upped my pace to a jog. I needed to get back to Marsh and tell him what I was seeing. Surely this must be where one of the missing boys' remains might be found.

I burst in the back door and startled Marsh, who looked like he hadn't moved from the spot on the carpet since I had left over two hours ago.

'What the hell are you so worked up about?' he said when he saw that it was me.

'I've seen something. I've seen where another body might be found,' I blurted, panting.

'Well, out with it,' he ordered.

'It's a small creek and there are a lot of people panning for gold,' I continued, still trying to catch my breath. *I have to do something about my fitness,* I thought as Marsh pondered what I had said and then took up one of the maps he had placed on the ground.

He pawed over the paper and then said, 'About the only creek they found any gold in is out of town at "Chinaman's Flat",' he retorted, his eyebrows raised to show his interest.

'Yes, that must be it, Chinaman's Flat. Cho, that must be it. We need to go there now!' I exclaimed with obvious excitement in my voice. I was excited, yes, but not in a good way. I dreaded what we might find when we got to the creek.

It took only half an hour to arrive at the area where there had once been a tent settlement of both Chinese and British prospectors. The settlement reached back in time to the 1890s when a very short-lived gold rush saw many hundreds come to make their fortune. Short-lived as there turned out to be no gold there at all. The riverbanks had been seeded by the farmer who owned the land on both sides of around two miles of the so-called bridge, if it had ever been a bridge, and he sold the land in small parcels, which saw him make a small fortune. His disappearance when the irate miners came calling was not really a great surprise.

Marsh parked close to the cement dip that now served as a crossing. The river seldom flooded and there was very little water, though it did always flow. We walked back to the dip, and I walked down into the lowest point. I felt long-lost memories of deaths that occurred in the tent city when starvation and an outbreak of cholera took many who had no means of being treated, having spent all of their earthly goods and cash to buy their worthless patch of mud.

'Well?' Marsh asked expectantly.

'This is a very sad place. There are bodies around us, but not the ones we are looking for,' I answered.

'What the hell does that mean?' he asked, firing me a contemptuous look.

'There are dead miners here, but none of our boys. Perhaps we should walk down the riverbank. They may not be close to the road?' I suggested, and we walked, downstream first and then, once I found nothing, we crossed and walked back up to the Ford.

'Nothing at all,' I answered the unasked question. It didn't take a medium to know what was coming from Marsh.

'Another bloody wild goose chase,' he said, but sounded more disappointed than accusatory.

'I think so, but we should go upstream to check,' I answered and began to climb through the barbed wire on the edge of the stream's bank.

We walked for nearly an hour, first in line with the creek and then, on finding some ruins of what looked like an old farmstead, we moved inland. This had obviously been a large building. There were some leftover brick piers that covered an area of at least ten yards in width and nearly twenty yards in length.

Standing where a front veranda might have existed, I got a strange sense of foreboding, and I knew, 'There are two bodies to the back,' I said and pointed.

Marsh, to his credit, took my direction, though I stayed exactly where I was. He pottered around for a few minutes and then shouted, 'There are two graves. It's hard to read the inscriptions but the surname is Hardy.'

'A mother and daughter, I think,' I answered.

'Yes, that seems to be right,' he concluded.

'Is there any reason for us to keep looking?' he said after another few minutes.

I shook my head. 'No, I don't think so,' I answered honestly. I had no feeling as to why I was drawn to this place, and somehow, I didn't want to leave, but this was not helping in the grand scheme of things. I had failed Marsh, and though I knew he was disappointed, he didn't express the same.

As we both got back into the car after what must have been nearly three hours, I had a feeling, the feeling of leaving something, perhaps someone, behind. I didn't like the feeling and had to get back out of the car to be sick. I stood, doubled over in convulsions for a minute or two, and then wiped my mouth with my handkerchief and got back in the front seat.

'What's that all about?' Marsh queried; his face contorted in a questioning way.

'I think there was a mass killing here. I can feel men, women and children, at least ten, maybe more,' I answered and signalled for him to leave. I was feeling as though I may be sick again. Marsh drove off and within a few seconds, I felt alright, normal again.

'I'll look up the records and see if anything did happen out at that farm,' Marsh reassured me. Not that I needed any reassurance from him.

Later, I looked to the internet to find that a family – that of Dawn and Fred Hardy, their six children and three farm hands – had been found in their ransacked home, dead. There had been no apparent cause of death, but poisoning was suspected. The means for identifying such a cause was lost in the time from the events and the discovery of the bodies, almost two weeks after their demise.

It was rumoured that Fred had at last found the gold reef he had been seeking, but there was no proof of this and no real gold was ever found in the area. As this all happened in the early part of 1857, it was obvious that it had nothing to do with the current cases well over one hundred and fifty years later.

Marsh had dropped me back to the Donne farm with the excuse that he needed some further papers from his office. We both knew he just needed to be away from me, away from my mad mind.

After finding the Hardy case on the computer, I lost interest in the day's efforts, and though it was only 4 p.m., I lay on the lounge and slept. There was no intent in my sleeping; I just slept and there were no dreams, an almost non-existent occurrence for me. When I woke, it was very dark and I couldn't for a moment gain my bearings. I sat up and allowed myself to acclimatise to the diminished light. Things began to come into view in what seemed to have been a completely black room. I remembered where I was.

My father came to mind. Why would I think of him?

Then I remembered why I was, where I was. It was not a pleasant memory. I gave myself the task of understanding why people killed, why this man killed. I wondered whether or not I had the information already, but the well-rounded education

I had, had, like most, only touched on the great minds, the Pavlov's dog or Schrodinger's cat, in one-line explanations of their theories, not to mention Nietzsche or that famous 'Sicko' Sigmund Freud and his psychosexual claptrap.

Yes, I knew all about these people from one-liners, and this was another point that seemed to drive my father mad: I wasn't very widely read. If I didn't become interested in something from the brochure, so to speak, I just dismissed it outright.

Father would rant and rave about such things, and that set my mind to not find out more. It seems to me that my early life at home was normal; Father was a person I saw mostly at weekends when he was getting ready to leave the family at home while he went galivanting around the countryside at some sporting event or another.

All this was running through my head as I sat down at the computer to find out, 'Why men kill'. I looked at many articles, briefly, but they all seemed to want to delve into the actual crime, the perpetrator, the victim and the gory pictures that heralded each terrible serial killer and their own picture when they had been apprehended.

Another memory of Father came to me, that of the day when I met John Cullen for the first time. John was around a year younger than me, and we met at Sunday school. The first thing I thought was that he was my brother. I couldn't wait to tell my father and mother that I had met my brother when they picked me up outside the church hall.

'I met John today. He is my brother,' my proud six-year-old self announced for all to hear.

'Bloody nonsense!' Father said, grabbing my hand and hauling me away. He blushed and I thought he was going to explode as he stormed down the street, leaving my mother and the gawking parishioners in his wake. 'You can't bloody say things like that.' His eyes were almost popping out of their sockets.

'But it is true, isn't it?' I asked innocently, still being almost dragged off my feet as Mother struggled to catch up.

'Of course it's not bloody true, you idiot!' he roared at me, but it was true, and I knew that he knew that I knew it was true.

Once my mother caught up to us, I could see that she was crying. That was certainly not what I had expected. I was too young to understand what this all meant, that my father had had an affair with John's mother. He was almost choking on his infidelity.

So, it was all my fault. I had driven a wedge between them. Yes, now Mother knew and that was something I always regretted. Mother, at first, threatened to leave him in the brawl that inevitably occurred when we arrived home. Father stormed out, saying, 'Bloody boy!' and we didn't see him again that day.

The next day, Father arrived home in a completely dishevelled state and though he didn't come near me, the large bunch of flowers he carried for Mother could not hide the stench of stale alcohol. So, from that day on, I was the cause of all of his problems. He not only blamed me, but he also hated me, and he didn't hide it for a moment.

I understand now why. He had realised that I was like my 'mad grandmother', my mother's mother, the one with the madness that saw him virtually ban her from our house. I can count on one hand the times my grandmother had visited, and it was usually after a funeral or some sort of perceived family difficulty.

My grandmother, whom I always knew as Nanna, was the most delightful person. My mother used to take me to see her as often as was possible to get away from Father, and I loved those times. She – Nanna – knew what I was going through and how to help me understand the things I saw and thought, the things that I knew to be real, even if my father was not a believer, and he certainly wasn't.

My grandmother used to call it 'the knowing' she encouraged me to see. My mother was a skipped generation; she saw nothing and had no feelings of that 'other'. That is not to say that Mother was not able to appreciate her mother's talents. She believed in her mother, totally, there was no doubt of that, but she wanted me to know when and how to use these 'talents', not to blurt everything out to anyone within earshot.

That was obviously not something that I was good at as a child, and to be honest, I am still often a victim of my own big mouth.

What most people don't understand is that often these things come to one like an open message, something conversational, if that makes it easier to understand. It certainly didn't make me easier to understand. I was brash and always wanted to say what I knew to be true. This infuriated my father, most particularly when he would berate my mother for voting for another party than the one he supported. I was never sure if she did it as a last display of her status as an independent woman.

So, I inserted myself into the discussion at the age of nine or ten by telling him that his wonderful party were going to suffer one of the largest defeats in Australian history.

When this proved to be true, it simply gave him another reason to despise me and though Mother did smile at the result, she also set up the second bedroom as her own and they never slept in the same room again, save in front of the TV in the lounge room.

It seemed strange that my mind would wander to these things when I was really trying to find out why men killed. I continued to go through the fifty thousand-odd sites that came up on the search engine answering the question, 'Why do men kill?'

The whole exercise was entirely unedifying and certainly did not enlighten me as to the reasons. It appears there was no consensus. Some gave long, rambling supposedly factual reasons about the hunter and the hunted, in what seemed to be some biblical sense, and others noted anecdotal evidence, some with backing and some which seemed to be, to me at least, flights of fancy. If all these learned scholars couldn't come up with a reason, why would I think I would understand? That I would immediately have the answer?

Well, I didn't have the answer, and I don't think I even came close. It seemed from what I read that there were different reasons in the minds of different murderers and there were triggers to their actions but similarities, though they existed, were never the whole story. In short, why they took the step over the line of the expected norms.

I had spent nearly three hours and was exactly where I had started: clueless.

As was often the case since staying at the Donne homestead, I needed to be out of the building. It was a fine house, don't get me wrong, but it was not my house and not my space in the world.

Leaving the kitchen door, I began to walk and found myself near the front gates to the property. This was the first time I had walked in this direction, though I had almost circumnavigated the property on several occasions. I had usually left the house and taken a route to either the east or west and followed the fence line all the way around until I neared the house. This cut off the front two paddocks, perhaps representing an acre each on either side of the entrance road.

I walked first to the left side of the road, then to the nearest fence, then clockwise to the front gate and then crossed the road and headed for the other outer fence. About halfway along the second paddock, there was a small, wooded area, which would have measured less than fifty by about thirty-five yards. I wondered why that was the only area where the trees, non-descript eucalypts, were not disturbed, indeed removed altogether like most of the ploughed land on the farm.

I determined to go through the trees, suspecting that there may have been a water source, a small swamp or some other reason for it to be still pristine. What I didn't expect to find was a small clearing at the centre that had several small graves, which were marked with crosses, each roughly hewn from sticks or waste timber from the farm.

There were around eight crosses and at least that many mounds, but it seemed to me that these were not human burials; the mounds were far too small. The name 'Alf' roughly carved on one of the crosses didn't really give me any more information as to its incumbent. Like the others, it was not that of a human. If there had been names on any of the other monuments, I certainly couldn't make them out. Perhaps they were lost to time.

I stood in front of 'Alf' for a short time. There was no feeling of fear for me in the area, but there was a sense of foreboding. I spent a few minutes reading the names I could make out; there were only three. Alf, Adam and Anna. *Strange*, I thought, *that they should all begin with A.*

This was quite a beautiful place, but I didn't find solace here. I felt uncomfortable so I wandered off toward the house.

I had no real reason to think that there was any problem with the little animal cemetery, and yet, I felt uneasy while there, and had the feeling that I should keep looking over my shoulder as I walked away. If something terrible had happened there, it was not something I could read, could understand. Still, I settled myself by thinking I would never go there again.

Chapter 16

I didn't see Marsh again until the next morning, when I smelt toast burning and went to the kitchen to investigate.

'Good morning. Sorry if I woke you,' he said, looking up from the task at hand, buttering the blackened bread.

'No, no problem. I don't usually sleep this late.' It was nearly ten o'clock. 'I was up late though, trying to understand what this is all about,' I answered.

'That is usually the problem. If you aren't a serial killer, you can't really think like a serial killer,' he answered, continuing to watch me as I sat down at the other side of the table. I nodded. There seemed no reason to say anything; I had come to the same conclusion.

'Where did you get to last night?' I asked.

Turning away to answer the hissing kettle, he said, 'I went to the office. I am on leave, but there were none of the homicide squad at the station, so I was able to use my computer. Only the overnight desk sergeant was there, and I told him I just wanted to download some stuff from my computer. He couldn't have cared less.' I nodded and he continued, 'You know, I thought of looking up the dates of the disappearances and comparing them to Donne's court appearances. You had me going there.'

'Find anything?' I asked perhaps a little too eagerly.

'Well, not at first. The first three, he was not in court, but he was on the day of the fourth disappearance. That day, though, he could have had time as the morning session of court was very brief, and the boy didn't disappear until after school. I got myself all worked up and started to think you may be right, but, on the next occasion, I found that he was on holidays and when I checked, Donne, his wife and his daughter were on a trip to New Zealand. I even checked this computer,' he said, gesturing to the home desktop, 'and there were photos of Queenstown taken by the three of them. He was there, so we can write him off the list of suspects.'

I let out a big sigh of relief. 'Thank heavens for that,' I said quietly, then I thought, *Why the hell did I think he was involved then?*

I buried the thought. I didn't want to concentrate on things that were not relevant and to be honest, I usually wasn't that far off the mark. Perhaps this was all getting to me.

Marsh had made tea, and I moved to pick the cup up with my right hand, forgetting the damage and the bandages. Naturally, the cup went tumbling across the table and made a hell of a mess.

'Bloody hell!' I exclaimed and jumped up to get a cloth.

'Hand still worrying you?' Marsh asked. Getting to the sink first, he threw me a tea cloth.

'Well, yes, it is very hard to sleep, that's when it throbs,' I answered truthfully.

'Do you need to see the doctor again?' he asked, sounding somewhat concerned.

'It probably needs to be cleaned and redressed,' I answered, knowing that he was loath to get a doctor out or to take me into town.

'What about Donne's daughter? She knows you are here, and I'm sure would do a better job than me,' he asked and gave me a knowing look.

'Well, I don't want to be more of a burden to them,' I answered.

'Oh, I'm sure *she* wouldn't see it as a burden,' he answered, smiling.

'Ok, if you think it best,' I conceded, thinking that it would be nice to see Sylvia.

He nodded and smiled again. I looked away, trying not to engage the inference he was making.

'I'll give her a ring,' he said and walked over to the phone. I decided to take the chance to have a shower. I went to the bathroom and reused the garbage bag and duct-tape to cover the bandages and then thought better of the shower and ran a bath.

I soaked for more than a half hour. By the time I got my clothes on, brushed my teeth and hair, and re-entered the kitchen area, Marsh was gone. He had left me a note saying that he needed to do some things in town and that Miss Donne would be out in the next hour or so.

I waited around, hoping I could hide my delight at seeing her, but when she came in through the front door, it was obvious that I couldn't. She carried a wicker basket, which contained some food and several new bandages.

'Morning,' she said with an obvious blush in her cheeks.

'Morning. Thanks for doing this,' I babbled. God, I was hopeless at this kind of thing.

'I made a steak and kidney pie and some apple strudel,' she said, unpacking at the kitchen bench.

'That sounds wonderful,' I said. I was not about to tell her that I loathed kidney.

She extracted the bandages and moved to where I was now sitting at the table. Once seated, she moved to unwrap a pack of gauze swabs and then started to unbandage my hand.

When she eventually got to the wound, she blew out through her mouth in a shocked way. 'Wow, you really did a job on it,' she commented and then, after getting a small bowl of water and adding some disinfectant, she began to gently sponge the dry blood and detritus that always seems to accumulate under any bandage.

'Oh, that looks sore and a bit infected,' she said as she uncovered the flesh nearest the wounds.

'Well, actually, I have little pain yet,' I answered and seeing the look on her face, I added reassuringly, 'No, really.' She still looked sceptically as she continued the job.

'I have had some pain at night, and that makes it a bit hard to sleep,' I admitted.

'That can't be good, and I think you need a doctor to look at this,' she said, pointing at the sorest part where the little finger had met the hand. It was very red.

'I don't have a doctor at hand. No pun intended,' I joked, and she shook her head in a disapproving way.

'I will talk to Marsh and set it up. If it gets too bad, you could lose another finger or worse,' she warned, and I nodded a tacit acceptance. She was in charge, and I liked it.

Not much else was said but she looked up into my eyes to make sure she wasn't hurting me as she washed each new part. God, she was beautiful, and she was caring for me.

When all of the cleaning of my wounds was completed, she began to bandage the hand again and it was evident that she knew what she was doing, for not only was the bandage evenly distributed and just overlapping the right amount, but it was also neat. She finished covering the small clip with a piece of tape to ensure it would not come off accidentally.

'There you go,' she said confidently.

'Thanks. You really know your way around a bandage,' I answered.

'Yes, Father has a friend who is a community nurse, and while at school I did work experience with her. Father thought it would be useful,' she explained.

'You seem to be good at everything,' I said and immediately thought how clumsy I sounded. We both blushed. I was so bad at this kind of small talk.

She placed the old bandages and the wrappings of the new one into a satchel, and got up to leave. I stood and then said, 'Do you really have to go? It is quite boring here.' I had not meant to sound so pathetic, but it did the trick, as she walked into the living area and sat down in her father's large recliner. I followed obediently and sat on the couch.

'Have you had any luck with the case?' she started the conversation again. I would have been just as happy to sit there and absorb her beauty.

'No, I have nothing. I have been trying to understand the motive, but it seems that no explanation fits the case,' I said in the rambling way I often spoke when in the presence of someone important or a member of the class just out of reach – and surely, she was out of reach. What could I offer her that she didn't already have in spades?

'Not everything has an explanation,' she said and seeing the look on my face, she added, 'That's what I think anyway.'

I nodded as if to say that I understood, ':Really that was the thing I was wrestling with; surely there must be a reason, not just a trigger.'

'What do you mean?' she asked, her eyebrows raised quizzically.

'I don't know exactly. You know, someone out there is not ordinary, not normal.'

'Someone who could murder young children, you mean?' she asked, sounding a little put out.

'No, not that. This bastard must fit into society, but, by definition, a serial killer must have something strange about them.' I couldn't be clearer as I didn't know what I was asking her, not really.

'So, people who do strange things?' she asked, looking introspectively for an answer to please me.

'Yes, or someone who has lost a child, or something.'

'Well, there is old Mary McMurtry. She is quite mad and often throws bricks at other people's cars if they are parked in front of her house,' she replied.

'No, it won't be a woman, and they won't be as visible as that or the police would have thought of them first,' I explained.

'Oh, of course. Well, Jed Jackson is... is a bit of a hermit. He hardly ever comes out of his home, but he doesn't have a car, I don't think.' She struggled with her thoughts for a few more minutes then added, 'The Bowens are a pretty strange bunch. They live just out of town, on the highway. They don't let their kids go to school, they home school and though they do have vehicles, when they come into town, they always drive a horse and cart. They seem nice, though.'

'Which way on the highway?' I asked.

'Oh, I suppose it would be to the north,' she answered, sounding unsure of north and south and positioning her hands as she was explaining it to herself.

I took a pen and wrote their names down. I didn't think this would be done by a family – surely it was some loner. Surely a serial killer wouldn't fit in with a family. Then my second thought was that, indeed, they often did fit in with other family members. Perhaps I had gleaned something from all the websites I had viewed.

'Anyone else?' I asked, hoping that she would say a name, and everything would just fall into place.

She put her hand up to her forehead and ran it down to her chin, thinking.

'There is a man who works at the hardware store, um, Jenkins. I don't think I've ever heard his first name,' she answered and resumed the search for the name as though she should know it well.

'And why is he different?' I asked, wanting more information than she could probably give.

'He's a bit of a loner and he never looks at you if you ask him a question. They say he has autism or something. I don't know – they call it something else,' she explained, tending to lift her eyes as though that helped her to remember things.

'Oh, Asperger's syndrome or something like that?' I asked, unsure of what I was saying. I was very unsure what Asperger's was. I had met people with autism but not, as far as I knew, with Asperger's.

Sylvia nodded in an uncertain way and said, 'Maybe, I'm not sure.'

'Well, that's a start. I suppose the police will have looked at all of these types of people, but I may look in a different way,' I said.

'I understand. Well, I suppose I don't, really. How does that all work?' she answered and asked at the same time.

'Usually, it is just a feeling of dread, of fear, but during this case, I have been seeing bodies and places where there are bodies,' I explained.

'Oh, how awful,' she said in a sympathetic but questioning tone.

'Yes, some people think I can control it. Some even think it might be fun to have "powers", so to speak. Well, I'm here to tell you that it isn't fun, and they don't feel like special powers. Some people look at you as though they would like to burn you at the stake or something,' I answered but I could see that she didn't really understand. 'Don't be shocked. I don't understand it myself. My grandmother had the same gift – if that is what one could call it – and she understood the scorn it brings. People who you haven't even met just hate you, fear you,' I explained, trying not to sound too pathetic.

'Oh, how awful,' she said again and then added, 'I don't fear you.'

I was delighted to hear it but could think of nothing more to tell her that wouldn't scare her off, so I kept my mouth shut.

Deciding she would make tea, Sylvia walked back to the kettle and after a few minutes, we sat drinking it, with homemade biscuits, on the lounge.

I usually didn't have trouble thinking of things to talk about, but with Sylvia, I felt like a schoolboy talking to the first girl I had ever met.

Eventually, she broke the silence, asking, 'Was your grandmother involved in solving crimes too?'

'A couple of times,' I answered shortly, wishing to change the subject but still finding nothing sensible to say.

'Tell me about them?' she almost begged.

'Oh, well, I don't really know much about them as my father tried to keep away from her. He hated the fact that I saw things and blamed her,' I explained but I could see that she wasn't going to be placated that easily. 'The first case was something to do with a friend of hers; I think her husband killed her, but that was all hush-hush. We weren't even supposed to ask about it. The second involved some famous artist who came to Australia to paint. It seems he was involved in some terrible Nazi things during and after the war. My grandmother went to one of his exhibitions and confronted him on the spot. My mother was with her, and she was too embarrassed to talk about it.'

I told the story because I felt I had to. She hung on every word.

'Grandmother even knew his name and title in the SS. She blurted it out in front of everyone. The man left and quickly left Australia, running scared knowing that he had been found out. He was found in his home in South Africa, just a couple of weeks later, shot dead. There were never any suspects or even an explanation given in the press, but it was rumoured that he had been taken out by a Jewish hit squad,' I explained and seeing that she was still captivated, I continued, 'Most people blamed my grandmother for his death and he was never outed for who he was, but the world knew, and he was dealt with.'

'Wow, she was a hero,' Sylvia said, looking into my eyes for confirmation.

'Yes, I think so too, but people like my father thought that this hocus pocus or witchcraft, which he used to call it, was shameful and to be feared, and certainly to be kept away from me.'

'That's terrible,' she said, deeply frowning, looking almost ready to scold someone.

'Yes, I suppose it is. My mother was reduced to seeing her mother when Father was at work or away on work. I knew when, sometimes on a Friday, I got up to find my good clothes set out for me to wear instead of my school uniform, that we were off on a secret visit to see Nanna,' I concluded, but again, she wasn't going to let it go so I felt that I had to go on.

'My father caught us once when he had gone to meet someone in the city, and we practically ran into him. Mother had a feeble excuse prepared, but he didn't buy it for a moment. It was so embarrassing, him standing out in public, roaring and shouting at Mother and her trying to walk away. In the end, he went too far and called Nanna a rude name and Mother turned and slapped his face. He was surprised and took a step back, looking like he wanted to reciprocate, but he didn't, which was lucky as a policeman who had heard the din appeared and asked my mother if she needed any help.

'Mother looked terribly set upon, and I'm sure the policeman would have carted Father off to gaol if she hadn't told him, "It's alright, Officer. He is my husband."

"That doesn't matter. I could still arrest him for disturbing the peace if you need me to?" He formed this sentence as an offer to Mother and a threat as he glared at my father. I must admit that I was pleased, but their relationship never came back to normal. They existed in the same world, and Mother played the good wife and still does. I wish I had been able to take her with me when I eventually left home, but it was as though she had made a life commitment, and she has never broken it.' I suddenly realised I was banging on about my private life and I felt embarrassed, so embarrassed that I could not look up for a few moments.

She seemed to be good at everything, and was understanding and compassionate.

Suddenly, Sylvia took my good hand. That was certainly not what I expected, but it wasn't a bad thing. It gave me the strength to look up. Our eyes met, and I knew that I was smitten. I also knew that she wasn't looking at me like other people usually did.

With timing I couldn't believe, the back door opened, and Marsh blustered in. Realising that we were on the couch holding hands, he began to back out again, saying, 'Oh, sorry.'

This made the happening very uncomfortable and we separated, with me telling him to 'come back'.

'Yes, I have to go,' Sylvia said, standing. She looked a little flushed but kept her composure. 'Mother will be waiting. She wasn't that delighted that I was coming in the first place.'

I didn't want her to go. I wanted that moment to last, and to hell with her mother, but I knew that it was the right thing for her to do, obeying the tyrant.

Marsh came back in the door and Sylvia left through the main entrance. 'Shit, sorry,' Marsh said with a slight knowing grin.

'It was nothing. She was just bandaging my hand,' I explained, perhaps a little too eagerly.

He continued to smile, and I thought to change the subject.

'What new information do you have about the case?' I asked, still feeling a little embarrassed.

'I went to check Donne's passport information. It seems that he and Mrs Donne and Sylvia *were* all over in New Zealand when the first disappearance occurred.' He paused then added, 'So Donne is not our man.'

'Thank heavens for that,' I blurted. This was all too hard.

'You like her that much?' Marsh questioned.

'That's not what I meant, but yes, I, um, do.' I bumbled my way through the sentence and felt even more uncomfortable than a juvenile me with my first crush.

Finally, he must have sensed my discomfort and changed the subject. 'What have *you* been doing?' he asked, looking at the pile of papers I had printed.

'I have been trying to understand what this animal is all about, and to be honest, no one seems to have any answers. There is a lot of psychobabble, which seems to chase its own tail. It seems to me that every case is different and that all seem to have triggers but beyond that, I can't work it out,' I explained.

'Oh, madness that way lies. I don't think you can hope to understand any one of them. It is not possible unless you have the same madness,' he both schooled and warned me. 'If you go down that path, you won't be much use to me. I need you with your eye on the ball.'

I nodded. I wasn't sure he was right, but he had been doing this for lots of years and I knew he had more of a chance of grasping any meaning out of the events. I needed to drop it and get on with trying to see something about the actual events, not some esoteric jargon proffered by someone whom I didn't really believe in at all. I steeled myself and resolved to leave the whys to someone much cleverer than I.

'So why do you think you suspected Donne?' Marsh asked, thinking that he may trigger something that he may be able to use.

'I have no idea. I just thought he was not telling me everything, but I often get that feeling with people,' I tried to explain.

'Any other thoughts on our perp?' he asked, watching me closely as the well-trained interrogator that he obviously was.

'It is all so dark. Sometimes I must just stop,' I admitted, looking down to break eye-contact.

'Well, if you like, you could do some of the legwork – that is, on the computer. Things I may or may not need to know but just don't have the time to do,' he suggested, and I was sure that he was just trying to placate me.

'Like what?' I asked.

'Well, you could put every name we know to be involved in some way into the computer and see if they are involved in any way. You know that there is some of that sort of thing in the file already, but I didn't have the manpower to keep looking at that when there was a need to have every man I had out in the field,' he explained and after making sure I looked as though I knew what he was talking about, he continued, 'Anything. Two of the parents going to the same school when they were kids, their children in the same sporting teams and any adult you can find who was involved with the victims. Teachers, coaches – you know, all that kind of thing.'

I nodded. I thought I would be wasting my time, I had looked at this before, but I had plenty of time to waste.

'What are you doing?' I asked in a non-accusatory voice. He still thought I was being smart though and became a little defensive.

'I won't be wasting my *leave* from work. I am going to follow the investigation team to see if they have anything we don't.'

I could tell that he was put out, as if I were rubbing it in that he had been taken off the case. 'I wasn't being a smartarse. I am just finding it frustrating that I can't pick anything else up,' I said, trying to reassure him that there was no malice intended.

He nodded. 'I know, but I know I shouldn't have been sidelined by these bastards from Sydney. They think they know everything. They are crossing all the Ts and dotting all the Is and wasting bloody time on irrelevant nonsense while the killer is out there waiting for the next opportunity to arise.' He spoke forcefully and from the heart, and I understood his frustration.

'I'll get onto the computer now,' I assured him. I got up and put my hand out and we shook. 'Let's do everything we can to catch this animal.' He nodded agreement.

Marsh made tea as I fired up the desktop computer and brought me a cup. Looking over my shoulder, he said, 'If you need clearance to get into anything, use my name, and here is my service number.' He wrote the number down on a piece of typing paper and when he left, I ripped it down to a size that would fit into my wallet. I placed it there with no other information on it; I didn't want anyone to know that I had been given a serving officer's personal information.

I immediately began looking up local clubs and their membership. Mostly they didn't have lists of members that one could access easily, but there was plenty of information one could glean if the time was spent reading the publicity pages, some of which were republished in the group's own publicity page.

Then there were the published notes of the council, where, as I mentioned earlier, two of the parents were elected Aldermen. From what I could see, there were very few contentious points, though, of course, there are always things to argue about in committee.

The two men in question were on opposite sides of the divide. Josh Marshal was the deputy mayor and a Liberal, and Peter Walsh was one of his Labour opponents.

The minutes were quite detailed, and I could see that their personal animus was very evident, that is, until Marshal's son was missing, then all members expressed their feelings in the most supportive of terms. This was done with Marshal not in the chamber; he was still searching the many bush areas where the boy may be. Walsh was one of the last to speak and expressed his sadness and support for his opponent in strong terms then moved that all business be suspended so members could join search parties and show their respect and support for the family. The motion was met with hearty 'hear, hears' from either side of the speaker, Marshal who closed proceedings.

The Marshal child was the first that Marsh and I had found and before that, the second and third child had been found dead, the third being Walsh's boy, Iain.

The two men had supported each other at each of the funerals.

Obviously, I thought, this was not about local politics with both sides being so horribly attacked. I moved on.

So many times, during the day, I felt useless, impotent. I was getting nowhere. The father and mother of one of the victims were seen as glowing members of a national weight-loss company. Another three were members of the local library. This information I prised from the local bibliographer Johnstone, a bent old man who seemed to have been carrying too many books during his life, which had resulted in a pronounced hunch-back. I had made friends with him when I first came to town, not through the library but through the local club where he set up a table every day, covered with tomes, making him look even more scholarly than he might have been. He would see people one at a time, like a fortune teller, but he dispensed gems of literary treasure, not those of the future.

I had found the membership listed on the library website under the heading 'library members' and the number of members, but it was not open to the public, so I rang the library and when I expressed my requirements, I was met with a flat 'no'. These were not meant for the public, Johnstone informed me. I explained that I was working with the police in the disappearances/killings. He expressed that he would like to help but that he could not unless a detective contacted him. I explained that I was working with Marsh and that the need for the information was imperative to the investigation, and he wavered.

'I will open the list and send you a copy, but I need some kind of proof that you are who you say you are, and that you are working for the investigation,' he insisted, obviously a stickler for the paperwork being just right.

'Well, Marsh has given me his service number if that will help?' I asked, and it did help. He sent me an email, using the police number offered and my email address as my identity. He insisted that Marsh see him to prove the information. I agreed.

The email took about fifteen minutes to come through but when it did, it was quite a large document.

Documents as requested. I have added the books borrowed as I am sure you meant to ask for them.

A.D. Johnstone,

Librarian.

This message explained the large size of the email, which was taking a long time to download. I waited, with little or no patience, and decided to use the time to call the local video store. Funny, we always referred to it as 'video store' even though nearly all of the movies were now on CD, and even that format was beginning to be phased out with the introduction of streaming and download services.

The phone rang for several minutes, and I thought I must have rung the wrong number. I took my wallet out with some difficulty, it being in my right trouser pocket, and I had to use my uninjured left hand to extract it. I fumbled through the many plastic cards until I found the shop's membership card – platinum, might I say – and checked the phone number.

It was the number I had called, and as I knew they were open until seven-thirty every night, I quickly re-rang the number. After the first two rings, I noticed the time on the computer screen. It was eight forty-seven.

Shit, I've worked through the whole day, I thought. It was like that for me; I would sit in front of a screen, be it a computer or TV, and just lose time, any amount of time.

Ringing anyone else that night would be fruitless, so I decided that the walk I had been craving was perfectly justified. I went to the kitchen, took a large glass of water and downed it. I then left the house through the back door and took one of my more regular routes to the back of the farm.

I was wandering aimlessly and quite slowly. I had nothing to get back for; I hadn't felt any pangs of hunger at all and thought that it wouldn't do me any harm if I skipped a meal. Eventually, I reached the rear fence and turned to see the car lights entering the front gate.

I quickened my pace. I could walk long distances, having trained for middle-distance races while in my late teens. True, I was now not in nearly as good a condition, but I had been lucky in the gene pool as to longevity. I rarely got tired while walking.

By the time I reached the homestead, I could see Marsh's car parked to the right of the main driveway, which circumnavigated the entire house and barn complex. Then I heard Marsh shouting my name.

I entered through the kitchen door and almost ran into him as he was heading out the same entrance.

'Oh, there you are,' he panted, and I realised he had been running around the house's rooms, trying to find me with some urgency.

'Yeah. What's all the fuss about?' I asked, noticing also that he was red in the face.

'They've arrested someone!' he almost yelled. He was excited and seemed upset.

'What?' I asked, not knowing what else to say.

'The bloody homicide squad have arrested Jack Pearson. You might not know him – he's a council worker. They say he reported hitting a kangaroo the same day the last boy was killed, and it was one of the council's work Utes,' he gave an almost ranting explanation.

'Oh, that's great,' I said.

This was the best news I had received since becoming involved in the case – this was my saviour. *I can let it go now,* I thought, but my delight was somewhat tempered when Marsh added, 'Not great for me. I interviewed Pearson as a matter of course, and I let him go. I didn't pick up any information from him that implicated him in any way. The bastards will be laughing at me, and six more boys were killed.' He hung his head.

'This is not on you. There was no way to have known,' I offered, trying to help but he was not appeaseable.

'Not on me? The whole bloody town will blame me. The parents and all the volunteers who searched for the boys. Oh god, I will be a laughingstock.' He slumped into the main lounge chair, that of Donne himself.

'I'm sorry. I tried to help as well as I could,' I continued to try to console him.

'No, no, it's not on you. At least you found bodies and one of the murder sites. It's me they will be gunning for. I have been summoned to the station tomorrow morning to see the regional commander and the boffins from Sydney. And they have information on you and your involvement – you are to come too.'

I could see that he was extremely worked up. The only positive thing I could think to say was, 'At least the killings will stop.' He nodded but looked like a man defeated.

Chapter 17

We arrived at the police station promptly at eight-thirty. Marsh had hardly said a word but as we drove through the front gate, I had to know what his course of action was going to be. I didn't think he should see these men alone and I had spoken to Donne, who said delightedly that he would be there to represent me.

'You should let Donne be in your interview, so they don't railroad you,' I counselled.

'No, there won't be much to say. I will just offer my resignation,' he said in a clear but certainly not strong voice.

'Bullshit, that is not fair. None of this is your fault,' I said, feeling my juices rising. I was ready for a fight, but it seemed that he wasn't.

'Someone will need to take the wrap, and it won't be anyone else,' he said, obviously knowing how these things went better than I did.

Donne met us at the front steps of the building, and we each shook his hand.

'Bloody good news. No more killings,' he said but he didn't put it in such a way that he sounded totally delighted. He obviously knew what hell Marsh was in for during the days to come.

'I will be in with you,' he said, nodding in my direction. 'They are going to interview you first.' He nodded in the same way to Marsh and Marsh nodded back. 'Do you want me to represent you as well?'

Marsh shook his head. 'I don't think I need a lawyer to do what I need to do, but if I do, I can call on one of the union's representatives.'

Donne nodded again and Marsh added, 'Thanks, though, for all your efforts.'

Marsh entered first and lifted the part of the front counter that allowed only serving officers to enter. He disappeared to the rear of the room, obviously knowing where he was to meet his inquisition.

Donne and I stood at the counter until one of the Sydney detectives instructed us to wait and pointed to the long pew-like seat that was bolted to the wall opposite.

We sat, but almost immediately, Donne said, 'I am representing Pearson as well. I have been doing his business for years, and I really can't believe that he would have done this. Either way, though, everyone deserves the best defence they can get.'

I had an opinion on his representation of the 'Boy Killer' as the papers had dubbed Pearson, but I knew it wouldn't be what he wanted to hear, so out of deference to him, I kept my mouth shut.

After a short wait, the desk sergeant reappeared and said to Donne, 'Come through, you can see your *client* now,' he sneered.

Donne turned to me and said in a whisper, 'Play along.' He then turned back to the officer and said, 'My associate will be coming in with me.'

'Not bloody likely,' the man fired back, still sneering.

'Oh, so you are refusing to allow my client to see his defence team. Judge Wilmont will be delighted to hear of this.' Donne began to twist the man around his little finger; he was so quick with words.

'He's not part of the defence team,' he blurted, not knowing what to do about his loss of face.

'Oh, even better. He will be even more interested in the fact that you are the sole selector of Mr Johnstone's defence team,' Donne said, slipping his antiquated mobile phone from his pocket and beginning to put a number into the keypad.

The officer watched for a moment and then moved to the door through which the public entered. He thrust it open, still sneering, but with his action admitting defeat.

To be honest, I wasn't delighted to be entering the cell that I had visited once before, but I was even less inclined to stay in the waiting area without Donne. I followed.

The door to the first cell was opened and empty as was the second, but sitting behind the third, on the ground, was a battered and bruised Johnstone. I had never seen him before, yet I felt pity for his plight. This beating he had suffered was nothing short of a travesty; this was not in any way what I thought of justice.

'Before God!' exclaimed Donne. 'Get this man some water and some towels so I can clean him up.'

'Prisoners are not permitted towels, nor sheets or blankets. They can use them to harm themselves,' the officer snarled back, knowing that they were the rules of holding cells in their station at least.

Donne reached once again for his phone. 'This man has been beaten while in custody. He doesn't need to harm himself.' He raised his voice, just enough to make his point.

'This fucker deserves whatever he gets,' the man continued to scowl.

'Well, this fucker,' Donne said, pointing to himself, 'is going to have you in court for violence against an unarmed prisoner.'

The officer thought to speak again but decided that he was simply outgunned and retired from the room, muttering.

Pearson was in a half-kneeling position now as he tried unsuccessfully to get to his feet. Donne reached for him and nodded for me to assist. I grabbed his left arm and between us, we lifted and placed him onto the bunk provided.

Donne began to speak. 'How are you? What have you said to them?'

'I didn't do it. You must believe me,' the answer came in gasps.

'So, we are pleading not guilty. That is all I need to know at this stage. You will not say anything else to anyone. Are we clear?' Donne instructed.

The officer returned with a roll of paper hand towels and a plastic bucket containing a couple of inches of water. He placed it at the door to the cell, which he now left open as he slunk away sneering but silent.

I dipped the first towel into the water and moved to wipe the small but bloody cut above his right eye. He flinched. 'Perhaps I should do that?' Donne suggested.

'There's no need. This man is not the killer!' I said knowingly, and Donne smiled.

In the interview room, I settled in front of the two senior Sydney detectives. Marsh had passed us on his way out but said nothing and didn't make eye contact. Donne waited until the door was open and began to speak forcefully.

'I hope you have good reason for bringing my client in here, again, today. I must say that it feels like harassment to me, or at least some sort of vendetta.'

'On the contrary, we wanted simply to let your *client* know that we won't be pressing charges for his actions posing as a member of the New South Wales Police Force. That is, if he ceases to do so.' He paused for effect and then continued, 'Detective Marsh has been stood down pending an enquiry into his conduct, and I assure you that he will play no more part in this, or perhaps, any case.'

I surprised myself by opening my mouth against the forewarning of Donne. 'You have no idea. This is the best man you have, and you will be the ones being *investigated* when you find that the blood on Johnstone's car is that of a kangaroo, as he informed you.'

Donne looked as wide-eyed as the men and after glancing at each other, the one who had done all of the talking so far said in a brusque voice, 'I would like to also warn you that if you are found to be knowingly involving yourself in this case again, you will be charged with obstruction.'

They both glared at me as if I were the dirt beneath their feet, but before I could take up the cudgel, Donne had stood and, taking my arm, he led me to the door, saying, 'This is how you treat people who are trying to do their civic duty. Well, you better hope the blood proves your case or you might find this bitterness comes back to bite you.'

We almost got out the door before the second man found his voice. 'We don't think it appropriate that you represent two clients in the one case – this *man*, and the accused.'

'Oh, now you come at me. Well, Mr Johnstone is my innocent client in this case, and as you have just informed Fitzpatrick here, he is no longer involved in the case. Be fully aware that I will be informing your boss that you tried to place pressure on me to drop Mr Johnstone as a client.' With that, he shut the door much more strongly than was necessary, emphasising his disgust.

'Well done, but I did say to let me do all the talking,' Donne whispered. Then he added, 'Can you find your way home? I might be a while here.'

'Yes, of course.' I nodded.

'Better still, go to the office. Mrs Donne will take care of you.'

I nodded and thanked him once again. We shook hands.

As I left the station carpark, I noticed Marsh standing next to a car on the opposite side of the road. He looked terrible and was obviously on his way to emptying his cigarette packet.

I walked over to him and said, 'How did things go?'

'Incompetent and insubordinate were the words they pressed. I am suspended without pay, and so I'm told, am lucky to have a job to come back to in a month,' he answered in what seemed to be a well-rehearsed statement.

'Oh shit, I'm sorry. But it doesn't matter – they have arrested the wrong man,' I said, hoping to console him.

'What do you mean?' he questioned, his eyes boring into me.

'That bloke couldn't hurt a fly, and they will be the ones looking incompetent when they are presented with the blood evidence,' I said, feeling at least a little triumphant.

His eyes widened and he tilted his head to one side in a questioning gesture.

'He did hit an animal. He said he did, but they were too busy slapping each other's backs to really look for the evidence. The van is not even the same colour.' I smiled widely.

'Well, what punishment did they lumber you with?' he asked, looking a little less upset.

'Nothing. Donne wrapped them around his little finger. You should have seen it. I am to stop investigating the case and am not allowed to pose as a police officer again. Even though I never said I was you, they were strong on that point.'

He now looked sideways as he often did when pondering something.

'It doesn't mean I won't keep looking, though,' I said.

'In the current climate, I don't think that is very wise,' he warned.

'Oh, they will have their time wrapped up trying to explain to their bosses and the press why they have arrested the wrong person,' I chided.

'Don't think they will let us alone because of that,' he warned.

'Well, the other good thing is that we have Donne on our side, and he is representing Johnstone as well. He is going to tie them in knots for days, if not weeks,' I said.

'You've changed your tune,' he said. I could see my hypocrisy writ large, but I didn't think there was much point defending myself.

'The one thing this all means is that you are still in danger,' he warned, and that sent a shiver down my spine. I hadn't thought of that, which only goes to prove that the saying 'pride comes before a fall' has plenty of merit.

I didn't find anything else to say. I did what I usually did and tried to work out how I could get out of the mess I had gotten myself embroiled in.

'I think I should drive you back to the farm?' he said questioningly.

'Donne must have thought of that. He told me to go to his office and that he would pick me up there later,' I answered, getting even more worried than I was earlier in the day.

'I'll take you there. Do you think they will give us access to a computer?' he asked, raising his eyebrows in an all-knowing way. He had believed me that Johnstone was not guilty, and he wanted to get back on the killer's tail as soon as possible. I was relieved, but I also doubted myself just a little bit. What were the ramifications if I was wrong?

We travelled the few blocks to the solicitor's office and though we didn't say much, I could feel a more positive vibe from my friend. It was as though a great weight had been lifted. He even gave a little smile when we stopped and alighted the car.

Chapter 18

Sylvia was waiting for us in reception. Her mother was, however, nowhere to be seen. Things just as I liked them.

After the usual greetings and a subsequent blush, she said, 'I have put you back in the conference room, if that is ok? I will bring tea in a few minutes. Are you staying, Detective Marsh?'

'Yes, we will wait for your father, if that is acceptable,' he answered and then as she went to leave us, he asked, 'Is it possible for us to use a computer?'

'Certainly, the desktop in the conference room is able to be used, though it may be connected to the projector, it is easily disconnected, or would you rather borrow my laptop?' she offered.

'Well, if it's not too much trouble, could we use both?' I asked, knowing that asking was a mere formality. She nodded her head and continued out the door.

A few minutes later, we were served quite a grand high tea. It even resembled the high tea I had been lucky enough to be rewarded with when I finished high school. On that occasion, it was by my extremely proud mother and grandmother.

The silver tower brimmed with two layers of quarter-cut sandwiches and two with a more than generous assortment of what looked to be professionally crafted pastries.

'Oh, you shouldn't have gone to so much trouble,' Marsh said, his eyes widening.

I succinctly said, 'Wow!'

Sylvia blushed a little then said, 'It was my pleasure,' and I could tell that she meant it.

'I'll just get the laptop,' she said and left blushing again.

'Bloody hell, you should put a ring on that one,' Marsh said, and I could now feel that it was me who was blushing even more than before. I just shook my head in answer.

When Sylvia returned, she handed the laptop to Marsh and turned to leave again, but Marsh asked, 'Would you be able to stay with us? We could do with a *native eye*, so to speak.'

'Yes, I would be delighted to help, but Mother is not back from the shops yet and I am manning her desk. She is born and bred as well, perhaps she would be more help?' she offered.

'No!' we both said together, and Marsh gave a little chuckle and added, 'What we mean is that, well, we want the eyes of a younger person. Being a detective, I don't really get to know many of the folk in town who are under thirty – that is, unless they are in trouble.'

Sylvia smiled and looked to me, raising her eyebrows questioningly and again, I coloured myself in a bright scarlet, renowned for my repartee. 'What he said.'

She laughed, thank goodness, and left us. Marsh smiled and said, 'She has you by the short and curlies.' I could tell he was enjoying my discomfort.

We got to work, Marsh on the laptop, and I began to unhook the desktop from the now antiquated projector. Most businesses had moved to smart whiteboards.

Once I got things going and entered the search engine, Marsh suggested that he look at all crimes in the area over the last ten years and I search before that time.

I nodded and said, 'Information from what source?'

'We better stay away from the official police site. I am suspended and I am sure my computer access will be suspended too.' I nodded and then he added, 'If I need access, I have another way in, but I will only use it as a last resort.'

I nodded again and we got on with trawling old and recent criminal activity through the local newspapers. Yes, strange to say there were two local news outlets in what was too small a town to warrant them.

The Advocate was published daily and was, as I learned from its narrative, very conservative. The Weekender, on the other hand, was obviously aimed at the more common folk and those interested in sport, especially the horse-racing guide in the Saturday edition. This, it seemed, must be how they were able to afford publishing two rags – advertising for the local racetrack, which hosted both thoroughbred horse racing and greyhound racing on a beautifully manicured establishment just out of town to the south.

It was a grand display of green and the colour of many thousands of roses to people who didn't take the bypass. It was situated just on the old highway around two miles out of the main street.

I searched back twenty years and thought to come to a time about ten years ago. First, I looked in the daily, and then the weekly.

I found many small misdemeanours mentioned but names were usually not mentioned, protecting the offender's right to privacy.

The only thing I had found by the time I got to the end of my search was a missing person from fifteen years previous. It was a strange report: a mother of two had disappeared from her home in the night, leaving two young children and their father with 'not even a note telling them why or where she was going' as the daily explained in a condescending way.

This was obviously not a member of the town elite that they were outing. The few stories that followed were full of blame and even some vitriol, couched as an editorial. The writer was, I thought, a jackass if not worse.

I couldn't find anything that ended the case. I turned to Marsh and asked him about it.

'Before my time,' he said and then added, after thinking, 'Use all reports after that time to check the family name and see if it leads anywhere.'

I nodded. I started with the family name and the date of the disappearance and then moved forward.

Soon, a light tap at the door made both of us look up, and Sylvia re-entered.

'What would you like me to do?' she asked, looking to Marsh for instruction.

'Could you spend some time with me?' Marsh asked, standing and moving to the conference table with a few papers that he had printed.

Sylvia followed him and they sat alongside each other with their backs to me. I think Marsh had positioned us this way so neither of us would become distracted.

'Thank you for all your help. We need anything we can get,' Marsh said and then continued on with the business, not allowing her to respond. 'What do you know about an old case of a missing woman?' Before she could reply, he turned to me and asked, 'How long ago was it?'

'About fifteen years ago,' I answered.

'Oh, you must be talking about Mrs Andrews?' Sylvia asked. 'Well, I can't see what that would have to do with this case. The woman, Mrs Andrews, just up and left, leaving a seven-year-old girl and an eight-year-old boy. She didn't even say goodbye to them. And for some time, no one knew what had happened to her but about two weeks later, the father got a letter saying that she couldn't live with him anymore and that she was not coming back.'

'Was she ever tracked down?' Marsh asked.

'Not that I know of, though I wouldn't think it would have been newsworthy if she were found. I was still at school, year ten or eleven, I think. You know, I never gave it another thought. It just wasn't on my radar,' she answered.

'Good, good. You can keep on with that,' Marsh said, nodding to me and I nodded back. I continued to scan the stories but found no further mention of the case.

'What I really want from you, Miss, is any information you have about anything or anyone who has come to your attention who might have been in trouble with the law or has done something that you think was unusual or strange, or violent for that matter,' Marsh pushed.

'The son, Aaron, Andrews I think, did get into some trouble, something about hurting animals I think. Some woman was involved but I don't remember the details,' she answered.

'Oh, this is unlikely to be a woman, but if you could, could you write a list of any women who act strangely as well?' He turned to the back of the little book, tore out a page and handed it to Sylvia. 'Thank you for your help,' he concluded.

Sylvia understood that she had been dismissed and collected the empty teacups, leaving the tray of half-eaten treats, and exited.

'Did you get anything from that?' I asked.

'Yes, well, the cruelty to animals thing is touted to be an early indicator of serial killers, but I think he is too young. He wouldn't have even had a licence when the first murder took place.' He paused. 'We will still look into his whereabouts, but I don't hold much store in that.' He again stopped and rubbed his forehead.

'Another story of some bloke looking up dresses – that doesn't seem as though it would manifest itself in killing little boys. He is worth looking at, though, for other things.'

'So, we are back at scratch?' I asked rhetorically.

Marsh shrugged and sat back in the big armchair to which he had moved. 'I don't think we have anything ... Yet,' he said, closing his eyes for a short time then saying, 'You keep on with this, and I have some other things to look into.'

'How can you do anything? You aren't carrying a warrant card,' I asked. I had heard of the police cards called a warrant on television, and though I didn't know if it was the correct term, I knew he would understand me.

'Yes, well, sometimes identification can put restrictions on how forcefully one can question a suspect,' he said, raising an eyebrow.

'Don't go getting yourself arrested. That's the last thing we need,' I warned, and he looked at me again, eyebrow raised.

I could tell he was not persuaded by my plea and knew he would confront the boy whatever I said, and that it would probably be when he was doing something illegal. Little did I know what would happen next.

Donne arrived at the office about half an hour after Marsh had left. 'What have you been doing all day as if I didn't know?' he questioned.

'We've been going through as much information as we can find on the internet,' I answered, nodding toward the computer and the papers on the table.

'We?' he questioned as he feigned looking around the room.

'Yes, Marsh was waiting for me when I left the police station, as we both expected, and his mood lifted when he heard that the man they had arrested was not guilty,' I explained.

'They have charged Johnstone, bloody fools. I would have defended him even if he were guilty, but I didn't believe it for a minute. They don't have any real evidence, just a dented car with blood stains, and that will backfire on them when the blood is identified as non-human,' he explained. After pausing to allow me to grasp what he was saying, just as he may have done when in front of a jury, he continued, 'I have already informed them that I will be acting for Mr Johnstone in his impending lawsuit for unlawful arrest and assault.' He smiled. He really enjoyed the game. That was why he was such a good lawyer, I suppose.

'Now what about you? You will need to stay in hiding,' he asked.

'I'm not sure. I don't know if I am in any real danger,' I answered uncertainly.

'Oh, you are. If that killer is even ten per cent confident in your advertised talents, you are in real danger. I don't think this man has any belief that the police know what they're doing. He operates right under their noses – he is probably known to them, and they don't suspect a thing,' he explained.

I didn't have anything to add to what he had asserted, so I nodded agreement.

'Back to the farm then?' he asked/suggested and I'm sure he was expecting my answer.

'You have been too generous. I don't know where I would have been without you and your family,' I thanked him after nodding. I knew he was right, and though I wanted this bastard caught, I knew I wasn't the person to do the legwork. I was just a liability in the field, but I could use whatever skill I had to keep Marsh chasing him.

It was then that I realised how much my arm was aching. I felt for my elbow with my good hand, and Donne noticed. 'I will get Sylvia to redress that before we get you back to the farm,' he said and left me holding his hand up to show that he wasn't about to brook any arguments.

Ten minutes later, Sylvia returned. She brought another cup of tea and the practice's first aid kit.

'I'll just need to get a bowl of warm water to bathe it in,' she said and left. Returning soon after, she started to unwrap my now throbbing hand.

I flinched as the last piece of padding on the main jagged cut in my palm adhered to the wound's congealed blood.

'Sorry,' she said, looking up from her task.

I just nodded. Such a master with words, not.

As soon as she saw the palm, her face paled and her eyes widened in surprise.

'This is infected. I'm not about to touch this. You need to see a doctor again,' she said and I nodded. I knew she was right. I did bathe it in the water she had provided as I thought it may help with the pain a little. Sylvia left to find her father and soon after, Donne returned.

'Sylvia is ringing the doctor now,' he explained.

'Thanks, so you think he will come here?' I asked.

'Like many others in town, he will do whatever I ask,' he claimed, looking pleased with himself.

He proved to be right as the doctor turned up within the hour.

'This looks terrible. It must be painful?' he asked rhetorically, and I nodded.

He washed the wound with another container brought by Sylvia, and as he completed his task, he placed some antiseptic, a vile-looking concoction, over the infected area with a square pad of muslin. It stung like crazy, but I tried not to show the pain in front of Sylvia and Donne, who had returned to the room.

He wrote a script and turned, handing it to Sylvia, and said, 'He will need to take both the antibiotics and the painkillers with food, but not at the same time or they will make him sick.' She took the paperwork and left without saying a word, heading for the chemist.

About two hours later, I was being delivered to the farm by Donne who had instituted the same ploy of having me load behind the seats, so I was not seen as we left the office. I was delighted when a few miles out of town, he stopped and allowed me to get up in the front seat. It was great to breathe again unhindered.

Sylvia had loaded two grocery bags into the rear of the Ute and left her laptop on the front seat so I could get on with any work Marsh may have been doing. I had saved everything I had found to a USB stick, humorously shaped like a chocolate éclair, that Sylvia had given me for the task.

On our arrival, Donne broke the silence of the last half an hour or so. 'It is still pretty painful then?' He nodded to my now heavier bandaged and slung hand.

'It's not great,' I admitted as I struggled to get out of the Ute with the laptop.

'I'll bring in the groceries,' he said.

I walked to the back door, where I had to wait as Donne had the key. Usually, doors in the area were not even locked, but in the current climate, everyone thought it necessary.

Donne quickly unloaded the groceries and unlocked the door. After quickly placing those foods that needed to go into the refrigerator, he moved to get rid of the bags and just left the rest of the goods on the counter. I could tell he was in a hurry. I thought he may have been getting sick of babysitting me.

'Sorry, I must head off straight away. I said I would go and see Johnstone this afternoon and I will only just get there before he is locked up for the night,' he explained as he headed out the door.

I followed him, saying, 'Sorry for keeping you.'

'Think nothing of it. My grandfather always used to say, "It never hurts to do a kindness, but it hurts to say no." I always try to help if I can. Perhaps one day you will be able to return the favour, but even if you can't, it still feels better to have helped,' he said, sounding like a great sage when he echoed his grandfather's voice.

'Still, I really appreciate what you have done for me,' I said and hoped I sounded sincere.

He began to reach to shake hands and then remembered my sling. We both smiled and I offered my left hand, and we shook.

Chapter 19

It was early the next morning when I heard Marsh's car coming up the driveway. I had tried to concentrate on the computer and had failed miserably. The drugs the doctor had given me seemed to ensure that the moment I tried to really put my mind to something, I began to fall asleep, and yet when I stopped and put my head on the pillow, I was as wide awake as was possible.

Marsh came in as quietly as he could, possibly thinking I would be asleep, but he smiled widely as he saw me still sitting in front of the glowing box.

'You still going at it? I wish *my* officers were as dedicated as you,' he said and smiled again. I could tell he had good news. He really was not one to show his pleasure so readily.

'What?' I asked.

'The bloody fools have had to let Johnstone go. The blood matched that of a kangaroo – the same roo they found at the accident site, right where Johnstone told them it would be.'

'Where did you hear all this?' I asked, knowing that he was considered 'persona non grata' at his station.

'Well, my sergeant rang and told me to come in. He had it all hitting the fan. When I got there, Donne was in fine voice. I won't be able to say word-for-word what he said but to say the least, he was holding them all accountable for the miscarriage of justice. He demanded the immediate suspension of the young officer who had laid hands on his client, and an assurance was given.

'One of the dicks from Sydney asked if there was anything else. That was a real mistake because Donne was really wound up. "I demand that the thug be made to apologise to my client, face to face, and grovel for his position, which I fear cannot be in any way guaranteed when I get you all in court."'

The man he was talking about was in the room, at his desk, and when all present turned to him, he looked shocked and began to say, 'I thought–' But Marsh then gave him and the other men within earshot a lecture that began the attack.

'"You thought, *you thought*. We all serve the law, and she is not an ass. She does not allow you to take liberties. When working with *any person*, it is not for us to carry out schoolyard justice like some bully boy, some common thug. It is our duty to treat all as innocent until proven guilty. You, young man, are a disgrace, and you need to feel ashamed of yourself." He went on, and no one in the place could get a word in edgeways.' Marsh was telling the story in what he thought sounded like the voice Donne used, and it wasn't a bad approximation.

'Before he was finished, he had ripped into everyone there, and none even defended themselves. He finished by saying that I was the only person present who had done the right thing. "And for that, he has been suspended. Well, I have recommended that Marsh here retains me as his representative at the wrongful dismissal suit I will bring, and I assure you, this will be a very public event!"

'Bloody hell, I was almost about to applaud when the lead detective said, "He was not dismissed and would now be reinstated with the suspension expunged from his record." And with that, he looked to me to see if I was going to accept his offer and perhaps calm the savaging they were getting,' Marsh explained and seeing that I was about to ask a question, he continued, 'I was enjoying Donne's rant, so I simply said, "I'm not sure yet, but I would like to be in the room when Johnstone receives his apology."

'The man sitting at his desk glared at me. He must have been surprised that I didn't support him in some way. Everyone now glared back at him, and his head dropped. I had problems with him from the start – he was far too cocky for my liking, but I did feel a little sorry for him as I could see that the boffins would not just land him in hot water but make him the fall guy for the whole event. So, I said that I would accept my position back only if I was reinstated as the lead on the case, without unwarranted intervention from anyone. I also added that I wanted to reprimand and deal with the breach of order by my own staff,' he rambled. I had never seen him so worked up.

'They quickly agreed, wanting to drop the hot potato and we all reconvened in Johnstone's cell, where the young cop did a pretty good job of apologising. I was delighted when Johnstone stood tall, walked past the boy and, with Donne, exited the station without saying a word.'

'Bloody hell!' I commented, amazed that Marsh was so bold with supposedly senior detectives.

'Yes, I have some friends too, and they knew they had cocked things up,' he said, smiling contentedly. 'I tell you something, Donne is one classy silk. Makes you wonder why he isn't in one of the top companies in Sydney or better.'

'I reckon that is down to Mrs Donne. She is the leading socialite here – she would be a small fish in Sydney or Canberra,' I answered, and we both nodded. She was someone who was hard to like but not to respect.

'I will need to go into the station tomorrow to get things back on track, but in the meantime, can you keep on the possible suspects?' he asked, and I nodded. I was so delighted by the news he had brought.

I sat myself down at the computer again. Marsh retired to the bathroom, and I could hear the running water. *He has earned a good bath*, I thought.

The next morning, Donne arrived bright and early. I was still in bed when I heard the car. It was very seldom that I was still in bed at 8 a.m. but then it was also seldom that I was up at 4.30 a.m. trolling the internet.

I met him in the kitchen. He had put on a kettle and was making coffee. *God, instant coffee. He must be desperate.*

He held the kettle up as an offer and said, 'Sleep well?'

'Better than the last few days,' I answered and shook my head at the offer of the coffee.

'Oh, yes, I forgot. You prefer tea,' he said. He reached for the tea bags and poured the cup, whether I wanted it or not. I did.

We sat, at his insistence, at the kitchen table. He glanced over at the pile of paperwork strewn over the table and floor in the lounge room. 'You were at it fairly late then?'

'We are still trying to find someone unusual, for any reason. Hoping to track him down, but we don't seem to be coming up with much,' I answered, knowing that he would want to know where we were at in our investigation. 'Sylvia gave us a few names to check,' I added.

'Ah, why did you go to Sylvia?' he asked.

'Well, I didn't. She just happened to be with me, fixing the arm,' I answered, lifting my arm.

'And who did my dear daughter suspect?' he continued, making me feel a little uncomfortable.

'Oh, the only interesting names she came up with was some bloke named Jaden Wells, and the Andrews boy' I answered.

'I know the young man Wells, and I don't think he can be involved in this?' I wasn't sure whether he was telling me or asking a question. 'My brother gave him some work, and he's still working for him. I haven't heard anything bad since – he's on a bond,' he concluded.

I nodded that I understood. I just knew that Wells was very unlikely to be our man – he was just an 18-year-old, and I thought that was simply too young. Most serial killers were of a certain age, mostly in their thirties and forties. Though I knew that there were exceptions, I had not heard anything about a teenager being that advanced, so I dropped that out of hand.

'The Andrews clan are well known for being violent and not just the son. He was still in jail for the first case and would have been too young at the time of his mother's disappearance to have been involved,' he explained. He paused, waiting for my nod to confirm that I understood, then continued, 'The father is one I would be looking at. He is a real customer. I thought, as most in town did, that he had got rid of his wife. No proof ever came to light and the police had nothing to charge him with. He engaged my services, though, before he was even questioned.'

'That's a bit strange, isn't it?'

'No, not if there is something to hide. These kinds of people tend to cover their backs. I represented him on another case where he had been accused of bashing a man. When it came to court, the witness declared that he wasn't sure who the thug was and that he thought that it may not have been Andrews. Andrews got off, and the man who had been attacked left town the next day,' he explained.

While I was listening, I typed the name Andrews and the name of the town's newspapers. Plenty came up about the case of Jaden but nothing else under the family name.

'What's the father's name?' I asked. When he told me the name was Don/Donald, I placed it in the same search.

There was no information on Donald Andrews; it seemed that he had never been in trouble with the law.

'I would widen that search. He wasn't a local originally – he came here just about the time his wife was giving birth to the son. He had registered the new address at that time with the motor registry for his licence etc. All seemed ordinary, in the scheme of things,' he explained.

'Anything else?' I questioned and continued to type. I had learned that skill when I worked for a short time as a telemarketer, though that was all I learned, and I must say, it was a particularly low period in my life.

'Yes, I have recently had him served with papers. He has never paid me for representing his son. He said that he would never pay me as I failed to get the boy off. I probably wouldn't have bothered about the money, but my wife isn't as generous as me and I would never have heard the end of it, if I hadn't got representation myself.' After another short break, he said, 'Having said all of that, I don't think he will be your man. He *is* a mongrel of a man, but he only acts in his own interest. He can't make money out of these poor children.'

'I am not finding the name anywhere; do you have any idea where he actually came from?' I asked.

'Well, no, but he did speak a bit about growing up in the country. Coonabarabran comes to mind, but I'm not sure that that is correct,' he answered, looking up as if looking for divine inspiration or checking the stored files in his brain. On reflection, I thought it was probably the latter.

I entered the name and added 'Coonabarabran'. Nothing came up.

'Well, perhaps Marsh will have a better chance. You know, through *official* channels,' he said.

Late in the afternoon, Marsh arrived home and moments later, Sylvia followed.

I had greeted Marsh at the rear door and was just letting him in when Sylvia's lights lit up his parked car. I was delighted to see at least one of them.

The three of us sat down at the kitchen table, and though I offered to make some tea, Sylvia said that she would do the tea-making. I acquiesced; it was obvious she wanted to play mother, and I wasn't about to get in her way.

'I questioned Andrews and was rudely met. I didn't think much of the man, but he has a solid alibi. He was at the local club at the time of the last killing,' Marsh said, sounding a little disheartened.

'Do you think it is worth me meeting him?' I asked.

'Couldn't do any harm. If he knows anything, we could get an idea at least,' he answered.

'Ok, how do we do that?' I asked.

'Well, he attends the club every day at four-thirty for a couple of hours. You could just sit at the next table.' He produced his phone and showed me a picture of Andrews. It was a bit grainy, but I thought I would recognise him. I nodded.

'If we get there before him, you could take up your table just before he enters. He always takes the table nearest to the entrance because he uses the betting machines to place wagers on the horses and the counter is right in front of the table,' Marsh explained.

'How will I get there?' I asked.

'I'll get you there,' he explained.

'Then you better pick both of us up,' instructed Sylvia, as she returned with the cups and a freshly made pot of tea.

'Oh, I don't think you need to be involved,' Marsh said very quickly.

'James would stand out like a sore thumb. Oh, sorry,' she said, recognising the irony of the reference to my hand.

'Yes, but why would you want to help?' asked Marsh.

'I would think any local person would like to help you catch the murderer,' she answered, sounding a little indignant.

'Yes, well, it could work. Could you get anything if you had your back very close to his chair?' Marsh asked. He adapted to changes in plan very quickly. I was still deciding if I liked the idea of putting my Sylvia at risk.

After considering his question, I asked, 'How close?'

'About three or four feet,' he answered.

'Sure, that would be fine, but I don't think Sylvia needs to be involved,' I assured him.

'What a pity *you* don't have a say in the matter,' Sylvia said, passing me my cup.

With that settled, Marsh asked if I had found anything else during the day and I had to inform him that I hadn't. He made his excuses; he didn't need to sleep at the farm now. He was able to go home to his own bed.

Sylvia stayed with me and made dinner for both of us and though it was pre-packaged fish and canned vegetables, she made it taste like it was from the best restaurant. We ate together, and after the meal, she washed the dishes and said her goodbyes. She looked excited to be involved in the next day's action as she leant forward and gave me a little peck on the cheek, saying, 'I can't wait to see you at work.'

Little did she know that watching me 'work' was nothing to be excited about.

Just after two o'clock the next day, Marsh picked me up in his work car, and when I got in, I was delighted to see Sylvia in the front passenger seat. She looked even more beautiful than usual.

On the way to the club, Marsh gave us advice on how we could look unnoticeable, though I remember thinking that no red-blooded man would miss Sylvia in that beautiful blue dress.

Marsh also handed me a small device; it was for recording the event.

'What do you want it recorded for?' I asked, taking the four-inch-long by one-inch-wide contraption. I could tell this was not a police issue; it was too clumsy.

'Who knows? He may speak to someone about something. Just put it in your shirt pocket, and here is a pen to put next to it to make it look normal,' he said, handing me the pen.

I put them in my pocket. They looked like a pen and a recording device.

'That will never fool anyone,' I protested.

'It will be fine. Let's face it, no one will be looking at you,' he answered, nodding his head sideways at Sylvia and I saw her blush.

'Ok, but I don't need to speak to him, do I?' I asked, feeling a little embarrassed.

'No, I don't think so,' he reassured me.

I nodded and Sylvia looked back at me to confirm she understood her part in the scheme.

Two blocks from the club, Marsh pulled up and said, 'I will be parked in the next street when you are finished.' He pointed to the upcoming street on our right and turned the corner. Once we had alighted, he parked in the first available parking place.

Sylvia took my arm as we walked. I would have been quite happy to have kept walking. Just having her near me was all I wanted.

On entering the club, we were confronted by a man who asked us to sign in if we were guests. Sylvia showed her membership card and signed me in, telling the somewhat suspicious-looking man that I couldn't sign for myself. He took another look at her card and then said, 'That will be fine Miss, er, Donne,' and dipped his head as if he were wearing a hat.

'What would you like to drink?' I asked Sylvia.

'Oh, I will have a vodka and orange, no ice, thank you,' she answered, standing next to me at the bar.

'Two vodka and oranges, please,' I said to the extremely short woman serving.

'Certainly,' she said and bustled off to the mixing counter.

We received our drinks and walked to the table Marsh had described. I sat with my back to the chair he thought Andrews would take.

We sat chatting about nothing and waited the twenty minutes until Andrews was expected. Almost to the minute, he entered and ordered a drink. On receiving it, he moved to the next table and sat down, but not in the chair that had its back to me. He seated himself on the right side of the table and looked toward the sporting screens, facing away from us back toward the bar. Damn, that might be too far away for me to sense him.

He sat with his back to us, not giving us a second thought. He must have decided that his usual chair was too close to us.

Sylvia was able to observe him as he took and completed a Keno ticket, then, getting up, he returned to the bar and placed his wager. Sylvia took the chance to whisper, 'Get him to help fill out a Keno ticket.'

I understood and took her advice. As Andrews returned to his table, I got up and moved to him. 'Sorry, mate, er, my girlfriend wants to play a Keno ticket, and we don't know how to fill out the ticket. Could you help?'

He glared at me, and I thought he was going to tell me to get lost, then he looked at the expectant Sylvia and she smiled. He took the ticket from my hand. I tried to brush his hand as he took it but missed. He placed it on the table and said, 'How many numbers?'

I hadn't anticipated the question and looked to Sylvia for inspiration.

'Seven, please. Seven is my lucky number,' she said.

'How many games? See, you put your games here.' He pointed, and I put my hand on the card, pointing to the area he had picked out. His hand was covering the larger numbers, so I bumped it to get him to move it a little, and he obliged.

'Ten games,' I answered.

He crossed the ten and then asked, 'How much per game?'

'Oh, just a dollar a game, thanks.'

He dutifully fulfilled my instruction. I thanked him warmly and passed his chair on my way to the bar. As I passed him, I realised that the next table was quite close and used this to bump his shoulder while moving a chair that was blocking my clear path.

'Oh, shit, sorry,' I mumbled, wanting to seem a little drunk. He didn't even look up but continued to write out a horse betting slip.

I stumbled to the bar and handed the short lady my ticket. I had connected with him, and now I began to feel sick. As the woman returned, I placed ten dollars on the counter and though I tried to hold back, I began to vomit. There was a drip tray running right along the front of the bar and I deposited my lunch into it, bending down low to avoid, as much as I could, hitting the carpet.

I looked across the room to Sylvia and then at the horrified bar attendant who knew that she was going to have to do clean up.

Sylvia got up and came toward me, saying, 'He really can't hold his alcohol.'

I continued to apologise to the woman behind the counter, who handed me the Keno ticket, and Sylvia bundled me out of the building.

Once on the street, I knew I needed to sit down, and the nearest of the taxi rank park benches was appreciated. We sat.

'What was that all about?' Sylvia asked, looking bewildered.

'Oh, I often get sick if I see something terrible,' I answered, still feeling squeamish.

'Saw what?' she asked.

'Just let me say, I need to see Marsh as soon as I can walk the two blocks,' I answered, trying not to repeat my earlier effort.

As soon as I could, we walked arm in arm to the street where we found Marsh parked. As we got into the car, he could see that I was unwell and asked, 'Are you ok?'

I wasn't but as quickly as I could, I said, 'He's not our man, but if you dig up the house's septic tank, you will find his wife.'

I got out and was sick in the gutter. Sylvia, looking very worried, handed me a tissue and I wiped my mouth. This was strange for me; I was rarely confident about anything I saw, but I knew I was right.

'Will you be alright?' she said, sounding really concerned.

'Yes, one of the little perks of seeing things. A weak stomach,' I answered, sitting back in the car.

'What's with you, water tanks and finding bodies?' Marsh said, obviously not missing the irony that we met the first time under similar circumstances.

The following morning, Marsh served a warrant on the property of Mark James Andrews. He had waited until he had arranged for a small mechanical trench digger to enter the property. There, next to the overflow of the septic tank, they found the dismembered body of what was later identified as Andrews's missing wife.

Marsh was beaming when he came to the farm to report the success the next day. He was the local hero again and we both knew that he was not going to be pestered by superiors again in a hurry.

'I had to tell a lie to get the warrant. I said I received an anonymous tip-off. I hope that is ok with you?' he asked, looking pleased with himself.

'Thank heavens he had been so easy to read, or we might never have got him,' I answered, knowing that he was right to leave me out of the request of the judge and the ensuing media storm.

'We looked at the date he had had the septic tank installed and it was only a couple of weeks prior to his wife going missing. He didn't deny anything but demanded to know where we had got the information,' he explained. I nodded.

'This hasn't helped us with the other case, but a long-term cold case solved will give us a little more grace,' he added.

After a short time, Marsh went back out to the car and returned with his arms full of Manila folders. Each was a local case of the last few years. He placed them on the dining table and said, 'Just a little light reading,' and returned for another load. The third bundle was not quite as big as the others and was, thank heavens, the last.

Each of the bundles was tied around four sides with one piece of string and looked secure. Marsh picked up the first and began to read the case notes. He signalled to the three bundles in an indication for me to 'dig in', and we began to read about the seamier lifestyles of the not-so-rich and famous.

Most of what I picked randomly were lesser cases, trifling fights between neighbours and the like. There always seemed to be a property tree line or something of that nature as a catalyst, the police only becoming involved when one side or the other lopped the other's tree that had inevitably been protruding over the boundary line. On occasions, an amicable agreement was reached and usually saw both sides give some ground. In a few cases, only a few, things ended up in court and at least one plaintiff was inevitably represented by Donne.

Marsh worked for hours without saying a single word. There were a few grunts and the clearing of his throat to let me know that he was still alive. We found very little.

The next morning, I got up early to the sound of Marsh's car starting and soon after, the sound of Sylvia's car arriving. I was not disappointed to see her enter with some more food and a bundle of papers, which she placed on the only bare corner of the kitchen bench.

'Morning,' I said as I started to clear some of the offending files.

'Good morning. There are a few extras in the bag, and the paperwork is from Father,' she answered and began to unpack the bag.

Bananas, oranges and three large red apples were positioned on the large leaf-shaped bowl near the sink. I was always delighted when she was with me, and I think the feeling was mutual, but making my next move was where I usually mucked things up.

I moved to her left side and took her hand. She turned to look up into my eyes. I leaned down and kissed her. She didn't recoil in horror, which was a good start. I broke my slight hold on her arm and stepped back a little. She looked up at me. Placing an arm around my waist, she drew me back in. We kissed again.

There was no time for this to go further as the sound of her father's car arriving broke the mood.

Moments later, she was back to unpacking, and Donne entered the rear door.

'Well, hello, you two. You may want these files as well?' He added them to the ever-growing work that I would have to get through. 'If anyone wants to know, I didn't give you these.' He tapped the top of the five- or six-inch pile.

'Thanks, what are they?' I asked, beginning to thumb through the top few folders.

'They are old cases that either didn't get to court or were thrown out.' He tapped the top file again.

'What's in them?' I asked, not delighted to see so many extra reems of cases I would have to go through.

'Well, as I said, they are old files and I don't even know if they will be of any use, but they are subject to client counsel confidentiality, which means that they are never shared with anyone unless ordered by a judge. I feel guilty even showing them to you.' Thinking a moment, he added, 'It's illegal, but we have to catch this bastard before he kills anyone else.'

'I will take good care of them,' I promised.

'When you have finished with them, don't leave them laying around. Lock them in the safe in my study,' he said, nodding toward the adjoining room. 'I will write the combination number down.'

I looked sceptical, and he noticed. 'Don't worry, there is nothing in the safe of any importance, no hidden treasure.' He laughed a little and began to write the code. He handed the paper to me, and I took it and folded it so I could not read the number, as if that was somehow making it safe.

'Now, I must go. The police have asked me to attend a meeting with Johnstone and an intermediary. They will try to settle his case out of court,' he said, bustling out the back door. As he did, he popped his head back in and said, 'Syl, don't forget that you have to relieve your mother at ten so she can attend.'

'I won't,' she replied.

As soon as I heard the car start, I moved back to her. I wanted more; I needed more. We kissed again and as I drew her in, she said, 'Pity I have to go. I will come back this afternoon.'

I didn't want to let her go. I didn't want to ever let her go again.

'Get to work,' she said, cracking an invisible whip and exiting. I nodded obligingly and she was gone.

Taking the piece of paper, I walked with the files to the study. I thought it was advisable that I lock all of them away, only looking at one case at a time.

The safe was positioned on the floor to the right of the desk. It was a giant old thing – must have weighed a couple of hundred pounds, brought from the offices of Donne and Williams, probably after they installed the new electronic security system, which had a brand-new electronic version.

I bent down and began to reach with my right arm, but the sling held it in place. Even this amount of movement hurt, and I winced as I thought what a fool I was. I opened the unlocked safe and knelt down to place the papers inside. As Donne had said, there was nothing of any real worth inside it, just a couple of family photo albums. I pulled them out and instinctively, I began scanning the pages. Sylvia as a primary school student, and many of her and her mother in special dresses for special occasions, which I knew nothing about.

Sylvia had always been a pretty girl but as an adult, she had grown into her facial features, making her, in my eyes, just about perfect.

The first book was finished; I moved to the second. It included pictures with the title 'New Zealand Trip', and the tourist photos were obviously of the trip they had taken to the South Island of New Zealand a little more than a year earlier. All of the shots were impressive: Sylvia and her mother in front of a beautiful mountain I knew to be 'the Remarkables Mountain Range', having travelled there with my parents once and my grandmother and mother another time as a teenager.

Every picture was of Sylvia and her mother, visiting the many beautiful sites of Queenstown, the giant trees of the botanical gardens, the open-air skating rink, the jet boat rides on the Shotover River and the restaurant at the top of the mountain. It all seemed idyllic.

The only thing I noticed was that Donne himself was not in any of the photos, not one. Wasn't that a bit strange? Yes, he may have been taking the majority of the photos, but there were several commercial 'we take you buy' pictures like the one on the jet boats or in Arrowtown and other tourist-driven venues, and he wasn't in any of them either. That was very strange, but how could I find out about his absence without upsetting him or Sylvia?

I had noticed a photograph on the mantel over the grand inglenook fireplace in the lounge room. I had admired the smiling face of Sylvia, though that of her mother was, as usual, not looking very pleased. Now I realised it was taken on one of the rubber rafts on the Shotover River. I resolved to bring it up with Sylvia when she came in the afternoon. I hoped above hopes that I wouldn't cock this up and spoil a good thing.

I went back to my study area and took one of the files left by Donne. I glanced at it and found that it was a deposition from a woman who said she had seen two men stealing gigantic rolls of coated copper wire from the local electricity company yard. The car she identified was a white van; it had writing on the side that she could not identify. They had cut the padlock on the gate and, having noticed that as she walked her dog, she had rung the police station.

I didn't see why she would have seen Donne and made a statement to him about something so obviously a police matter. As I read on, it was obvious that the police had attended the yard and checked the locks, and that nothing looked out of place. The woman argued that the locks had been cut, that they had used bolt cutters, and she even described the offenders. She then went on to say that the police had warned her against giving a false statement and that is why she came to see Donne and make the statement.

This all seemed strange to me. Why would she have been treated like this if she was just an innocent bystander?

Donne had made some handwritten notes and as I read them, I began to understand what this was all about.

Mrs Swift, again warned by the police for a false report, on the 17th of Feb. This time she was so worked up as she swears that what she says is true.

Took her statement to protect her in case they charged her with wasting police time with a false report. Don't think they will take it any further, was scrawled right at the bottom of the page. Below the lines, I read another entry:

As it happens, Mrs Swift was right. When two men turned up to stocktake at the yard, they reported that the locks had been changed and that there was a considerable amount of copper missing. The police had to apologise. The young constable, Aitkins, is a proper dill, so unprofessional. 21st Feb.

Aitkins, he was the cop who beat up Johnstone. What a dick, I thought, and I suddenly understood why I didn't like him from our first meeting at the lookout when he was ready to arrest me. I hadn't really thought about it; there had been too many things happening.

I don't know why but I started to get tired and within a few minutes, I was sound asleep. I shouldn't have been tired but apparently, I was and I slept until after midday. When I awakened, I looked at the mess around me. The papers I had last been reading had fallen from my hand and were all over the other papers and evidence sheets supplied by Marsh.

I didn't want to get things mixed up, so I set about recovering each sheet to return them to the safe. I sat back on the couch and went through the sheets, sorting them into the right order, then I realised that the last sheet, with Donne's notes on it, wasn't there.

I got back down on my hands and knees and started to look for where it had fallen. There on the first pile, under the paper clip, was the missing piece. How could it fall and land under the paperclip and so perfectly in line with the other sheets?

Well, I thought, *I have seen stranger things. Or did I put it there before I fell asleep? Whatever.*

I picked up the file to separate them, and it was as if I had been hit in the chest. It knocked me back into the lounge. I felt sick.

The top sheet and the bottom file must have something to do with each other. It was like they were whining at me. I pulled them apart with some difficulty, then looked from one to the other, trying to see if they bore any resemblance or were involved in any way.

The report was that of a burned-out car and the sheet about the woman, Mrs Swift. I kept looking back and forward and then there it was, both cases involved Constable Aitkins.

Chapter 20

I had almost worn a groove in the carpet in front of the fire. I needed to tell Marsh, but when I rang his number at the station, a voice informed me that if I wanted to leave a message, I could speak after the beep. I wasn't sure I wanted to leave a message, so I hung up and continued pacing. After about half an hour, I rang again and gave an answer to the recorded message with a message of my own. 'Marsh, where are you? Get back to me. It is urgent. I think, um, Aitkins is involved.'

I was about to hang up when the sound of a receiver being lifted was audible.

'Hello?' a tentative voice said.

I recognised it immediately. It was the man himself, Aitkins. Gaining in confidence, he added, 'Marsh is not here. Would you like to leave a message?'

Bloody hell, no, I didn't want to leave a message and most certainly not with him. 'No, thank you,' I said hesitantly, and I should have hung up right there and then, but I didn't.

'Is that you, Fitzpatrick?' he probed.

As competent as I was with a phone, I didn't want to answer him, but how could I just hang up? Had he heard the message?

'Shall I get him to ring you back?' he asked and paused as I remained silent. 'Where will I tell him you called from?' he added but I wasn't about to tell him that. Still, for some reason, I didn't hang up.

'What do you need?' he said, raising his voice as though he thought I was hard of hearing or a long way away.

'I will ring back,' I answered and as I hung up the receiver, I could hear him speaking further, but I didn't catch the words. Was it possible to trace the call? Could they triangulate the signal? That seemed pretty unlikely, it being a landline. God, I had been watching too many cheap thrillers.

Almost immediately as if by magic, the phone rang. It startled me so much that I felt as though I would hit my head on the ceiling. I picked it up and very tentatively said, 'Hello?'

There was no answer. Someone was on the line, but there was nothing to tell me that, not even heavy breathing. I said hello a second time but still there was no reply, so I slammed the receiver back in its cradle.

What the hell was I supposed to do now? Should I run?

Being a cop, perhaps Aitkins could redial the last number in the memory of Marsh's phone and redial it to get the number and possibly the address. Oh shit, I needed to run. I went to the study and recovered the pistol Donne had shown me. I really didn't know what I was going to do with it, but it was a kind of insurance at least.

Moving to the kitchen, I took a small bottle of water and as I pulled on my jacket, I tucked it into one of the pockets and the gun in the other.

I charged out of the back door. I could hide in one of the outbuildings, I thought, though I hadn't had any reason to go into them yet. At least they would offer me cover and let me view the house with some certainty that I wouldn't be seen.

I rushed down to the first building, an old, hangar-looking construction that was about twice the size of a double garage. The main door was locked, so I walked to the huge sliding door on the side of the building, which faced the house. I'm sure that this door had not been opened for years. It took me all my might to heave it just a few inches so I could squeeze through the gap. Once inside, I couldn't move it back or further open to give me some purchase to ram it shut. It appears I had pulled it off the rusted runner at the top.

Leave it, I thought, and I rushed to get to the windows that were at the end of the building, which faced the house and driveway.

I scratched around for a while, looking for something to clean one of the panes so I could view anyone who might approach. I found only a few pieces of old weathered newspaper, so I fashioned them into a makeshift cloth, spat on them and rubbed the glass. It made a little difference, and then I realised that much of the detritus was on the outside. I quickly made my way back through the jammed door and gave the pane as good a cleaning as I could.

Once back in my little hole, I began to think rationally for the first time since the phone call. Why the hell was I rushing? If the bent cop was on his way, he would take at least an hour, and that was assuming that he was able to leave the station immediately after I had called.

There was an old, beaten-up wooden bar stool to one side. I recovered it and gave it a brush with my hand. As I sat on it, it lurched to one side, and I had to catch myself to stop from falling. Naturally, I did that with my injured hand. The shooting pain was unbelievable, perhaps even worse than when I had first tangled with the cow. I swore loudly, got to my feet and wandered up and down, shaking my arm, which had been forced out of the sling. Bloody fool.

Once the immediate pain subsided a bit, I began to return the arm to its sling, and it was then I noticed the blood. It was flowing freely from my hand to my elbow and seeping into the crook of the arm sling.

I noticed that there was another similar stool against another wall, and I recovered it. This time before sitting, I tested that it would hold my now unsteady bulk.

I sat, a million thoughts running through my head. Oh, my head. I was in pain – I was bleeding and now I was feeling faint. I put my head down on the workbench in front of me, and I'm not sure if I fell asleep or passed out but either way, my consciousness left me.

I was awakened by the turning headlights of a car arriving at the front of the house. I fumbled for the gun in my coat pocket and found it difficult to get out with my opposite hand. Reaching across my body, I dropped it, and it hit the floor with a thud. I bent down in the darkness and felt for it. Once I found it, I got up and looked through the window. I couldn't see the car very clearly and didn't know who had arrived.

I heard the kitchen door slam and realised that whoever it was, they had entered the house.

I waited and saw nothing. I heard nothing. After ten minutes, during which time I thought I would burst, the back door opened, and Marsh came out. At that moment, I could have kissed him. I was safe again.

I made my way out of the shed, hearing Marsh call my name.

'Here,' I shouted back and broke into a jog, meeting him halfway across the yard.

'What the hell are you doing?' he asked incredulously.

'Did you get my message? I rang. Did you get your phone back? It was Aitkins,' I babbled, not making much sense.

'Yes, I have my phone. No message came up,' he reassured me, pulling it out of his pocket and looking at the screen as it lit up.

'Was it important?' he asked, clicking on the message. My voice blurted out its message. When the recording finished, I looked up at him. He was standing on higher ground as the yard sloped down toward the sheds.

'Aitkins, but that is mad. He was with me on two occasions when kids were taken,' he explained and fumbled in his back pocket. After a few seconds, he pulled out another small journal, like the one he had shown me the other day.

'You must go through one of those a week,' I said, looking at the bulging pages. It had an elastic band around it.

'One every two weeks, whether I need it or not,' he confided and then added, 'Well, I can't read it out here.' He turned and we went back into the house.

We seated ourselves at the kitchen table. He removed the band and took out many small pieces of paper. They were many business cards given to him in the course of his day-to-day business as well as many phone numbers he had written on scraps of paper and had later decided to keep.

He scoured the pages, looking for the incidents in question. 'Here, he was with me when, oh god, the girl was killed.' He looked at me, startled that his memory had failed him.

'You see, I got a hit when I found his name attached to one of your files and some paperwork left for me by Donne,' I stated my case.

'What were they to do with?' he asked with some urgency in his voice.

'The case was one of stolen electrical cable and the other about a Mrs Swift. I think they may be the one case,' I answered.

'Oh, yes, I remember that case. We didn't get anyone for it,' he said. 'So how do they tie in with this?' he asked after thinking for a moment and gesturing toward the heaped paperwork all around the room.

'I have no idea. The two pieces of paperwork found each other and when I tried to separate them, they resisted, then they showed me violence and blood,' I answered.

'What do you mean they resisted?' he asked, looking bemused.

'Oh, I don't know. They didn't want to come apart. Um, well, I can't explain this shit – they just did,' I answered, sounding more annoyed than I was.

'Ok, don't get your knickers in a knot,' he said and smiled to break the tension. He rarely smiled and it looked strange on him.

I waved him off and said, 'We must look at him. He is the only thing that brings my visions together.'

'So, how do you think we can do that? Just walk in and ask him, a serving officer, if he is involved in a crime?' he asked and looked as though he was considering the question he had posed. 'I suppose we could ask the woman?'

'Yes, that sounds the best way to go. We could visit her tomorrow,' I suggested.

I nodded agreement. As I did, the lights of another car flashed through the windows. It was approaching the house. I jumped and glared at the lights as they turned in front of building.

'That could be him,' I said in a voice that sounded very agitated and somewhat frightened.

'Settle down,' he said but I noticed that he reached for his chest-holstered pistol.

The door of a car could be heard slamming and then a shadow was noticeably coming past the side windows, heading to the kitchen door.

We both stood there expectantly, then the unexpecting Sylvia entered. She was, to say the least, startled by the sight of Marsh re-holstering his weapon.

'What's going on?' she asked.

'Oh, nothing, I was just showing Fitzpatrick my gun,' he lied.

Sylvia looked at him, raising a quizzical eyebrow.

'Well, I brought dinner. There is enough for three,' she said, holding up a brown paper bag, which I recognised as coming from a chain chicken shop.

'Ah, no thanks. I will have to go,' Marsh said and began to leave.

'You could stay. There is plenty, honestly,' Sylvia offered.

'No, no, thank you. I will see you at nine in the morning?' he answered and nodded back at me when I nodded agreement.

We ate the chicken and chips she had served on two plates on the couch. Really, it was the only place there was room without moving reams of paperwork.

The usually greasy southern-style chook was exactly the right meal. I'm not sure if that was because it was served by Sylvia or because I hadn't had anything to eat since breakfast.

On glancing around the room, Sylvia saw the photo albums I had taken from the safe and asked, 'What have you been up to?'

'Oh, yes, I had to return the paperwork I haven't looked at yet. Your father told me to, and I came across those photos. I hope you don't mind?' I said awkwardly.

'See anything you like?' she said cheekily.

'Plenty,' I answered, playing the game.

'Well,' she said, getting up and recovering the two albums, 'we better see what you were looking at.'

We finished eating and she sat close and opened the first album. We spent a nice time going through the pictures of her early years, and though it was very pleasant, I longed for the second book to come up for inspection. There were so many things I wanted to know.

She started with the cover page in large bubble letters she had obviously written, 'New Zealand Trip'.

Then she turned to the shot of her and her mother in Queenstown with the Remarkable Mountain Range in the background. She explained the shot and turned the page.

On the next page, she went into detail about her and her mother's travel on a bus to Lake Wanaka. There was still no sign of her father. Next, on the white-water rafting outing on the Shotover River, no Donne. Finally, it got the better of me.

'Where was your father in all of this?' I probed, feeling uncomfortable about asking.

'Oh, he had business and didn't join us till the second week,' she explained.

'Oh. I wondered why he wasn't in any of the pictures?' I said, feeling a little clumsy.

'Yes, but he usually insists on taking the pictures of us anyway. He is a good photographer, and he really hates having his photo taken,' she explained.

'Me too,' I said, but really, I was thinking, *What if Donne really is involved?* I knew I had to find out more, but I just couldn't push the point here for fear of making Sylvia suspicious or something worse.

We talked for another half an hour and then Sylvia stood and said that she needed to get home.

'Do you really have to go?' I asked not very tactfully.

'Yes, I have work in the morning. Mother is going to Sydney, so I have to put on my best *legal secretary* act,' she answered.

I stood and made it plain that I was going to kiss her. She didn't resist. Our embrace was passionate and excited, and my hands began to wander as my hand slid down her back. She stepped away and gave it a slight slap, saying, 'Naughty boy.'

I stepped forward again but this time, my injured hand got caught between us and it was so painful that I had to stop.

She smiled supportively, seeing that I was hurting. 'I have to go,' she said and started to head for the door.

I didn't feel that the encounter was over. I wanted to kiss her again, but she was determined and got to the back door. After saying 'bye, bye', she was gone.

Chapter 21

I pined for Sylvia most of the night. My arm was painful, and I resolved that I should try to see a doctor the next day. Finally, I fell asleep at around four in the morning. I had been reading more files but was distracted by the thought of Sylvia.

As I often did when I couldn't sleep, I decided to go for a long walk. I took my torch from the bedroom and then went to the kitchen to get a bottle of water but to my surprise, there was none left. Donne had warned me against drinking the tank water without boiling it so I thought of taking some of the orange juice from the large plastic containers, but there was nothing around to put it in and I would have looked a bit funny carrying a gallon bottle around. Then I remembered that I had taken a bottle with me to the shed the previous night. I decided to retrieve it. As I opened the back door, I had second thoughts and went back inside and recovered the pistol Donne had loaned me.

As I neared the shed, I had a cold feeling, and the door – the sliding door that I couldn't close the previous evening – was closed. What the hell? I stopped in my tracks, and it took a little while for me to gather the courage to try the door. It slid open as easily as possible.

Shit, what is going on? I thought, my mind racing, trying to convince myself that I had shut it, but I knew that that was not true. Could Marsh have shut it? Well, no, why would he have done that? There was no reason for him to even go near the shed when he was leaving, and I had watched Sylvia walk to her car and give me a little wave before driving off.

I shone my torch inside and picked out the two vehicles that were covered with very large tarpaulins. I had been in such a flap the previous night that I had hardly given them a second thought.

The nearest car was obviously a convertible of some kind, as the tarp showed its shape. I liked sports cars, perhaps because I had spent hours as a young boy pretending to be James Bond or whoever was the raging favourite in the world of Corgi toys at the time. The other vehicle looked bigger, and I really wasn't interested in it.

I lifted one corner of the tarp and found just what I wanted to see. Oh god, it was a Corvette Stingray, an early model, and though it had appeared to be a convertible, I found that it was actually a hard-top, but it was very low to the ground.

I could tell that the car had once been red, though there was little of the original paint left. It was obviously a barn find, and some restoration had begun, sanding the paint back and filling some of the rust holes on the bottoms of the doors. I vowed to come back and have a look a better look in daylight.

I moved through to the room with the windows and recovered the bottle of water. I left the building, sliding the door shut again. It slid perfectly again. I must have shut it the previous night. I was pretty worked up, and who knows what I could have done.

I walked. I saw nothing other than the flashes of Sylvia in all those beautiful, exotic locations in the photos. My mind was clever enough to cut her mother out of the vision.

Soon, I realised I had almost walked into a dam. I was smitten, and I felt like a young schoolboy again, unsure, insecure and loving every minute of it. Love is such a crazy thing.

I skirted the dam and reached a large pump. I noticed that the hose had become detached. I didn't have any real idea what the pump was used for, but I presumed that it was some kind of overflow into the front lower paddocks. I wondered if I should get down closer and try to reattach it, but I could see that the area close to the pipe was very thick, deep-looking mud.

I stood, looking at the scene, wondering if I was going to be able to pull up the hose and connect it with only one good arm. My position meant that I was looking back at the house, and I was soon surprised to see the lights of another car arriving.

I had remembered to lock the house and felt for the key in my pocket. It was there, so I hurried back toward the newly arrived car, knowing that if it was Sylvia or Marsh, they wouldn't be able to get into the house.

I came down the slope behind an old tractor, which I think was more of a garden ornament than a working vehicle. The tractor blocked my view of the house area, and just as I started to come out into the open, I saw Aitkins knocking on the back door.

Quickly, I ducked behind the tractor's rear wheel and hid myself from view. I was still able to see him, but his back was to me, and he was speaking, though I could not quite hear what he was saying. Suddenly, he seemed to lose interest and backed away from the building.

Seeing a rock, he bent down and picked it up. I thought he was about to smash the glass in the door, but to my surprise, he turned the rock over and looked at it closely, then put it back down on the ground where he had found it. He turned to look around and I ducked for cover as the torch he was carrying lit the area where I was hidden, though dimly.

I waited for the light to turn away. The few seconds it took seemed like an hour. As I saw the light finally turn, I looked out again to see Aitkins walking down the left side of the house, not the side he had arrived on. It was obvious he was casing the building, looking for another way to enter. I began to panic.

Was he here to silence me? Had I locked the front door? Had I locked the double glass doors that fronted onto the veranda?

I saw the light emanate from the front right side of the house as I looked at it. He was on the front veranda. Both doors must have been locked as he quickly appeared in sight again and turned up the side of the house, heading in my direction. Then the light paused, pointing at the tractor, right where I was hiding. I had drawn back from the edge of the wheel and was sure he was not able to see me, but the pause sent a chill down my spine.

I stopped breathing and was relieved to see the light turn from left to right and back again, then past the other side of the tractor, I could see it settle on the outbuildings. He was heading toward the first shed.

I wondered if I should take that chance to get to the house and get inside, then I could ring for help, but my feet wouldn't move. Now I knew what it felt like to be frozen in the spotlight.

I could see Aitkins quite clearly as he tried the doors and then found the sliding one and slid it open. I felt for the gun in my coat and was relieved when it was there. I fumbled with it but got it into my left hand and readied myself for whatever was to come next.

I could see the torchlight picking out each of the windows and searching the shed from side to side. He must have satisfied himself that there was no one there. He walked around the next two buildings, and I held my breath again when he came back. He walked back toward the house, and the movement of his torch seemed to show that he was indeed heading for his car.

The door slammed and the lights came on, pointing almost directly at me. The car started, turned around and left. I sat on the ground with my back up against the tractor tyre. I felt exhausted. I didn't move for what felt like an hour, probably it was no more than a few minutes.

When I became brave enough, I skirted the yard and headed to the back door. Realising that I still had the gun in my hand, I put it down next to the rock I had seen Aitkins pick up. It didn't look right; there was something about it that didn't look like a rock. I picked it up and realised that it was a key hide, and it was empty. Had the key been there, Aitkins would certainly have gained access to the building, so it must have been empty. *Well,* I thought, *it must be the key Donne gave me. Thank heavens for that.*

Immediately, I grabbed the phone as I re-locked the door from the inside. The line was dead.

Chapter 22

I raced about, trying each door to see that they were locked. When I finished, I started on the windows. Everything that had a lock was secure.

I heard a noise outside and though I thought it was a cow calling, I panicked and grabbed for my gun. It was not there. 'Oh. Christ, where did I put it?' I said out loud. Then I remembered that I had set it down near the steps at the back door.

'Oh, you stupid bastard,' I said, putting my hand to my forehead.

I was really frightened. I knew that if Aitkins had cut the phone lines, he would be back. I knew that I had no other option but to open the door and regain the gun. I knew that there were many other guns in the den, but I would have had to break into the gun cabinet to get at them. I knew that they were rifles and shotguns, and I only had one arm, making them virtually unusable. I went to the kitchen and peered out of the window. I couldn't see much. I turned the light off and looked out from side to side. Nothing seemed to move, and I thought that if I got out of the door quickly enough, I might regain the weapon safely.

I prepared myself, took a deep breath and burst out. I grabbed the gun and turned. As I reached the doorway, I heard another loud noise and though this time I knew it was a cow, it still scared me half to death.

I fumbled with the lock and eventually got it in place, then I went around turning all of the lights off, even those illuminating family portraits and landscapes on the walls. It was now much easier to see out, and I was certain that if I were in the right place, I would see if someone came toward the building. It may have seemed to an onlooker that I was doing things in a calm, methodical way, but nothing could have been further from the truth. I was panic-stricken.

I decided, whether right or wrong, that getting upstairs was a good idea, so I almost ran to the stairs and darted up them two at a time.

At the top, I turned to the right knowing that those windows would have the best view over anyone approaching via the entrance road. The room I decided on was the Donne master bedroom. Everything was pink. There was a tall boy dresser near the door. I upended it with difficulty and pushed it into a blocking position. The door opened inward; this would make it harder to get through.

There was a double love seat near the most advantageous window, and I turned it around so I could be seated looking out of the window. I parted the lace curtains slightly to give me a better view.

I could feel my heart almost beating out of my chest again, and I was breathing very hard. I had never been so frightened.

I just sat there watching, my mind racing and reacting to every noise, my senses tingling at the sounds a house makes or some animal noise or the wind even though it was a slight zephyr.

I must have lasted hours before the inevitable happened: I fell asleep. I had no idea how long I had slept but I was awakened by the sound of a door crashing in. I stood up and wheeled to face the door. *It won't be long now,* I thought. My heavy breathing retuned as I pointed the pistol at the door.

I could hear my name being yelled, but I wasn't sure who was yelling. Suddenly, a loud knock on the door. Should I shoot or should I wait to see who it was? Thank heavens I waited, as a voice I recognised rang out, 'Fitzpatrick, are you alright?' It was Marsh.

I moved to the tall boy and tugged at it, but it was wedged tightly between the two door jams. I couldn't budge it.

'I'm here, but you will have to push hard on the door as I can't get it open,' I yelled.

'Stand back,' he yelled back, and I could hear strong force being applied. The tall boy moved just a little, then a little more. Marsh's head stuck in through the gap. 'You ok?'

I couldn't find any words; I just nodded, and I could see in his eyes that he didn't believe me.

'It won't take us long to get you out,' he said, and another big shove saw the door open about halfway, then further. Standing there was Marsh and peering over his left shoulder was Aitkins.

'Oh god,' I said and backpedalled. I caught my heel on the edge of the bed and fell backwards, landing face-up in what was an extremely painful effort. Still, I raised my pistol and pointed it at Aitkins from the ground.

'What the hell?' Aitkins said, though he didn't move knowing that I was more likely to fire if he tried to retreat or pull *his* revolver.

'Put the gun down,' Marsh was able to say. Then seeing that I didn't lower my weapon, he added, 'He's cleared. He was on a training exercise with me when the second boy was killed.'

I still didn't lower my gun. 'What about cutting the phone lines last night? He came here to kill me,' I blurted.

'What the hell?' Aitkins said again.

'No, no, I asked him to come and check on you when I couldn't get an answer on the phone. He lives halfway out here, so I knew he could get here faster than I could.'

The gun stayed up, and Marsh said again, 'Put the gun down.'

'What about the two reports about Mrs Swift and the lost copper wire?' I insisted. I was sure this cop was bent, and I wasn't about to give him any chance to get at his gun.

Marsh, seeing that I wasn't going to let things go, told Aitkins to wait for us downstairs. The young man had looked stunned when I had mentioned the wire and the old woman, but he obeyed, and his footsteps could be heard going down the corridor and stairs.

'Christ, you've got yourself worked up,' Marsh said, taking the gun from my hand. Then he added, 'We will check the phone lines to see what happened. It might just be a coincidence.'

'But what about the wire and Mrs Swift?' I asked and I couldn't believe how hard I was breathing.

'Well, I stopped checking those when I proved that he wasn't the killer. But I'll look into it tomorrow,' he reassured me.

He helped me to the bed, and I sat down, feeling quite the fool.

'There you go. I will tell Aitkins to go home and come back for me in the morning,' Marsh reassured me and walked out to give the young man his instructions. Moments later, I heard the sound of a car leaving.

I didn't move. I still felt such a fool and my hands just wouldn't stop shaking. I really wasn't cut out for this kind of thing.

Marsh re-entered and said, 'Come downstairs. I've put the kettle on.'

I just followed as instructed. This was all such a blow to my self-esteem; I was so embarrassed. Once downstairs, I sat in the lounge room and Marsh went to the kitchen, returning a few minutes later with two cups of tea.

We sat quietly for a short time, then I found words.

'I don't understand why I was so wrong. I read the two papers. Both named Aitkins and I saw blood and violence. I don't understand. I don't just imagine things like that.' I covered my eyes with my hand.

'This is not scientific. You've told me before that it isn't always clear, what you see,' he said, trying to reassure me.

'I know but I don't just see blood without a reason,' I said. I took my tea and sipped it, then covered my eyes again when I put the cup down.

'Mate, I wouldn't ask for any more from you, but there are lives at risk and we have no real idea who this mongrel is yet,' he said.

I dropped my hand and looked at him. Now there were no words; I just nodded.

I had hardly slept a wink when the sun lit up the lace curtains of the guest bedroom. I took a few minutes until I could hear Marsh rattling around in the kitchen and then walked down the corridor and descended the stairs. I was still feeling a bit of a fool.

'Morning,' Marsh said, turning some bacon on a skillet pan. 'Bacon and eggs ok?'

I nodded but said nothing as I noticed a chair under the back door handle. He saw where I was looking and said, 'Oh yes, I know how right you are usually, and I got a little spooked as well. It never hurts to be careful.'

I nodded again and said nothing, though it did reassure me to see that he still regarded me as worth listening to, which may have been the reason for the chair.

We sat and ate, quietly. Near the end of the meal, which I thought wasn't a bad effort for a bachelor, he asked me if I wanted to go with him, first thing, to see Mrs Swift.

I nodded. I was still aware that I had looked foolish the previous evening, but I was still sure what I had seen and felt about Aitkins.

I took my clothes and retired to the bathroom to shower. When I returned, Aitkins was in the lounge room. I noticed that Marsh had at some time between last night's events and this morning, cleaned all of the paperwork up and it was nowhere to be seen.

'Morning,' Aitkins said, looking to see if his superior approved and he received a little nod.

'Morning,' I replied. I supposed I was expected to return the pleasantry but there was no way I was going to apologise.

You could have cut the atmosphere in the room with a knife. Marsh, seeing that I was still not giving up the animus, said, 'Aitkins is going to drive us to his house where we can pick up my car.'

I nodded. I was still not sure I wanted to be around this man, but I had little or no reason to back it up.

'Oh, and get the phone lines fixed ASAP. I don't know what happened there, but we will need them to be up and running,' he instructed Aitkins.

Marsh opened the rear door of the bright green Ford, and I got in thinking that it was a bit of a hoon's car, not something a more seasoned cop would drive. As he took off, it was obvious that he just couldn't help creating a little dust. Marsh, sitting in the passenger seat next to him, just gave his head a little shake of disapproval.

We travelled far quicker than was necessary to the young man's house. It was a little secondary building near a farmhouse but it had its own turning circle in which Marsh's own car was parked.

I was much happier when we had switched cars, and he had driven off in the direction of the town.

'What a dick,' I said, and though Marsh didn't say anything, I could tell that he agreed from his slight smile.

We arrived at Mrs Swift's house. The old woman let us in and asked if we wanted tea or coffee. We both said that we were fine.

'What I wanted to follow up with you, Mrs Swift, was the claim about the two men who broke into the work yard opposite?' Marsh started.

'I have handed that over to my solicitor. He has my statement,' Mrs Swift broke in before he could say more.

'I see, that is a bit strange. Why do you think you need to have a solicitor?' he asked.

'For protection, naturally,' she answered.

'But protection from who?' he continued, wanting more information.

'Protection from the thieves and protection from your lot,' she answered bluntly.

'Sorry, I can't see why you would need protection from the police?' Marsh goaded her to give more information.

'It's not right. I was just trying to help. I saw those two men robbing the place and had to wait for two hours for someone to turn up, and then he threatens me!' she answered quickly as though she had practised her words.

'Who? Who threatened you?' he pushed.

'Your great Detective Aitkins told me I was a public nuisance. Me, who never does anyone any harm,' she said, throwing her arms around.

'You must have misunderstood. Aitkins is not a lead detective, and he has no right to tell you not to contact the police,' Marsh reassured her.

'Well, that was how he introduced himself and he was in plain clothes, but that was only the first threat. As he threatened me, one of the men turned up across the road and opened the gate. I wasn't sure what he was there for, but Aitkins told me to stay inside and crossed to challenge the man. I stayed inside but I could see everything.' She pointed to the large front windows.

'What happened then?' I asked and received a stern look from Marsh.

'What happened then? I'll tell you what happened then. He proceeded to beat the hell out of the other man, and who are you anyway?' she both answered and questioned me.

'That's not important. What happened next?' Marsh interrupted.

'Then he picked the other man up and threw him into his car. He threw something in with him – it looked like paperwork – then he pointed to the road. The other man accepted the instructions and took off as fast as he could get out of there.' She paused for effect. 'Then Aitkins looked across and saw me, just minding my own business. He came over and burst in the front door and threatened me with all sorts of things if I said anything. That's why I gave a full statement to Mr Donne. If anything happens to me, he will give it to the papers. Threaten me, will he? Well, you now have a threat you can give him.' This was a rambling rant, but I admired her tenacity. I smiled – that was just what Aitkins deserved.

Marsh thanked and reassured the enraged old biddy, telling her that she may be called to repeat the statement in the case that may be brought against Aitkins. 'Rest assured, he will feel the full weight of the law if we can prove anything,' he promised.

Mrs Swift looked at him for a moment, looked up and down then concluded, 'I have your word for this, and I know that means something.'

'Well, I will see what can be done. He is a constable, not a detective, and he must have been off duty when he came here. It will be hard to prove the assault if we don't have a victim, but I can investigate that. He can still be charged through internal affairs for misrepresenting himself as a detective and for threatening you,' Marsh explained and seeing that the woman looked sceptical, he added, 'It would be your word against his, and that is not a good thing, but he has a record of being quick to turn violent. Even if it didn't immediately see him dismissed, it would stay on his record.'

Mrs Swift nodded and walked us back to the front door.

Marsh thanked her again and we left, her eyes never leaving me. I'm sure she was sizing me up, working me out, trying to understand if I was the famous medium, she had seen and read about in the paper.

I had gained some view of blood/violence when I was in her home. I'm not sure if it was the house that I was getting it from or if it came straight from her, but it seemed plausible that what I had seen was exactly what she had described.

'Well?' Marsh asked as we got into his car.

'I saw what she was talking about. I think she was telling the truth, but there is a lot going on in her memory. I don't think she would be a good witness,' I answered truthfully.

'I hate this kind of thing. I must register the complaint with internal affairs and then they act and the men working around you hate you for the rest of your career,' he said, looking out the front window without starting the car.

I thought for a moment. 'What if I was to report it, anonymously, on paper?' I asked.

'You would do that?' he asked.

'Yes, if it would help?' I offered.

'That could work, ah, if you were able to stay anonymous. Could you do it on a computer that is not yours?' He thought for a moment. 'No, that would not work. If they question Mrs Swift, they would know I covered it up. No, I will have to do the report.'

I nodded. 'It will be the right thing to do, as long as he is found guilty.' I didn't know what else I could do to help.

'It's not your problem. I don't want to involve you further. I will send the complaint from Mrs Swift to them this afternoon. Then the place will be crawling with outsiders. That is not what we want, but I can't do anything else. I promised her, and it is my job,' he said, though he sounded more like he was trying to convince himself not me, so I just nodded my support.

Marsh took me to the Donne office and left me there for the day. I don't know if he knew that Mrs Donne was going to be away for a few days, though I expected he did.

'I will pick you up here this afternoon,' he said as he pulled up outside the building. It was then that I remembered that I had to tell him what I had found out about Donne and the holiday in New Zealand. I had forgotten with all the events of the previous day.

'Oh, I forgot to mention, Sylvia told me that Donne was not with them for the first week of the New Zealand trip,' I blurted.

'Oh shit, that makes it even harder. I will, um, I will investigate it during the day. When the check was done, I only asked for the dates of the trip. Maybe I got that wrong – I can't remember. God, I will investigate it today,' he concluded.

I was never sure whether he thought life would be easier without me around.

Once Sylvia had settled me into the usual meeting room and loaned me her computer, I started to think about other things. What future would I ever have in the area, now that I was outed as some kind of seer? I knew that they would never let me settle; there would always be someone who wanted something, someone who thought of me as an evil unholy being. Someone to rail against.

The only other real friend I had in town, other than Sylvia, Marsh and Donne, was my boss, Bob, and I had let him down. I knew that he would have been picking up all the extra work I had left him stranded with. True, I wasn't the greatest genius in the world but I was good at my job, and he was the only one who could step into my shoes at such short notice. I decided to give him a call.

I heard the phone pick up, and Bob's voice started the blurb we were always taught to use with customers. 'Good morning and well –'

'Bob, it's me,' I interrupted.

'Bloody hell, I thought you were dead or something,' he answered.

'Not yet, but I am unable to come back to work. I, er, I won't get any peace if this case is not solved,' I explained.

'I don't care about that. How are you?' he asked, knowing about earlier times when I had lost it when in this situation.

'Thanks, mate, but they won't let up. You know what those bastards are like,' I answered, referring to the reporting fraternity.

'Where have you been staying?' he asked.

'Oh, I'm with friends. I had an accident, smashed up my right hand. I can hardly use the bloody thing,' I answered, trying to change the subject.

'What have you done? Is it permanent or what?' he asked.

'Well, I'm not sure. I basically de-gloved the hand and it is a bit of a mess. I have lost the little finger, but the pain is not too bad,' I explained.

'Bloody hell, you are in the wars. How can I help?' he asked.

'I don't really need any help, but I know I have left you in the lurch with the shop, and I don't think I will be able to come back any time soon,' I answered.

The feeling that I had let him down must have been understood in my words as he answered, 'Not a problem. I am going to put the manager of our first shop in here for a few weeks until I can train someone to take your place. I will always have a position for you. I owe you everything,' he concluded.

'Mate, you owe me nothing. You are about the only person who would ever employ me, and I loved what we were doing,' I answered but cut short as I could feel the emotion getting to me and it was obvious in my voice.

There was a slight pause. 'Any time, just give me a ring. Where should I send your last pay packet to?'

'I'll get someone to pick it up,' I reassured him.

'And what about the house?' he added.

'I have someone clearing it in the next few days. There isn't much stuff to clear, and I have paid the rest of the month's rent,' I explained.

'Where can I catch up with you then?' he continued to push, but I didn't want to have him in the loop for fear he would be another target.

'I'll get back to you as soon as I get back from Sydney,' I answered, thinking that he would leave it at that.

'So, you are in Sydney?' he continued.

'Yeah. I might be back at some time or contact you at the other shop or at home, if that is ok?' I answered, leaving him nowhere to go with the questioning. I felt bad about lying to him, but I thought it was for his safety as much as mine.

I settled down and waited till I got my head in the game again, and then I rang my parents. Thanks for small mercies, my mother answered.

I reassured her that all was well, and I didn't need anything; I just didn't want her to worry. Worrying was of little or no use; it didn't change anything. I wished someone could have convinced me of that.

I had fulfilled my commitments on the phone, and I was relieved that my father was not at home.

I started the work of searching for incidents that were relevant or at least had some rough chance of being seen to be relevant.

I put a few things aside to discuss with Marsh but there really wasn't any other way that I thought I could help. I really didn't find anything; perhaps there was nothing *to* find.

I decided to stretch my legs and walked to the main office where Sylvia was dealing with some customer. A man of little consequence to me but he was being treated very kindly by Sylvia; indeed, she was holding his hand in what seemed to be an offering of sympathy.

The old man turned when he heard me enter. His eyes were bloodshot and he looked embarrassed.

'Oh, sorry,' I said as he nodded to Sylvia and turned to leave. He didn't say anything, just passed me and began to shut the door behind him as Sylvia said, 'I will get Father to call in on you tomorrow morning, Mr Field,' and we were alone.

'Poor old thing lost his wife this morning. She was only seventy,' she explained, wiping a tear from the corner of her eye.

Being such a craftsman with words as I am, I uttered, 'Oh.' Succinct and brief. Oh god, I was pathetic. She smiled. It was as if she understood me without me saying anything else.

We chatted for a few moments before a knock came on the door and Sylvia said, 'Come in.'

The door opened and a middle-aged woman entered.

'I'll get out of your hair,' I said and turned to go.

'I will bring lunch in in about fifteen minutes,' Sylvia said.

I said, 'Thanks.'

Wow, I really was impressive.

I sat looking at the mantle clock. The fifteen minutes seemed like a lifetime; it almost looked as if the hands were going backwards.

When Sylvia knocked and entered, it was obvious that it was going to be an extremely opulent midday meal as she turned and pulled a small cart into the room. This was less of a luncheon and more of a high tea. The three-tiered cake tower carried an extremely large assortment of the best pastries, and there were also trays with quarter-cut sandwiches. Two teacups were in the nicest saucers, and a matching tea pot showed steam from its spout.

'Wow, you shouldn't have gone to so much trouble,' I said, giving a little whistle.

'Not at all. This is what Father has us serve to all important clients. I don't really think it is for the clients – even when we don't have anyone, the cakes still disappear,' she joked.

I couldn't believe the trouble she had taken. Yes, some of the cakes were purchased, but many had the Donne ladies written all over them, and the sandwiches must have been prepared while I was in the meeting room, they were so fresh.

We ate and we chatted about nothing – the weather was hot, there was a promise of rain, but that never seemed to come to fruition in the current El Niño event. Where her parents were and what they were doing. I was such rubbish at this kind of thing.

When it was obvious that I had eaten my fill, she stood to clear away the plates. I stood with the intent that I would help, but my main reason was to close the gap between us. I took her in my arms, and we kissed. At almost that exact moment, the door opened, and Donne's head came into view.

'Oh, sorry,' he said and stepped back out.

'Oh, shit,' I said.

'It's alright,' Sylvia said, walking to the door and beckoning to her father to re-enter.

Donne came back in and looked sheepishly at me as though he had something to be apologetic for.

'Oh, sorry, we were just...' I started but he interrupted.

'I think it's fairly evident what you were just,' he started and then turned his gaze to Sylvia and continued, 'If I were you, I wouldn't tell your mother, you were just...' He smiled and she walked over to him and gave him a hug. Like many daughters, she could twist him around her little finger.

She looked over her shoulder at me and said, 'I had better get back to the desk,' and left me there. What the hell was I supposed to say? Was he going to punch me on the nose?

I stood for a moment, thinking of what to say. 'I'm sorry, I –' I started but he silenced me with a raised hand.

'You are both adults. It is none of my business, but let me just say, don't hurt her or I will release the kraken, and you don't want to take on Mrs Donne.' He gave a slight smile then looked away toward the papers I had printed and placed next to the laptop.

'Where have you got to with the case?' he asked, changing the subject to my relief.

'Ah, well, we are at a stalemate. We thought that Aitkins may be involved, but it seems that the old woman, um, Mrs Swift, had seen him beating up some guy,' I answered.

'Oh, she told you about that?' Donne said, sounding surprised.

'Yeah, she seemed to trust Marsh,' I said, and he nodded for me to continue. 'Seems that Aitkins waited for someone to turn up and belted the piss and pick handles out of him,' I continued and felt a bit embarrassed at my ineloquence.

'Yes, well, she gave me a statement to use if she was accused of something by him. She said he threatened her?' he answered and questioned in the same breath.

'It seems so. Marsh is contacting Internal Affairs this morning,' I answered.

He immediately picked up the phone and dialled a number, saying, 'Well, we will put a stop to that right away.' He waited for the number to answer and when it did, he asked to speak to Marsh. Turning back to me, he said, 'It would end his career if he did that. No one will work with him. Ridiculous, I know... oh, Marsh. It's Donne here. You haven't done that report yet?'

'No, not yet.' Marsh's voice was audible as Donne had pressed the conference call function on the extension.

'Good, good. Come here and I will make an official report. I am just a well-meaning member of the public – after all, as is my client,' Donne instructed.

There was quite a long pause, then Marsh said very quietly, 'I'm on my way.'

Donne hung up the phone and said, 'He was reluctant to owe someone, but he had nothing to lose really. I have friends in all parts of the law, and they will take my word that I made the report to Marsh.' He raised his eyebrows and gave a questioning nod.

I nodded back and he went on, 'You know, there are other things Aitkins could go for, but everyone is a bit frightened of him. His connections are, shall we say, on the darker side.' He again raised his eyebrows to solicit my response.

'What about you?' I asked innocently.

'Well, he wouldn't dare. My connections are on both sides of the aisle. I know judges and politicians – equally, I know thugs and underworld figures whom I have defended, successfully if I do say so myself,' he concluded, smiling. He was obviously enjoying the tussle. We both stood for a while. We looked at each other and he must have been able to see the doubt in my expression.

'Ah, the age-old question is in your thoughts. Why defend these low lives? Well, it may be hard for anyone to stomach, but it is the law that any person, innocent or guilty, is entitled to a vigorous legal defence. Everyone is innocent until proven guilty,' he explained, and I nodded again, but he decided that the lesson was not over. 'I have defended drug bosses, brothel owners, murderers down to the lowliest scum of the earth, and they all got my best defence. That doesn't always make one popular, but the law doesn't care about popular. If this killer we are chasing asked, I would defend him, but for the fact that I have been involved in the investigation.'

He paused for a moment. 'I am delighted to be on this side of things in this case as it would be very hard to even sit next to this bastard, let alone defend him.'

As always, I felt like a lower form of life when he gave one of his lessons. I admired him; I'm sure he had a stronger character than I did. I knew that I could never do what he did. I nodded.

Marsh arrived about an hour after his call from Donne. He entered and knocked on the conference room door.

'Come in,' Donne and I said in unison.

'Talk about singing from the same hymn book,' Marsh said as he obeyed the double invitation.

'Now, look here. I will ring a friend in the IA branch and tell him that I have come across a statement that besmirches one of our local police officers. I will tell him that I have a statement, from *a client*, that places Aitkins in a fairly bad situation where he has broken the law. I will say that she does not want to talk as she is frightened of what he might do. I will add my own feelings, that I believe him to be bent, and the investigation will begin without you being implicated. Understand?' he instructed.

'Well, yes, but they will question her and ask why she didn't go directly to the police?' Marsh questioned. It was obvious he had thought things through; I hadn't even thought of that.

'I will advise my client to tell the truth – the part of the truth that will benefit her own defence, that is if they even want to question her. I will try to keep her name out of it if possible, saying that she fears for her life and will not give any evidence, as I would advise her if she were subpoenaed. I'm pretty sure I can pull that off and it will keep your name out of it. You know what happens to cops who call in IA?' he answered, counselled and questioned all at once.

We both nodded dutifully, bowing to the greater knowledge and planning of a man who was used to dealings with people on both sides of his beloved law.

Two days passed before the visit to the station started. Two Internal Affairs officers arrived and took Aitkins into an interview room. Around an hour later, two other officers arrived and escorted Aitkins to a waiting car. As he walked head down and handcuffed past his colleagues, who had gathered at the front counter, he said to Marsh, 'Contact the union.'

Marsh nodded, not knowing whether he should or shouldn't obey the instruction.

Marsh was now taken into the same interview room by the two men. The first of the two who followed him into the room introduced himself as Butler and his offsider as Milton, though he omitted both of their ranks. They had all the power, something most of the police force and their unions resented.

'What do you know about the officer in custody?' Butler asked.

'Are you aware that this man has been threatening witnesses and has at least once been violent on the job?' Butler probed.

Marsh knew about the incident they were asking about but he also knew about the incident in the cells just the previous week.

'Yes, he was reprimanded for being violent with a suspect last week. He thought the man had been the child killer. The man has since notified that he will not be making an official complaint,' he answered, looking from one man to the other.

'Do you think he was dealt with appropriately?' Butler asked.

'We all make mistakes, and he is young,' Marsh answered, avoiding giving his opinion.

'Yes, but how do you think he should have been dealt with?'

'It would be inappropriate for me to say. I am not his commanding officer,' Marsh continued to avoid.

'Oh, so you know how to play the game?' Butler stated.

'We're talking about a man's career. I wouldn't think that it should be called a game,' Marsh answered, showing an amount of scorn.

'Just so. We are here about another incident,' the second man interjected.

'What other event?' Marsh asked, trying to keep his temper.

'Do you know of any other events?' Butler asked pointedly.

Marsh thought for a moment. 'I think I would like to call my union delegate in, if you have further questions?'

'Do you realise what happens to an officer if they are found to have hindered an internal affairs investigation?'

'Yes, and I know what happens to an officer if he gives up another officer,' Marsh came back.

The interview was closed until the union were able to send one of their lawyers, and that was not until the next afternoon.

Marsh told me about the interview; he knew that I may be brought into the investigation if they could find me.

As it happened, Marsh was ordered to produce me, and he notified me the next day that I would need to speak to the investigation team. He arranged a meeting with them for 2 p.m. that afternoon.

Donne picked me up early that morning, and we went to his office where he schooled me in how the inevitable questions were to be answered.

I hated all of this, the lying, or as Donne put it, telling the truths you need to tell. The hiding behind a solicitor, and knowing that if I got it wrong, I could be not only sealing my own fate but that of Marsh as well.

I tried to find a way of getting out of the meeting, but Donne kept reassuring me that I could do what needed to be done. He seemed to have undying confidence in me, a confidence I thought was unwarranted.

I fronted up with Donne, and he had deliberately made us ten minutes late.

'It is better to keep them waiting, put them off stride a bit,' he told me. I thought it may just make them angry.

As we entered the station, Milton, who was attached to a phone at the front desk, hung up the receiver and said in an irritated voice, 'Not a great start, keeping us waiting?'

'Not a great start, giving my client and I such a short amount of notice. I do work for a living, you know,' Donne fired back and Milton bit his tongue as he joined us in front of the main desk. He opened the door that led to the cells.

'Excuse me, but I don't think so,' Donne said as we reached the first offender interview room.

'What the hell do you mean?' said Milton, beginning to become riled up.

'Is my client being charged with something?' Donne demanded. He was so good at getting under this man's skin that I thought the young IA officer was going to burst.

Hearing the commotion from inside the room, Butler stood and, striding to the door, said, 'What seems to be the problem?'

'I want to know what my client is being charged with?' demanded Donne indignantly.

'Fitzpatrick is not being charged with anything, *yet,*' Butler returned.

'Well then, we are not going into the cells to be interviewed. It could brand my client with guilt by association. If anyone saw him being interviewed in the cells, they would think him guilty of something, and by my deductions, you have already branded him as not guilty of anything by not charging him with anything.'

The two officers looked at each other. Milton turned a shade of crimson that was almost unbelievable.

'Well, as you are here on your own volition, where would you like to be interviewed?' Butler asked, keeping calm, and it was obvious why he was the senior man.

'Well, really, I would like to tell my client to come back to my offices to hold the interview, so there will be no misunderstandings,' Donne rattled off the answer as though he had been practising it for hours.

'That would be possible, but it would only delay the investigation. We will question you,' Butler said, now looking to me for an answer to his problem.

'I will do whatever my lawyer tells me to do,' I answered in what could have been a well-prepared answer – actually, Donne had not told me that the relocation was part of his plan.

'So, you don't want to help us?' Milton blurted but was silenced by his superior.

'We don't know what it is that you want help with. We were not given any forewarning nor any information. My client will not be answering anything that could incriminate him,' Donne concluded.

Milton flushed an even redder colour, but Butler took it in his stride.

'Shall we say fifteen minutes then?' he conceded.

'No, I will need at least half an hour to prepare a meeting room, to make sure that one of my colleagues is not using the room,' Donne informed him, knowing full well that he was a single solicitor business. It was hardly likely that Mrs Donne was going to be holding some kind of symposium.

Butler looked as though he knew that this was only a stalling tactic but nodded his head in agreement.

When we arrived back in Donne's car, the first thing I thought to say was, 'You didn't say anything about going back to your offices?'

'No, I decided that on the spur of the moment,' he confided and continued as I raised my eyebrows. 'Always fight the enemy on your terms, on your own ground, if you can.'

I must admit that I had never heard this before but decided that it was probably something said by some great leader, like Churchill. To not show my ignorance, I just nodded knowingly.

On our arrival at the office, we were met by Mrs Donne and Sylvia.

'Set up the meeting room for five, please,' Donne instructed. Sylvia and her mother just disappeared and set about the work.

'Why five?' I asked, knowing that there would only be the two of us and the two of them.

'Always try to have an advantage in numbers. Sylvia will be taking minutes, if I get my way,' he explained, smiling widely, then added, 'That won't upset you too much, will it?'

'No,' I answered succinctly. I was delighted to have Sylvia with me wherever I was, and her support, I knew, would be just what I needed.

Donne left me for a few minutes. He re-entered with Sylvia and directed her to a seat at the end opposite to him. He directed me to sit next to him, and I obeyed. This left two seats vacant for our grand inquisitors.

'The position of the chairs is so very important. They will have their backs to the door. A high percentage of people are uneasy with their backs to the door,' he explained.

I really didn't know if all this was bullshit or not, but he was in charge and I could find nothing intelligent to say, so I fell back on the thing I knew would not get me into any trouble: I said nothing.

When Butler and Milton were shown into the room, both of their eyes darted toward Sylvia and then to Donne for an answer to the unasked question.

'Yes, this is my daughter. As we don't have recording devices like you would have had at the station, she will be taking notes. I presume that will be acceptable?' As usual, Donne answered his own question and accepted the nod from Butler as an affirmative answer.

Donne nodded to Sylvia and started proceedings by asking all present to state their names and reason for being present. He nodded to Butler who smiled; it seemed that he was almost enjoying the theatre-worthy performance of Donne.

'I am Inspector Adam Butler, Professional Standards Command. My colleague is Senior Sargent George Milton,' Butler answered and then Donne introduced himself and pointed to me.

'My name is James Fitzpatrick, and I have no idea why I have been requested to attend,' I answered, trying to look at ease as Donne had instructed.

'And?' Donne said, pointing to his daughter.

Sylvia didn't look up but stated, 'Sylvia Donne, acting as Stenographer.'

'To answer your question, Mr Fitzpatrick–' Butler began but was interrupted by Donne who raised a hand.

'Sorry, Inspector, but I must make a few comments. Mr Fitzpatrick is here of his own free will and can leave at any time, is that correct? Or is he to be charged with anything?'

'We have no need to charge Mr Fitzpatrick, unless he confides that he has committed a crime,' Butler answered cleverly.

'Oh, so you would say that this is a fishing expedition then?' Donne returned.

'Not at all. We simply need some information that Mr Fitzpatrick may have,' the inspector explained.

'Well, pursuant to that, I will be advising my client to refuse to answer anything that I think may incriminate him,' Donne said but before the words were out of his mouth, Milton exploded with indignation.

'This is all bullshit. Just answer the bloody questions,' he said rather louder than was necessary in the small room.

'I don't think you understand the process here, Mr Milton,' Donne answered, also raising his voice slightly. Butler shot Milton a withering look. Yes, they had set up to play 'good cop bad cop' but not with Donne. Milton took the admonishment and sat back in his chair.

'Please repeat the last comment of Mr Milton,' Donne instructed Sylvia, and she obeyed.

'This is all bullshit. Just answer the bloody question,' she read strongly, almost mimicking Milton's tone. I thought that if he turned any redder, he would have a stroke or something.

'Yes, yes, I see how this is going to play out. Officer Milton will refrain from asking any other questions. Now, may we get on with the interview?' said the older and much wiser Butler.

Donne waved a hand as if conceding the floor. He had made his point and now would be dealing with Butler one on one, if I could keep to the facts. He had the legal side of things well in hand. It is always nice, when in any challenging situation like this, to have a leader who you knew would handle the trickiest dealings.

'Now, Mr Fitzpatrick, what I want to know is if you were involved in the investigation with Officer Marsh?' Butler took his chance.

Bloody hell, that wasn't one of the questions I was told to expect, and it was the very first.

'Which investigation?' I asked, trying not to give anything away.

'So, you were involved in an investigation then?' he fired back.

'Sorry, that is not really what you want to know, is it?' Donne spoke up, trying to protect me as both questions were a bit unexpected.

'It is a simple question,' Butler answered, though his eyes never left me.

'Are you investigating Aitkins or Marsh?' Donne said, again trying to protect me from answering.

'Well, we take notice of all involved officers when there is a complaint,' Butler answered. It was obvious that Donne was not going to get things all his own way.

'I did give some help to the officer as requested,' I answered, feeling that I was on message.

'Exactly what kind of help do you offer?' Butler pushed.

'I tell the officer what I see,' I answered a little cryptically.

'So, let me be clear, that is what you see in your mind?' he challenged.

'My client has answered the question,' Donne interjected.

'Well, no, he has only partially answered the question. Please give me an indication of what you mean when you say "see",' Butler pushed.

'I notice things that others may not,' I answered.

'You mean that you *see or notice* things in your dreams?' he pushed further.

'That is simplifying things a bit, but yes, I am a medium. Is that what you want me to say?' I answered, getting a bit defensive.

'I only want you to answer the questions you need to answer, to show where you get your information. You know there are a lot of shysters out there who prey on the vulnerable,' he explained.

'Are you accusing my client of being, how did you put it, a shyster?' Donne interjected, feigning insult.

'Certainly not, but it is fair to ask what the source of the information is, surely?' Butler fired back.

'Well, you have your answer, and let me tell you, as a witness to my client at work, he has shown himself to be extremely accurate with information in cases where he has been consulted.' Donne answered.

'Yes, Officer Marsh says you are uncanny in the information you are able to give.' Butler continued to play the word game. Donne was getting as much as he gave.

'If you don't believe anything my client says, why are we here?' Donne queried.

'Well, that is the nature of the beast. We ask questions and then work out what the truth is and what is not,' Butler answered, seeming to be careful with his selection of words. 'For instance, how did you know about the misconduct of Officer Aitkins?'

I thought this was a good question. I knew I had to answer, and yet I felt I had to be guarded with this man.

'I didn't need to see much of him to see that he was a thug. Bashing prisoners in their cell doesn't impress me in the slightest,' I answered in what I thought was a fairly strong voice.

'Yes, but what about the other incident he is being investigated for?'

'That information I gained from the old lady who saw the incidents and suffered his threats,' I continued to answer as carefully as I could.

'But why were you questioning the lady in question?' he asked, and this question threw me a bit.

'I wasn't, I wasn't questioning her,' I answered, and even I was unsure if it was a complete lie or not.

'So, some complete stranger came up to you in the street and gave you the information?' Butler said with a slightly sarcastic tone, and his subordinate smiled widely; it was obvious he was enjoying watching me squirm.

'No, I knew she had reported the incident and had made a statement to Mr Donne, to protect herself,' I answered.

'So, Mr Donne just gives you access to all his confidential files?'

'That is a scurrilous accusation. I think we should leave,' Donne said in a most indignant voice. He began to stand but was re-seated as the officer waved his hands.

'Alright, alright, I won't follow this line of questioning any further,' he reassured, and Donne just raised his eyebrows in a most indignant pose.

'Now, you say you gave the information you have to Officer Marsh?' Butler continued.

'Yes,' I answered, suddenly remembering the instruction I had been given, that one-word answers were the best defence.

'So, what exactly did you tell Marsh?' he continued, obviously knowing what I had been instructed.

'I told him about what the lady, Mrs Swift, had told me,' I answered.

'So, you just reported what the witness had said?'

'Yes,' I concluded.

'Nothing other than that?' he quipped.

'Yes, I told him that I thought the officer was violent and should be investigated,' I returned.

'And nothing you saw in dreams?' he pushed.

'Well, yes,' I said slowly.

'Yes, you did see something in a dream or yes, you told him what you were told by the witness?' he asked. It was a clever ploy; I was unsure how to answer.

I pondered for a short time and then said, 'Yes to both.'

Donne looked at me. He had told me to try not to admit anything about my psychic abilities. He paused for a moment and then said, 'Are you trying to trap my client or do you want information? Because if it is the first, I will advise my client to answer no further questions unless you charge him with something.'

'You are here as good members of the community, doing your civic duty,' Butler said.

Seemingly placated, Donne nodded, then having decided his next ploy, he said, 'Why don't you confine your questions to what the information is rather than where it came from?'

'Yes, well, we don't want to upset you,' Butler said in a slightly mocking tone. He glared at me, and I could tell that he was not impressed.

'What information did you give Officer Marsh about the missing children?' he asked in a slower and more demanding voice.

'Excuse me, we are here to answer questions about the officer who is under investigation. We are not here to speak about other ongoing cases,' Donne answered before I could even open my mouth. I was always amazed by his acuity and dexterity of mind when under pressure. I supposed that one could learn how to prepare a defence but I'm sure that Donne's speed of thought was a gift.

'Ongoing cases? So, you now think you are involved in ongoing cases?' Butler fired back.

'Listen, Mr Butler, we really are wasting time. My client has been very successful in helping the local police in their investigations and one can only surmise that that is why his assistance has been sought about other matters,' Donne answered.

'That's Inspector Butler, and I am interested in what other help your client has offered,' Butler answered, feigning indignance again.

'Perhaps we should refer you to the officer who has used my client – Detective Marsh,' Donne said shortly.

Butler sat for a moment. I think he realised that he was getting nowhere with the questions about the missing and murdered children's cases, so he returned to the case of Aitkins.

'So, do you have any further insight into the officer being investigated?' he queried, and this time I answered without thinking.

'Yes, I had a feeling that there was a death in custody in the cells here and I think Aitkins was involved.'

'You think he was involved? You just think he was involved?' Butler pounced. I had let my guard down.

'Yes,' I answered, going back to what I knew.

'Do you realise what harm you could do to this man's reputation, not to mention his possible case against you for accusing him of such crimes?' he asked quickly, hoping to get me to speak further, but before I could answer, Donne said, 'There is no legal case against my client. He has made no allegations – he has just expressed to the police his feelings. Police, I might add, who listened and have been using his "feelings" to solve several cases since this all began.'

This seemed to throw Butler as he may have thought he had the upper hand with me, which, to be honest, he did, but Donne, as always, was ready for his ploy. He fumbled with the papers in front of him as if looking for something. I'm sure he was just regathering his composure.

Suddenly taking control, Donne stood and said, 'I think we have helped you more than enough. You can contact me again if there are any charges you wish to level against my client for his efforts in assisting police with their duties.' He nodded to me, and I also stood.

'Yes, you can go, and *thank you* for your assistance. And, er, where can I contact you if I need to speak to you again?' Butler said, knowing full well the answer he was going to get.

'You may contact me if you wish to speak to my client again,' Donne said strongly and led me to the door of the room where we both stood, allowing Sylvia to exit first to her office, and then seeing the two officers out the front door.

As they exited, I heard the less-competent detective say, 'That's bullshit,' but he was put in his place by Butler who fired back at him.

'Your interruption immediately put them on the defensive. Bloody clumsy. You need...' His voice trailed off as the door was closed behind them by Donne. He then opened the door to the public waiting room and showed me in.

He signalled for me to sit, and I obeyed then he gave me a metaphorical pat on the back. 'You did quite well. It is always better to know what you are going to say in an interview before you say it. There is no taking it back or saying that what you said wasn't what you meant. It is all there in black and white.'

I knew what he was saying was true, but I also knew that without his interjections I would have fallen into all of the verbal traps Butler had set. I admired him greatly. How could I have thought him to be involved in these terrible child killings? I felt like a fool. I knew also, though, that I would have to find out through Marsh where Donne had been while his wife and Sylvia were touring New Zealand.

Chapter 23

Donne left me at the office with Sylvia who had prepared freshly cooked pastries and moved with the tray into the conference room. Donne said that he had to do a few errands and that he would be back in a couple of hours. I wasn't terribly disappointed to be left alone with Sylvia; he could have stayed away forever.

'How do you think your interview went?' she asked after we both settled down at the conference table where the pot of tea was steeping.

'Oh, ok. I'm glad you and your father were both there, though,' I answered. She just nodded and smiled.

I hadn't realised how parched I was, the dry throat made worse by nerves, the nerves that can destroy you if you are being interviewed by a professional.

I drank two cups of tea and had two of the best Neenish tarts I had ever tasted. As usual around new friends, I was a fairly awkward, speaker and was finding it hard to think of things to say. I always brought up some subject that must have been very boring to the other person, and I would usually see their eyes glaze over and make any excuse to escape my presence. Sylvia wasn't like that; she seemed genuinely interested in me, and that started to loosen my tongue a little.

Eventually, our talk turned to the case, and she asked me what I knew now that I had had a bit of time to think things through.

'I can't picture the killer,' I told her.

'I thought you said you don't see dead people?' she queried.

'No, well, he's not dead though,' I explained.

'Yes, how silly of me. It's just that it is a lot to take in, you know, the clairvoyance. Is that what you call it?' she answered.

'I suppose so, though I really don't call it anything.' I paused and then continued, trying to explain what I meant. 'It's not like TV. People who have died don't just come up and start talking to me. I get a feeling of the violence, the gore, the intent of the killer. Then I have sometimes seen one of the killed boys. Only the one. I don't understand it, but that is what it is. I have tried to hide it away, but the mind won't be silenced, even if I am asleep.'

She let this sink in for a moment. I thought she must be thinking me mad, then she said, 'It must be terrible sometimes, but it is like a gift.'

'Yes, my grandmother called it "The Gift", but it is rather an affliction sometimes,' I answered, but seeing that look of confusion on her face, I felt the need to explain further.

'It's because there is no off switch. They are not like voices as some people think. No, for me, it is like cascading thoughts and sometimes pain.'

Sylvia still looked confused, and why wouldn't she be? I had lived with this all my life and I still didn't understand the half of it.

'I have been seeing one of the boys, just every now and then when I close my eyes. He is not doing anything, just standing there. I don't even know which boy it is. He doesn't look like the pictures of the boys I have seen in the press or in the files Marsh lent me,' I explained. She still looked quizzically at me.

'Yes, I know I'm strange, but that is what I am seeing,' I said, feeling that I was losing her.

My hand was on the table close to her, and she covered it with her hand in a reassuring way and gave it a couple of pats.

I didn't know what to do. Should I stop there, should I continue? I bit the bullet.

'I want to help solve the case to stop this animal so I can rest,' I concluded, hoping that there would be no further questions. I suppose I knew that that was not going to be the case.

'When you are away from all of this, does it stop?' she asked tentatively.

'Yes, there can be some quiet moments, but there are so many disturbances, so much violence. Sometimes I will witness car accidents when I'm on the road and I have to stop until the feeling leaves me. I try not to go to funerals or churches or graveyards, and even times with my grandmother, when she went to a retirement home. So much death,' I explained.

'It must be horrible?' she said rhetorically.

'Well, not always. I could feel my grandmother near me, kind of protecting me, at her funeral. My father didn't want to take me to her funeral. He didn't approve of her, and he thought I would make a spectacle of myself. Strangely though, I just felt like smiling. Everyone who spoke said nice things about her. She was loved, and perhaps a little feared, but mostly loved by the people around her,' I explained and felt myself smiling even then.

Sylvia squeezed my hand again. She made me smile, too.

After a little while, she took the tray of cups, saucers and the tea pot and started to walk toward the small kitchenette.

'Let me help with that,' I offered.

'Certainly not,' she answered with feigned indignance.

Though a bit sexist, I knew that she, like her mother, thought of the kitchen as their domain, and they certainly didn't want us mere males messing things up. That was probably fair enough if she had seen my own kitchen after I had prepared a meal.

I sat for a moment with my eyes shut and remembered my grandmother's face. I think she was the only person who really understood what this was like, always seeing terror, one might say evil. Then, as if on demand, the small boy stood before me. He just stood there; he didn't seem to be injured, and he was not saying anything or even moving. He just stood there. What the bloody hell was I supposed to do about it? What did he want, and why did he think I could help him? *Did* he think I could help him? Why me? That's what it usually came down to – why me?

I tried to concentrate on the case for the rest of the day. Sylvia and I had a very pleasant lunch with miniature quiches and a rainbow sponge. I worried that if my relationship with Sylvia were to continue, I would have to up my physical exercise tenfold or buy a new wardrobe.

At about 2 p.m., Marsh picked me up to return me to the farm.

'Have you been before the IA team yet?' I asked him as we walked down the hall having said farewell to Sylvia.

'Yes,' he answered shortly.

'Well, what was it like?' I asked.

'Pretty unpleasant, as you would suspect. It's not easy to break rank and put a fellow officer in shit,' he answered, looking glum.

'He was no fellow officer of yours. He was just a thug or worse,' I said, and I could tell that he felt that way too, but it was still much harder to report on someone you have worked with, someone you knew about. His wife and one-year-old baby, what were they to do now that they had no breadwinner?

I understood how hard it must have been for him and decided to change the subject as we entered the car.

'I have been seeing a boy. That is, when I shut my eyes. Um, I don't think it is one of the boys who has gone missing here. He is a little older – perhaps thirteen or fourteen – and he is just standing there. I don't understand. I don't usually see dead people. Well, that is unless they are in terrible agony, and even then, it's not like this,' I blurted all of this as he covered me over in the back seat of the car, so I wouldn't be seen.

'What is your gut telling you about him?' he asked, though I'm sure he didn't understand how oblique the premise was to me. I could see him but there was no feeling there. Oh sure, I was worried for him, frightened to know what had happened, but I wasn't seeing that: I was seeing him, just standing there.

'I don't have any feeling for him. I just see him. I don't understand. It's times like this that make me wish I could just be a normal bloke,' I said.

'I don't really understand, but it is amazing, what you do. When we first met, I thought you were some fraud or some kind of nutter, but you get things right, and I would never have closed the cases I have in the last couple of weeks without your help.'

Though I couldn't see his face, I knew that he meant what he said. He wasn't one for giving out praise without good reason.

I lay on the cars floor, as uncomfortable as it was, not saying anything. Every time I closed my eyes I could see him, the boy, just standing there. I tried for a while, just lying with my eyes open but that only made me feel carsick.

Once we were on the road to the farm, Marsh told me that it would be ok for me to sit up and I asked him to stop. I felt I would feel less unwell if I were in the front seat.

Once I got out, though, I felt sicker and had to go to the shoulder of the road to divest myself of the beautiful luncheon Sylvia had prepared.

As I leaned over in the gutter, I felt even sicker, and I knew that this was not from the travel. I could feel terror and kind of see blood. Oh god, someone had been hit by a car, right there. I couldn't see the boy when I closed my eyes now. Was it him? I couldn't stand up straight; it was as though I had been hit by the car. And then the smell came, the smell we all know of death: carrion. It was so terrible that I heaved again, though there was very little left in my stomach.

Marsh got out of the car and walked around to my side. 'What's going on?' he asked, giving me a slap on the back.

'Oh god, there is death here, from a car. Oh shit, it can't be him,' I babbled, but pointed to where the smell seemed to be coming from, a small copes of acacia just a few metres from the edge of the road.

Marsh sniffed the air and nodded. 'You stay here,' he said and wended his way through the roadside weeds. The blackberry bushes and a fallen tree made him change direction a couple of times. He almost fell as he found the lowest point and began to go up the other side of the gutter area.

For a moment he was out of sight, but as he returned, he looked less distraught than I thought he would be.

As he arrived back at the bottom of the gutter just in front of me, I stuck out my hand to help him up the bank.

'There is a victim, the victim of a car accident, but it's a horse.' He smiled.

'Oh, sorry, but I was seeing the boy. I feel like this is involved somehow. I don't understand. I feel like a fool, sorry,' I blurted, not knowing what to say. I couldn't have felt any stupider if I tried.

'It's alright, it might have been prompted by the smell. You are under a lot of pressure. I can't say I understand but at least I didn't have to find another body,' he concluded.

'You know how I mentioned that Donne was not with the family when they were in New Zealand? I asked Sylvia and she said he wasn't with them for the first week. I don't think he has anything to do with it, but it is in my head, and I just can't forget about it,' I blurted, not wanting to sound stupid, but it was still nagging at me and this was all one thing in my head, even the dead horse.

He gave a little whistle, trying to sound like he understood. I'm sure he didn't. 'I will look into it,' he added quietly.

We silently got back into the car, and I cupped my hands to my face. What a fool I must have looked. Then he was there, the boy was there again. I didn't want to say any more to Marsh at that moment. I thought he might have me committed or something. No, I would have to work this out without help.

The drop-off was short. Marsh didn't come in, saying, 'I will come back in the morning, well, maybe lunchtime.' I thought he must not want to spend time with a lunatic.

The night passed slowly. I couldn't sleep; he was just there. I tried to watch some TV at around 3 a.m., thinking that the rubbish screened at that time might force me to fall asleep. It didn't; even the inane babbling of one of the most annoying voices in advertising didn't do the job.

I paced up and down in the lounge room and hallway, worrying that I would wear a groove in the carpet. But sleep just didn't figure in my evening. I thought to go for a long walk outside but when I neared the kitchen door, I saw that it had begun to rain. It was not very heavy but heavy enough to stop me from going out.

He was there; he was just standing there. I felt as though I would lose my mind, when every time I closed my eyes, he was standing there.

A thought came. What if he wasn't dead?

What if it was some kind of warning? But then, that wasn't my usual MO. I felt the suffering and the blood would sometimes be as visible as if it were right in front of me. But not warnings – not something I could do anything about. The feeling that it was a warning wouldn't leave me though, and I decided to ring Marsh.

It took almost five minutes for Marsh to answer but when he did, I just started as though we had just been carrying on a conversation.

'I think he is alive. I think the boy is alive,' I blurted.

'What the hell? Do you know what time it is?' he said in a rough voice.

'No, not really,' I answered.

I heard him fumble for a moment, changing the ear he was listening with, then he declared, 'It's bloody three-thirty.'

'Oh, sorry. When I get like this, I can't stop. We must do something. It won't let me go,' I ranted. I knew I was sounding a bit mad, but I also knew that I was being forced to act.

'Ok, let me get up,' he groaned and then after a few seconds, he came back on the line. 'Alright, what do you think we should do? I didn't know you got warnings like this.' His comment was right; I didn't usually get messages, but I didn't usually see the dead just standing there either. I was totally second-guessing myself, and he must have heard the doubt in my silence as he added, 'You're not sure, are you?'

'No, this is not usual, but I think he is still alive,' I answered, sounding a bit frantic.

'Ok, well, keep calm. I can go to the two schools and get full student photos,' he suggested, then realising that this had not placated me, he added, 'There is no chance I can get into the schools before about eight-thirty, so we will just have to wait till then.' He waited for me to answer but I was so distracted by the looming figure in my closed eyes world.

'Are you still there?' he questioned.

'Oh, yes, um, that seems the best thing to do, but I think it is fairly urgent,' I answered in a very uncertain tone.

'I'll get there as soon as I can,' he answered, and I heard the receiver replaced in its cradle.

I paced again for a while, then it hit me. What if I were to search the internet for photos put into the local paper? The community pictures of sports and awards won by local students.

I quickly got the search engine up and running and started looking at all sporting photos, hoping that I would happen upon the face that so forcefully dominated my mind. I trolled all mention of the schools and found nothing. I then started the search for sporting events, which were sometimes accompanied by a picture, but still found nothing. I became frantic and was trying to rush the computer. I found myself double-clicking the mouse when it was not appropriate; I was taken to pages I didn't want, and had to back arrow to return to the page I was looking for. In short, I was a mess.

Something possessed me to look at the time, and I saw that it was already seven o'clock. The next time I looked, it was eight. I still found nothing. I racked my brain for any other event or pastime that might have pictures of students, then I read one of the site headings: 'Music prodigy Matthew Wells'.

I flicked to the page and there, as I had been seeing him for nearly twenty-four hours, was the boy, Matthew.

I dialled Marsh's home phone and got no answer. I waited for several minutes before looking at the time once more; it was after eight and I knew he must be on the way to the school. I rang his mobile and immediately got a recorded message, which meant to me that he had his phone switched off or something. Shit, what could I do? I kept ringing, but the machine continued to invite me to leave a message. I paced for a few minutes, then tried again to no avail.

Let's face it; I had lost it. I was in a total panic. What else could I do?

I could ring Donne. I paused then I decided to ring the Donne home line. I was fairly certain someone would answer, and I was delighted when Sylvia's voice stated the phone number in a practised way.

'Oh god, Sylvia. It's me. I need some help!' I blurted.

'What's happened?' she asked, sounding sympathetic if a little surprised.

'I rang Marsh. I can't get Marsh. He was going to the schools, and he is not answering his mobile. I need him, urgently,' I continued to rant, thinking that she must think I was mad.

'Well, do you want me to try him?' she asked.

'No, I can do that. Can you go and find him? It's a matter of life and death,' I instructed, hoping I wasn't sounding too rude, too demanding.

'Yes, I'll get in the car. Do you know which school he is heading to first?' she asked, and I could tell she was anxious, trying to get things right.

'I don't know, probably the one nearest to his home or the police station?' I half answered and half questioned, knowing she had a better grasp of the local area.

'That will be the private school. I can get there in about fifteen minutes,' she asserted.

'Thank you. Tell him to ring me, and he is looking for Matthew Wells,' I said, still sounding frantic.

'Matthew Wells?' she asked, meaning to secure the name in her memory.

'Yes, sorry to do this to you, but it seems very urgent,' I explained.

'I'll call you back later,' she said and hung up.

I immediately rang Marsh's mobile again, but it rang out and I was again left feeling impotent in what was happening. This could be our best chance to catch this bastard.

Almost half an hour passed before I heard the phone ring as I was on one of my many laps of the hallway. I ran to answer it. 'Marsh here,' came the voice I was waiting for.

'Oh shit, I hope this is all right, and I am not running you both around for nothing,' I said apologetically, hoping that he would not be too annoyed.

'Better to be safe than sorry. I'm at the school and they are just calling the kids into class. I'll get back to you as soon as I check that the boy is here and safe,' he rang off without saying any more. I knew he believed me, but he had his eye on the prize and wasn't thinking of anything but the boy.

I paced and an agonising half an hour later, the phone rang again.

This time it was Sylvia.

'Hi, I'm with Marsh at the school. Matthew Wells hasn't turned up for school yet and we are trying to get in contact with his parents. Marsh has called out all of the local police and all of the students are in the school hall with the principal. That has allowed us to send teachers out to look for him. Marsh wanted to know if you had anything else. We don't have anything else to go on.' I could tell that she was very anxious; her voice was urgent and higher pitched than usual, and she spoke very quickly.

I closed my eyes and tried to force something to come forward, but it was just Matthew, standing there. 'No, he is just standing there. God, I don't know what to do. I'm just sitting here,' I answered.

Soon, Marsh came on the line. 'We haven't been able to raise the boy's parents. I have men going out to the house. Can you give me anything else?' he said hurriedly; it was obvious that he had been well trained as his voice was calm and controlled even though he was speaking more quickly than usual.

'Oh shit, I don't have anything, but he is still standing there, so he must be alive,' I blurted. I was so worked up that I could feel tears trailing down my face and I was glad that no one could see me.

'My mobile is not working for some reason. If you need to ring me, ring Sylvia. She is with me.' He again hung up curtly. I knew that he was just being efficient, but it made me feel all the more panicked. Another hour passed and no one called. I decided to sit and try to calm myself, clear my mind. But everything changed. Matthew was not standing and there was blood.

Chapter 24

I wanted to be composed when I called Sylvia, but I just couldn't get myself together. I was a blubbering mess when I called. 'Sylvia, get Marsh,' I instructed in a terribly almost pathetic voice.

I could tell that they were in the car as I could hear road noise, and it took a moment for Marsh to pull over and answer.

'Yes, what?' he asked with urgency but without panic.

'The bastard has him. There's blood. He's not dead though. Oh shit, why can't I see where he is? It is very dark. That's all I can see – that it's dark.' I was panicking enough for both of us.

'Ok, keep calm, and keep trying. I'm putting Sylvia back on. We are about to arrive at the Wells' house,' he said, and I could hear the car wheels squeal as he tore off from the side of the road. This time, the police siren was audible.

'Are you alright?' Sylvia asked, sounding as though she, too, had shed a few tears.

'I just can't do anything. I feel so useless,' I answered, my self-loathing being obvious. I was not in control, and it was a lot to bear.

'You've got everyone out looking for him. No one else could have done that,' she reassured.

The siren stopped and I heard the door of the car slam. I could hear a screaming voice, though I couldn't tell who it was. It was a woman. I only caught one phrase, 'Oh god, oh god,' being repeated. I took the voice to be the mother of Matthew.

'Sylvia, what's happening?' I asked but she had alighted the vehicle too.

Holding the phone, she had taken it upon herself to comfort the older lady, and I could only hear her soothing tones and not the actual words, the phone being muffled by the embrace.

After several minutes, Marsh came back on the line. 'He's not here. Do you have anything?' he demanded.

I closed my eyes. The boy was there. He was on the ground and covered by something and yet I could tell he was moving. I told them what I could see.

'You are his only hope. Put the fear of failure behind you for now and get me something,' he spoke harshly, and I knew what he was trying to do, trying to scare me out of the spiralling depression.

It kind of worked. I knew I had to shut down the blubbering mess that I was and get on with trying to find Matthew if he had any hope.

I had never before spoken to a vision I was having, but something told me to call his name, so I did, and it seemed to me that he reacted even though he was covered and in darkness. I spoke again and asked if he knew where he was. Naturally, he didn't answer but again he seemed to stop struggling as I spoke.

Marsh, who had heard me speak, must have thought I had lost it completely, as he handed the phone to Sylvia, saying, 'Talk some sense to him. We need something.'

Sylvia came on the line and said, 'Try to gather yourself. Take deep breaths and tell me what's going on?'

'I can see what he is seeing. He's covered, in a rug or something. It's very heavy and wrapped around him tight. When I spoke to him, he seemed to hear as he stopped struggling. I think he can hear me,' I explained as calmly as I could.

'I heard you say to Marsh that you thought he was in a car?' she asked.

'Yes, well, he's moving. It might be a Ute or a van, I can't tell,' I answered, trying to keep the vehicle and its precious cargo in my mind. I usually tried to shut things out; now, I was in overload. I was doing all new things, things I had little or no control over.

'I am hearing him, though I don't think he is speaking. He's terrified – well, naturally, but I think I am making it worse for him,' I said.

As this new feeling that I could hear him flashed through my mind, I worried that I must sound like a lunatic.

'Tell him who you are and that you are trying to help him,' she suggested and added, 'Speak calmly!'

Strangely, I nodded even though I knew that she couldn't see that.

'Matthew, Matthew. I am James, and I'm trying to help,' I said. I used my voice; I didn't just think it. He stopped struggling.

'If you can hear me, know we are looking for you. If you can tell us anything to help or let us know where you are, tell me now. Do you know what car you are in?' I waited and though he seemed to stop moving again, I could only hear terror, a fear of everything. He was in greater pain than he had ever suffered before. His thoughts were almost incoherent. I thought he may be losing consciousness.

'Matthew, Matthew, don't go to sleep. I am trying to help you. What car are you in? Can you hear me?' I asked, trying not to scare him anymore.

There was a slight calming in his thoughts, and he said, 'It's a van,' then he was gone.

'Oh shit, he's gone. I can't see him. I can't see. I've lost him,' I babbled, and tears flowed again.

'Oh, keep trying. Can you try anything else?' Sylvia asked, sounding very worried.

'He said it was a van, then he blacked out. Oh god, did he die?' I babbled.

'Marsh, it's a van. That is all he got,' I heard her relay to Marsh.

Marsh's voice was audible, saying, 'All units, stop every van. I mean *every* van. You see and search it. We think it may be a van. Use caution, he may be armed.' There was no way of knowing if the person was armed or not, but the caution was understandable.

'Fitzpatrick, can you hear me?' he asked.

'Yes,' I answered, not thinking of anything to add, I was so distraught.

'Get a map and try to find him. We are coming to get you,' he said. 'We may have a better chance of finding him if you are here.' I knew that he was right but mostly I just didn't want to be alone.

The map did nothing for me. This was the same map we had used last time, but now I felt nothing. I waved my hand over it, thinking that I may draw some inspiration, but none came. I even held it up to my head. I felt a little foolish; this had never worked before. What would make me think it would work now?

I heard the car coming up the front drive, though it seemed to be hours since I had spoken to Marsh. I ran outside and met them before they could even get out. I had brought the map and was pulling on a coat as I had felt cold, though I think the cold shiver was something else, for as soon as I got into the front seat, which Sylvia had vacated for me, I felt far too hot and had to remove it again.

'Have you got anything?' Marsh asked with no formalities. I would have expected none.

'Nothing, I still can't see him, and that's not good,' I answered honestly.

'Well, I'll take us back to the home and work from there,' he continued as Sylvia placed a supporting hand on my shoulder from the rear seat.

'It may be better if you can keep calm,' she said, and I thought how wonderful it was to have her there as calmness was not something I felt in any way.

We turned into the road in which the boy lived, and I could see along the way that many police were out on the side of the road scouring the area, looking for anything that may help.

About half a mile down the road, a uniformed officer flagged Marsh down and came to the driver's window, which Marsh wound down.

'Here, Sir,' the fresh-faced junior said, showing appropriate deference.

Marsh quickly got out of the car and moved to where the young man crouched, pointing at what must have been blood stains. I'm sure he expected me to be next to him, but I stayed seated. He gave orders to the other man and then came back to the car.

'You don't need to get out?' he asked as he opened his door.

'No, he was hit here, and we need to go back toward the town centre,' I answered, avoiding eye contact. I was a little embarrassed. I knew I would have wasted time being sick if I got out.

'Fair enough,' he said, and I think he knew that I was not being difficult but merely trying to cut out unnecessary 'white noise'.

He turned the car and headed back toward the town centre. As we turned the next corner, I could see that police had pulled over a white van and had the driver beside it at gunpoint. One officer was frisking the other man while his partner covered them. As we approached, I recognised that the van was our work van and the man was Bob, my boss.

'Oh god,' I muttered as the officer with the gun moved to the back of the van and jerked the lifting door upward.

This time, I was out of the car before Marsh, and I nearly ran to where Bob was now kneeling. I looked to Marsh as he approached and said, 'Fucking hell. This is not the man.'

Sylvia arrived at my side and clutched my arm. 'Keep calm,' she said in a supportive voice.

Marsh reached down to Bob and helped him to his feet. He turned to face me. 'What the?' he asked, looking surprised and scared.

'Sorry, he has another boy, and he is in a van. They are stopping all vans,' I explained as quietly and calmly as I could. Like him, I wasn't used to guns being drawn.

The officer who had opened the rear door of the van came toward us and said, 'All clear.'

'Sorry for the inconvenience,' Marsh said then looked to the two young officers. 'Try not to be quite so rough but continue stopping every van you see.'

'Yes, Sir,' they both answered. Marsh didn't waste a single second more as he almost ran back to the car, followed by Sylvia and me. As I left, I said, 'Sorry, mate,' to Bob who nodded, still looking startled over the whole incident.

We soon arrived at the intersection where one could continue to the shops or divert to the left, which took traffic to the rear of the shops on the other side of the railway station.

'Which way?' Marsh asked and turned to look at me as he stopped almost in the middle of the road.

'I have nothing. Oh shit. And I can't even feel his presence. We better go back,' I answered very uncertainly.

Marsh swung the car around in a U-turn and narrowly missed a car coming toward us. The car realised that we had lights flashing, though our siren was not on. The driver slammed on his brakes and pulled over. Marsh roared back the way we had come, and as we neared a small cross street, I said, 'Here, I think,' and pointed to the right.

The car crossed the intervening distance and bounded as it hit the dip in the side street where water was redirected to the gutters. From there, Marsh had to slow his progress as the street was narrow and there were parked cars on both sides.

We came to an intersection. Marsh skidded to a stop and looked for direction. I had nothing. 'I don't have anything again,' I told him, and I again avoided his searching eyes.

He turned around and headed back the way we had travelled. This time, he took things more slowly, looking into each yard as we passed. There was no sign of a van.

We again reached the small intersection we had earlier turned at and this time continued straight across; therefore, heading the opposite direction to the one we had taken last time.

'I think this is right,' I said but doubted myself as I really didn't have much of a feeling for the boy and the van. We drove along this small road until it reached the next corner, which was the highway. I sensed nothing.

'Which way?' Marsh asked urgently. I sat for a moment, then I shook my head.

'I can't feel anything,' I answered. Sylvia's hand reached for my shoulder again, and I wished that this would have helped, but it didn't.

Marsh got on his radio and ordered all his officers to do a sweep of the area we had just been through. 'Show credentials and ask to look through all buildings and garages where a van may be hidden,' he concluded.

'Is there any way other than this that you might be able to help?' Marsh pleaded.

I shook my head. 'I don't think so, but if we continue to drive from here and look at each of the streets that branch off the highway, I might get a sense of him,' I answered very uncertainly.

'We will start, but there are dozens of turns in each direction,' he answered but started to turn to the left, leading us away from the town to the north.

I had no sense of Matthew, and it had now been at least two hours.

We drove, turning each corner to the left and travelling along for a short time until he looked to me for a decision. I shook my head for the first six times. As we approached the seventh side street, I was filled with the terrible feeling that I was going to be sick.

'Stop,' I instructed and almost before I could get out of the car, I was vomiting. Not that I had much in my stomach. I hadn't really eaten much in the last twenty-four hours.

Marsh jumped out and followed me into the gutter, and Sylvia also came to my side.

'Have you seen a direction?' Marsh asked urgently as Sylvia clutched my arm in support.

'No,' I answered then I added, 'He's not dead. He's laying right in front of me, and he knows I am with him.'

Chapter 25

Back in the car, I put my head down onto my knees. I felt Matthew's pain.

'Can you tell me where you are?' I asked, saying the words. I was not in touch with this new part of my 'gift', and I didn't know if I had to speak or if I could just think my questions.

I heard Matthew cry in pain, and I cried just as hard. Then he uttered an answer. 'In a van. It is not moving,' he almost whimpered.

'I am trying to sense where you are. Did you go to sleep before?' I asked and I could feel that the question confused him. 'I think you may have passed out?' I added.

I sensed that he had never passed out before and therefore had no point of reference with which to answer.

'Ok, what can you see?' I asked.

'Nothing,' he whimpered again.

'Alright, can you hear anything?' I asked, trying to sound as calm as I could.

'No,' he answered.

'Try hard, mate. Are there any cars passing? Anything?' I said persuasively.

'No, I heard a dog bark but nothing else.' He again made a crying noise. He was in terrible pain and naturally was the most frightened he had ever been.

I began seeing a woman that I thought must be his mother, then a man, and back to the darkness.

'I think he is going to pass out again,' I told Marsh and Sylvia.

Then I had the feeling that he was trying to get up. His legs failed him, and after a short few moments of extreme pain, he was gone from my sight.

'Oh, god. He's gone again,' I blurted, crying like a baby.

'What do you want me to do?' Marsh asked, grabbing my arm. His grip was strong, but it was to support and not intimidate.

'We better keep driving,' I said, struggling to my feet. They each took an arm and escorted me back to the car.

Once back on the road, I told them that Matthew had said that he didn't hear cars and could hear a dog bark. I knew that this didn't help much, but I was trying to show them what I was working with.

As ridiculous as it sounds, I was feeling that this was all my fault. Oh yes, I understood the concept of blame, but one is not rational when in such a desperate situation. I was seeing and feeling all new experiences, and they were certainly soul-destroying.

We drove and drove. I saw nothing more. It was crippling. I was in quite a state when we finally arrived back at the Donne office to drop Sylvia off.

There was nothing positive to say. Matthew was gone and there was nothing anyone could do about it. Even the ever-positive Sylvia seemed flattened.

I went to get out, but Marsh said, 'If you want to go back to the farm, I will have to drive you much later. I have a feeling that we will have to be at it all night.'

'That's alright, I will take him,' Sylvia said, giving a little smile. I was pleased. I would rather have had her company than anyone else's.

Marsh left, assuring us that he would ring if anything else happened.

I remembered thinking that he meant if they found a body.

When we got inside the office, Mrs Donne was all over us. What happened? Where had we been? Why hadn't Sylvia rung? Along with a myriad of other questions, which in the end, Sylvia couldn't take any more, and she burst into tears and left the room.

The old woman just glared at me, and I really couldn't think of anything else to say. I just moved to one of the chairs in the waiting room and sat down. With my head in my hands and my elbows supporting it with my knees, I tried to see the boy, but he was gone.

This stalemate, of a kind, continued for around five minutes, then Mrs Donne arrived in the waiting room with a cup of tea, which she placed next to me. She didn't speak, but it was some sort of concession at least. I nodded a thank you, still not sure I could speak, and she nodded back.

Strangely, I had the sudden thought, *Where is Donne?* and it worried me. After thinking hard to find the right words, I asked, 'Where is Mr Donne?'

'He is in court in Sydney for the day,' she answered, though neither of us could see the other. 'Was there anything you wanted me to tell him when he gets back?'

'No, thank you. I will catch up with him tomorrow.'

Another few minutes saw Sylvia return, having got her composure back, and though I couldn't really see them, I could tell they embraced.

'I'm going to take James back to the farm,' Sylvia informed her, and her mother answered, 'We will talk when you get back.'

Once on the road, I watched her in the driver's seat and felt guilty. Why should she have any reason to follow me through all of this?

'I'm sorry I dragged you into this,' I said and hoped that I wouldn't sound too pathetic.

'No, I wanted to help. I would have been more involved, only Father said I should keep my distance while the case was happening,' she assured me. She always supported me. I felt blessed – well, just for a few minutes, then the self-loathing returned, and I felt like such a failure.

Sylvia stayed to make us a cup of tea, which we drank in the kitchen. We didn't speak much; it was so difficult, under the circumstances, to find anything to say. As she left, she gave me a little kiss on the cheek and I wished it could have been more, but now there were other things to occupy my time.

The afternoon moved at a snail's pace. I wandered up and down the floors of the house; occasionally, I even walked up and down the stairs to try to settle my mind. I'm sure I was suffering an amount of OCD. There were certainly some compulsive traits in my make-up, and they were always worse when I was under pressure.

Just before four o'clock, I had the feeling that Matthew was still alive. He was not in my head when I closed my eyes, but I had a sense of him. I know that sounds a bit mad, but that *is* what I felt.

I had the urge to go searching for Matthew again but besides not having a vehicle, I knew I needed to stay close to the phone. I was still hoping that Marsh would ring with news, good news.

I decided I could afford to pace the front veranda. From there, I could still hear the phone yet still be outdoors. I paced. The veranda was made of new-looking floorboards, though there was still a bit of spring in them, and they made a little noise at two different places.

Basically, I was torturing myself. I'm sure I could have gone insane. A psychological practitioner of one kind or another would have locked me up and thrown away the key. I paced.

At one point, I was driven to look toward the shed and was surprised to see that the large door was again shut. When I last entered, the door had jammed, half-opened. As happened the first time, I was drawn to the door. Who could have put it right? I dismissed the thought; it was just my mind going ten to the dozen.

Eventually, though, I just couldn't resist. I knew I had to go and check it out. I jogged over to the door; it was locked, so I entered through the small door near the front of the building. I switched the light switch, but nothing happened. As before, the lights seemed not to work. There was a small amount of ambient light, lighting the inside of the area furthest from the house, the area with the two vehicles, which as before were covered by tarpaulins.

I walked in and went to the rear of the vehicles. I don't know why but I had the urge to see them.

Perhaps I could use one to go out searching for Matthew. I knew that this was not rational. For a start, my hand was still too messed up to have steered, and secondly, I knew I had to be here when Marsh rang or came out later in the evening.

I lifted the first tarp and saw the beautiful little sports car.

It was a mottled, sanded colour from what I could tell with such little light. I placed the cover back in position. I didn't want Donne to think I had been snooping around his buildings. The second vehicle was positioned in the same place as last time I had been there, though the tarp appeared to be a little less dusty. I walked to the back and suddenly saw Matthew in my mind. He was back. I quickly rushed outside, trying to get him to talk to me.

'Matthew, Matthew. Are you alright? Can you talk?' I blubbered. Still, I did try not to sound too mad. It would have heightened his fear.

'I can hear you,' he answered.

'Oh, thank god. I have been so worried,' I continued.

'No, I mean I can really hear you,' he cried.

Chapter 26

An immediate terror spread through me as the hair on the back of my neck tingled.

My first thought was, *What does this mean?*

Then I knew. He was in the car in the building. I ran back to the rear of the vehicles and lifted the second tarpaulin. There stood a white and pink ice cream van. Strangely, the rear door had a padlock bolted closed. I grabbed at it and heard Matthew groan in fear inside.

'I'm here, mate,' I said quietly as I thought to myself, *It was Donne all along. Oh god.*

The padlock didn't budge under my efforts, and I started to panic. What if Donne was here somewhere? I needed to get to the boy.

I moved to the driver's door and tried it. It was locked. The window where a myriad of children had been served over the years was locked, and then the passenger side door, it too was locked.

I knew that I had to get the door open right now. There was no time to waste. I grabbed for a piece of timber I saw leaning up against the wall. Placing it behind the bar on the lock, I pulled and nothing happened. I pulled again and I almost fell as the piece of timber shattered into splinters. My injured hand hit against my body and the pain made me groan.

I heard Matthew give a little gasp of fear.

'I'm still here, mate. I'm trying to get you out,' I reassured him. I could hear him crying and my own pain moved aside.

I fumbled around the back of the building, trying to find something to use to prise the door open. Eventually, I stumbled over a piece of roofing tile and rushed back to the lock. I immediately brought the tile up and smashed it against the latch. It did not give.

Matthew screamed in fright. I should have thought to tell him what I was going to do.

'Sorry, mate. I'm trying to smash the lock,' I said and could feel his breath as if it were my own. I brought the tile down again and it shattered into several pieces, but this time the lock gave, and the door moved just a little.

I grabbed at the handle with my injured hand and let out another loud groan as the pain shot up my arm and made me let go. I moved myself to a better position and used my other hand to drag the difficult door open.

There on the floor, I could see Matthew, huddled up against the back of the panel that separated the front of the vehicle from the back. He was covered with a light-coloured bed sheet but still I could see that he was trying to get away from me.

'It's me, it's me, it's me,' I reassured him as I entered the rear door. I knew I had to get him out of there.

I dragged back the sheet and could see the injuries to his legs. There was blood, and it appeared that both were broken as they lay at a strange angle.

'Oh shit, I will have to carry you,' I said, and he almost screamed as I tried to lift him. I struggled with him to the doorway of the van, and then getting onto the ground, I found it easier to get under him with both my arms.

'I have a smashed hand. You will need to hold on, so I don't drop you,' I said. He grasped me around the neck so tightly, I was surprised at his strength, considering the situation. He was a fighter.

I lifted and he groaned in pain as I backed away from the van and started to head out of the shed. As I got outside, I could suddenly hear a car coming up the road. I turned and rushed behind the building so we would not be seen, in case it was Donne returning to finish off the job.

The car sounded like Donne's. It had a low pattering sound that I had noticed before, it being a hybrid electric/petrol model of some kind.

Matthew gave a little groan, and I decided that there was no time left; I would have to make a run for the back door. I needed to keep the boy safe at any cost, and the house was safer. I needed the pistol. I had left it near the phone in a small drawer, hoping never to have to touch it again, but now it seemed like a lifeline.

I could hardly walk let alone run while carrying my load. My arm throbbed like someone with a knife was working away at it from the inside out.

I stumbled near the back steps, and though I caught myself before hitting the ground, Matthew let out a yelp of pain. I struggled up the steps and could hear the car getting closer. The light from the headlights crept around the corner. Another twenty feet and he would be able to see us.

I fumbled with the door handle and couldn't open it. I knew that I couldn't put Matthew down, and though I knew that it would probably hurt him, I pushed forward against the rear wall and held his body weight with my own and my injured hand. I gave almost as loud a groan as he did, but my good hand was freed just long enough to open the door.

Once inside, I placed Matthew on the rug in the kitchen where I knew he would not be seen and locked the door then rushed to the phone and grabbed the pistol. I could hardly even grasp it, I was shaking so hard, and I rushed back to Matthew, dragging him up against the furthest wall where I could see the only entrance to the kitchen. This is where I would have to make a final stand, if I could.

I saw the car lights go off and then thought of Donne finding the locked kitchen door. He would just get a key out, so I jumped up, ran to it and flipped the little silver button, which made the use of the key impossible. As I did this, I heard footsteps approach the door and the handle turned, then as I hid next to the door where I could not be seen, the door gave a little shake and a voice called, 'Fitzpatrick, are you there?'

It was Donne.

I nearly had a heart attack. I don't think I had ever been so terrified in my life. I just stood there, knowing that he couldn't see me, hoping that he couldn't see me.

Keys rattled and slotted into the lock, but it didn't turn.

'James, it's Donne,' he called loudly.

I was frozen to the spot, then a terrible thought crossed my mind. If he didn't get in here, he would go to the front door and simply unlock it.

I regathered my wits. Ducking low, as if that made me invisible, I ran toward the front hall. At the corner, I slipped and fell heavily, naturally landing with my injured arm under me. I tried not to make a sound but there was no doubt in my mind that I sounded like a bull in a china shop. I got back to my feet and charged to the door, clicked the safety then I slowly slid the chained lock into place.

Soon after, the screen door outside could be heard whining as it always did when being opened. I was terrified, but there was nothing else I could do so I ran back to the boy on the kitchen floor. Luckily for him, he had again passed out. I positioned myself next to him and dragged the large mat up over our legs. I knew I needed to keep him warm so the chance of the shock worsening or even killing him was negated. It strangely gave me a feeling of safety, as ridiculous as that was.

Matthew gave a little whimper. He was still little more than semi-conscious, but it was obvious that he could feel the pain. I hugged him close to me with my injured arm and clutched the pistol in the other awkwardly. My terror was heightened by the fear that I had no confidence that I would ever be able to pull the trigger.

Matthew woke and began to cry, not really remembering where he was immediately. He looked up at me and noticed the gun for the first time. Tears were streaming down his cheeks, and he fell weakly against my shoulder. I could feel his body shaking, but no more than my own.

Every noise made me jump. Donne called out a few more times, and then all was silent. We waited and waited.

Then suddenly I heard what must have been some metal tool working at the back door. Thankfully, it didn't give way. Donne's voice kept calling ever more urgently that it was him and he was trying to get in, and was I there, and should he call the police?

Call the police, that was an idea I hadn't thought of. Them coming to save us was not something I thought of as useful; they were more than forty minutes away, even with all lights and sirens ablaze.

I tried to steel myself. Only I could take care of this kid; it was me or no one. If Donne came through that door, I would have to use the gun.

There was a lull, a quiet time, and perhaps that was even more terrifying; the thought of what was to come. Then the sound of smashing glass came from the front of the building. Oh god, he was inside.

Then there was another call, 'Fitzpatrick, are you there?'

It sounded frantic and yet somehow benevolent. It was Donne. He had been my friend, my confidant, my saviour to some extent. Oh, it was too terrible to think about.

I could hear him coming through the house. There were tell-tale sounds of him entering each room, then I heard him in the living room. Matthew heard him also and let out a little whine. He looked scared and so fragile. Oh, god could I do this?

Movement stopped for a moment. It was as if Donne had heard the boy and was waiting for the next sound to hone his direction.

I put my finger to my lips to show Matthew that we must be quiet, but he was not looking at me. I gave his arm a little shake and he looked up. To say that he was terrified was so much an understatement that it didn't really bear any resemblance to the truth. I put my arm around his shoulders to show him that he was safe. The look he gave me showed that he was not sure that I knew what I was about, but he gave me a little nod. Then we both jumped as a chair scraped across the wooden floor, just a little noise.

The doorway filled as Donne stepped into the gap lit by the light behind him. He faced out the back door, not immediately knowing that we were there cringing against the back wall of the kitchen. Then he turned and saw us.

The look of disbelief that crossed his face amazed me. He had not seen me with the boy, of course.

He turned to face us, and his mouth moved to say the words, 'What the–' but the words were drowned out by the sudden smashing, splintering sound of a chair as it struck the right side of his head and he fell out of view. Nothing for a moment. We had both jumped. This was unexpected; we had been saved. These thoughts flashed through my mind all in a matter of a few seconds, and then the void where Donne's head had been filled by that of his brother.

He knew why he was there, and it only took me a second to realise why when Matthew began to squeal in fear. Oh god, it was his brother.

I raised the gun as best I could and pointed it in his direction. A smile, an evil smile, crossed his face. His eyes were those of a rampant beast, all humanity gone. I knew I had to do this. I had to pull the trigger. I shook uncontrollably, and then the click as I squeezed. But the gun didn't fire. I froze. Oh, the safety. Donne had told me about the safety.

The bastard's smile broadened as his hands came up. He was holding a large knife. I fumbled with the gun, trying to unlock the safety switch but my injured hand was now so traumatised that it was like trying to use a stump.

I could not immediately disengage the switch but continued. I looked back at the figure standing there. It seemed to grow straightened himself to full height as he savoured the moment. Finally, I felt the catch give and looked back up, knowing that the bloody thing would now fire.

He started to move, then Matthew and I both screamed as an ear-piercing roar came and the man's head literally disintegrated in front of us, and he too fell out of our view. Oh, but how? I had not been able to pull the trigger.

The moment of sheer terror lasted only a few seconds before Sylvia, my Sylvia, stepped into the void. She carried a double-barrelled shotgun, and it was emitting smoke from the upturned barrels.

She started to move toward us, throwing the gun aside. It clattered on the kitchen floor tiles. Matthew cringed, trying to get away. Of course, he didn't know who Sylvia was.

'She is a friend, mate. A friend,' I said, but my voice trailed as the crashing shot seemed to echo in my head. He held me tight as Sylvia knelt next to me. She was beside herself. Her tears streamed, and she whimpered. I placed the pistol on the floor and pushed it away as she fell into my good arm and the three of us clung there for a few moments. She had saved us.

Finally, I said, 'The boy needs an ambulance.'

Sylvia fumbled for her mobile phone and rang Marsh's number, then handed it to me.

'Yes, it's Marsh here,' he answered.

For a moment, I couldn't speak, but when I did, it came like a torrent. 'I have Matthew. We need ambulances. God, we are at the farm. Oh god, it was Donne's brother. Oh, get here quickly. The boy is hurt,' I babbled almost incoherently.

'What? Do you mean you can see him?' he looked for clarity in what I was telling him, but clarity wasn't something I had in great abundance at that moment, nor did I have any poise.

'Fuck no, I have him. He's here,' I tried to explain, my words turning to blubbering like a baby.

'We're coming. Where is the killer? You say he is Donne's brother?' he said, rushing his words, trying to understand if we were still under threat.

'He's dead,' I blurted as I was almost drowned out by the sobbing of Sylvia to my left and Matthew to my right.

'We're coming, hold on,' he promised. 'Keep the phone line open.'

I put the phone down as we three clung to each other and jumped as one as we heard a groan from the other side of the kitchen counter.

'Father!' Sylvia suddenly cooed. And though there was no answer, it soon became obvious that he was not coherent but alive. I think we had all just assumed he was dead; such was the force with which he had been dispatched.

Sylvia started to move; it was, however, almost as if she were glued to me. She couldn't let go. She was still terrified to see what she would see, what she had done.

'I'll go,' I said and started to move. Matthew was not letting me go, though. 'It's ok, mate. Sylvia will look after you,' I said, leading Sylvia's hand to his. He took it tentatively and then folded into her arms. I crawled a little way but found this incredibly difficult with only one hand, so I struggled to my feet as I rounded the corner to be confronted by more blood than seemed possible from only two bodies.

Donne was on his back, his brother's lifeless body draped across his lower legs where he had fallen.

Blood and brain matter covered the bottom two-thirds of the glass back door. Donne had so much blood covering him that it was hard to see that he could be alive.

I kneeled in the blood, and with my good hand, rolled the body from his legs. The almost headless body rolled onto its back, and the gore was so awful that I began to dry retch. I stopped myself for a moment to calm. God, how could one calm amidst all this carnage?

I reached for Donne's throat, but didn't need to take his pulse as he gave a little cough. I knew I had to get him onto his side so he wouldn't drown in his own blood. His face was a mess; the chair had shattered his cheek and nose, and now even the jaw seemed to stick out at an oblique angle.

I rolled him toward me, to his injured side. I was not sure that this was correct – all those years of training to be a first aider as a teenager seemed to be a long distant memory. He coughed again, and a small amount of blood ran from the corner of his mouth.

Sylvia's voice weakly said, 'Is he...' then stopped, frightened to say the words.

'No, no, he's alive. I've placed him on his side. I think he will be ok,' I reassured her, though I'm sure she knew as well as I did that I had absolutely nothing on which to base that assumption.

'Should I come?' she asked very tentatively.

'No, no, stay there,' I instructed, sounding more urgent than I had intended. I heard her whimper and added, 'Marsh is on his way with help.'

Donne seemed to be breathing normally, so considering the circumstances, I decided to crawl back to Matthew and Sylvia. We three lay there trying to keep warm under the kitchen rug. I positioned myself to Matthew's right so he would have one of us supporting him on either side. This was also a way of keeping his body temperature warm should he go into shock any further.

About forty minutes passed and though I knew that there was little hope of Marsh getting to us within an hour, I could hear the faint sound of a vehicle. When it became stronger, I could tell it was the rotor of a helicopter. Within minutes, it had landed in the front paddock and Marsh was with us.

'In the kitchen, we are safe,' I yelled in as loud and strong a voice as I could muster. He soon rounded the corner and, seeing the two bodies near the back door and us huddled on the floor, he lowered his weapon.

'What the hell has happened?' he asked, rushing toward us. Matthew cringed as he neared and clung even tighter to me.

'It was Donne's brother. He had Matthew in the outbuilding in a van. He hit Donne and Sylvia shot him,' I answered. I was obviously babbling a bit incoherently as he knelt in front of us, putting his revolver away.

'The brother?' he questioned.

'Yes, Donne is still alive. We need ambulances. Matthew is hurt, and I'm not much good either,' I answered and fell back against the wall, exhausted.

Marsh jumped up and rushed back to Donne. He was out of sight but announced, 'I think he will be ok.' Then after a pause, he uttered the words, 'Jesus Christ,' and I knew he had seen the other man's lifeless and almost headless body.

'We still had the search copter in town, so I got here as soon as I could. There are police units and ambulances following – they won't be far behind me.'

He rushed away and returned with some blankets. He quickly covered us with two then threw one over Donne, still in the recovery position. Next, he was on his mobile phone and explaining what the arriving officers and ambulance staff would be confronted with.

Soon after, the sound of sirens was audible, and the roaring of vehicles was quite loud as they raced to the site. We were all saved.

The first ambulance officer came near us as the second moved to Donne. They assessed those of us injured and decided that Donne was the first to be moved.

'I should go,' Sylvia said as she saw the stretcher being moved out of the room. I nodded and she stood as the other ambulance officer asked her if she was injured.

'No, I'm not injured,' she answered him and turned as he continued to examine Matthew. She left us, looking back and trying not to see the body of her uncle.

The boy let out a loud scream and clung ever tighter to me as the officer examined his legs. 'How long has he been injured?' he asked, turning to me.

'Well, I suppose it was about eight this morning,' I answered uncertainly.

'Oh, and he has had no treatment?' he continued.

'No, nothing,' I answered more strongly, showing how proud I was of the boy's bravery. The officer moved away for a short time and returned with a small tube.

He handed it to Matthew and said, 'Breathe through this. It will help with the pain.'

Matthew did as he was told and soon gained some relief. It was then, though, that I realised that I was still hearing him think. That was not normal, even for me.

Everything will be alright, I thought, and he answered, looking into my eyes with a nod. Oh god, he was still hearing me, too.

Donne, they decided, should be taken away quickly. Such a head wound was life-threatening, and the decision was made to load him onto the helicopter, which was fitted with a basket for such patients. Sylvia walked out with him and then took a passenger seat and quickly, they were gone.

With much discomfort, Matthew was loaded onto a wheeled stretcher but would not release my arm. It was obvious that he was not letting me go, and the officers decided to work around that rather than upset him further.

Once in the ambulance, he was given some stronger painkillers, and he soon went off to sleep. 'Now for you?' the man said as he undid the boy's grip on my arm.

I was covered in blood – mostly, it was not mine, though it was obvious that I was bleeding through the bandages on my injured arm.

'Oh, it's been nearly a week since they did the surgery on it,' I explained.

'I think I will just double bandage it to stop the bleeding. It will need to be a doctor who looks after you,' he explained, and I was happy to concede as I was not looking forward to the discomfort I knew I was in for when the bandage was removed. He then offered me one of the pain relief breathing tubes, which I took gratefully.

I was positioned against the side wall of the ambulance and though it was uncomfortable, I soon fell into a deep sleep, a sleep that I had not been able to get for several days.

Chapter 27

I woke briefly when we arrived at the hospital, but realising where we were, I simply allowed myself to drift off again.

I was awakened by a hand stroking my uninjured hand. It was Sylvia.

'Oh, good,' she said quietly.

It took a moment for me to gain my bearings, then I suddenly saw Matthew, sleeping soundly, in my thoughts.

'It's been nearly twenty-four hours. They had to operate on your arm again. Matthew has had two operations on his legs, but he is ok,' she cooed.

I held her arm tightly. That was not all I needed to know – what of her father?

'Father is still in an induced coma. They say he will be alright, but he looks so terrible, the tubes going in and out everywhere,' she explained, trying to keep her composure. Even in the worst of times, she had such poise.

'I'm sure he will be alright,' I heard myself saying, and thought how dismissive I sounded, and then I thought to add, 'And how about you?'

'Oh, I am not sure it has all hit me yet. Marsh says there will have to be an inquiry into the death.' She was anxious and a single tear followed the tracks of many shed in the last hours.

'You were magnificent. He would have killed us all if you weren't there,' I gushed.

'I don't feel magnificent,' she said, dropping her head, and more tears flowed. I sat up in bed to comfort her and was struck by a feeling of dizziness that I hadn't expected. I fell back onto the pillow.

'Yes, you will have to rest for a while. The arm was infected again.' She paused, fluffing my pillow and fumbling with the blankets as if to tuck me in. In truth, I was tucked in so tight that it almost cut off my circulation. My head seemed to spin, and I felt sick. Sylvia pressed a button, and a nurse appeared and quickly rushed away to get a bowl.

I was not sick. I would have been so embarrassed if I had been. Even now, I was thinking of how I looked to Sylvia. She had seen me at my lowest and yet she was now at my side. She hadn't run a mile as so many others had.

Some hours later, I woke at the request, it seemed, of Matthew. Sylvia was gone and I didn't have any idea what time it was. I could hear Matthew calling to me, though I couldn't actually hear words. I started to get up and felt so unsteady that I had to sit back down. I almost fell and another patient, seeing what had happened, pressed his service button, saying, 'Just wait there. The nurse will come.'

I didn't look at him, though he was in the next bed, but I did manage a 'thank you'.

When the nurse appeared, the man pointed to me and said, 'He tried to get up and nearly fell.'

'How can I help you?' the nurse said as she tucked at the edge of my blankets. What was with all this tucking? It was like being in a straitjacket.

'The boy I came in with, I heard him calling,' I said, not really looking her in the face.

'I don't think so. He is in another ward – the paediatric ward – and it's all the way on the other side of the hospital,' she answered curtly.

I wanted to argue with her, but how could I dispute what she had said? She left me looking as bewildered as she must have thought I was.

Matthew's voice came to me again and again, and I struggled to get up from the bed. I felt so unwell, however, that I sat down in the visitor's chair, trying not to pass out. I was only there for a short time before the nurse came bustling back into the room with a wheelchair.

'I have been instructed to take you to the boy. He will not settle until he sees you,' she informed me, helping me to the chair. She could have no idea that his state and the calls I had heard were the same thing.

She wheeled me to the nurse's desk and handed me over to a wardsman with the instruction, 'To paediatrics.' He did not query her but raised his eyebrows. 'That's right, paediatrics,' she said, turning her back as though she was disgusted to have her authority questioned.

The man began to push me in the direction he had been given. My head spun and I felt at each corner that I would be sick. As we moved toward a T-intersection, I heard Matthew calling again, then it struck me: I had never heard someone call me like this. The connection with him seemed to be initiated by him, not me. Oh god, it was him, not me.

As I was wheeled into the two-bed room, which I felt I already knew, Matthew's voice was calling to me, again, I could not hear actual words. This was so strange, even for me. No one had ever been able to contact me like this other than my grandmother, and I only saw her; I didn't hear her.

The boy reached out for me as I was wheeled around the end of the dividing curtain. His mother and father stood on the opposite side of the bed, and I could see that the father looked annoyed. Matthew grabbed my hand and held it with both of his, almost dragging the drip and cannula from his arm.

'Oh, thank you, thank you. I didn't get to thank you,' he said, breaking down and weeping.

'It's alright, mate. You were the brave one,' I answered, not really knowing what to say. I felt so awkward.

He held on as tightly as he could and his mother stepped forward, taking my arm and saying, 'Matthew has told us how you saved him,' then she hugged me to her and started weeping uncontrollably. She kept repeating, 'Thank you, thank you.' I felt a bit embarrassed; this was all too much.

As the woman stepped back, she was replaced by her husband. He did not look so delighted. He shook my good hand as if by duty rather than him wanting to; it was a solid shake but there were no words.

In my mind, I heard Matthew again saying, *My father doesn't approve of psychics, and I don't think he likes me very much either.*

I looked at the boy and nodded. He nodded back. *It was the same for me with my father,* I thought, and he nodded again. When he spoke, without speaking, his voice was loud and strong. He seemed so confident, not the blithering idiot I was at his age.

Before any other discussion could take place, another wardsman appeared with a wheeled bed and a nurse by his side. 'It's time,' she said, and Matthew nodded resignedly, though I could tell he was quite anxious. His mother bent to kiss him, and he took my hand again and said, 'Thank you. Will you be here when I wake up?'

'I think I will be in the hospital for a few more days at least,' I answered as the two wardsmen transferred him painfully to the trolley.

Matthew's mother followed the bed out of the room but as his father passed me, he bent down and looked me in the eye. 'I know what you are. You leave my son alone,' he snarled.

I had met plenty of bullies in my time and knew he was used to getting his own way, but I wasn't about to give any ground, so I just stared him down. I'm sure that this was not the response he was expecting. He turned and stomped out of the room like a three-year-old in a tantrum, saying not too quietly, 'Bloody freak.'

Now I was left alone. My wardsman had gone with Matthew. I tried to move my own chair but it was a waste of time with only one hand free, so I just sat there waiting. After a few minutes, I saw Matthew's eyes close to avoid seeing the needle he was about to be given.

'It will be alright,' I said, and he responded, 'I will be alright,' then he quickly dropped away from me and I knew that he was asleep.

Eventually, a nurse came walking by and I called out to her. When I told her I needed to get back to my ward, she asked which ward I was from, and having no idea, I just pointed in the direction.

Once back in the ward, I suddenly had the feeling that Matthew was there in my presence again. Then he was in the back of the van, and then he was being struck by the car. He was dreaming, reliving the terrible experience as the anaesthetics took him out of his conscious state. His thoughts were all over the place, jumping from the trauma to the memory of the first operation then to the van again.

I felt that I needed to help him. 'It's alright, mate,' I said out loud and the man in the next bed asked, 'What's alright?'

'Oh, sorry, I was just thinking out loud,' I apologised. He looked at me as though I were crazy; it was a look I was used to. I had seen it almost all of my life.

Be calm, Matthew. You are safe, I thought. I sensed him relax a little, so I continued thinking the same thoughts repeatedly.

After a short while, I was asleep, and I felt I was in the operating room with him. I could see his head and shoulders. Tubes protruded from his nose and mouth and though his eyes were closed, I felt that he knew I was there.

I could see the backs of two doctors and a nurse, but thankfully, I couldn't see the legs that they were operating on. I, like Matthew, was spared that at least.

I don't understand what happened next; there was nothing, I wasn't sure if the drugs had taken him further or if I were dreaming out of step, but there was nothing.

When I next woke, it was morning. I felt very much rested, and my painful arm seemed to have settled quite a bit. I immediately thought to look in my mind for the boy. There was nothing. I was surprised and anxious. What had happened? Had he passed away? There was nothing.

I rang for the nurse, and when she appeared, I asked about Matthew's condition. 'I'm afraid I can't discuss another patient's condition,' she explained, though in a sympathetic tone.

'I, um, I just need to know if he is still alive?' I asked uncertainly.

'Well, as I said, I can't discuss another patient, but I can tell you that no one has died at this hospital in the last few days,' she answered, raising her eyebrows as a question – did I understand?

I was so relieved. I lay back down and soon drifted off to sleep again. This was the good sleep I needed. I was hearing and seeing nothing.

Chapter 28

Almost six months have passed. I have been recovering at what can only be described as an asylum. Oh, not the kind you see in the movies. This is a hospital caring for those suffering from post-traumatic stress. There are many soldiers here; some from recent conflicts, a couple from the Vietnam War and even one from the Second World War.

I try to keep away from all of them for fear of seeing the atrocities they witnessed. I have not always been successful in this, which led to several moves of room and a few sleepless nights.

Sylvia has visited each week and speaks of what we might do when I get out. Matthew and his mother also visited, only once though, as I gathered his father did not approve of them coming. It's strange to say, though, that he, Matthew, is in constant contact with me. I remembered how hard my teenage years had been, and knew just what he must have been going through, his abilities being much stronger than mine.

I had a visit from Marsh in the first week I was here. We had little to talk about, but he did tell me that Donne and his brother had been with their grandfather when he had run over the man and his dog on the lookout road all those years ago. They had been made to help the old man get the suffering body of the man and the deceased animal into the back of the Ute, and they were with him when he buried the bodies at the lookout.

Donne, it seemed, had grown normally, but the brother had been so broken by the incident that he had taken to killing the family pets and burying them in his makeshift cemetery at the farm.

No one could understand why he transitioned to humans and why boys, though the method of running them down in his vehicle was very understandable. It seemed that he liked to watch them suffer in their final death throes.

Donne had not visited. I sensed his guilt – he felt that he should have put things together and realised his brother's involvement. I know that he still has much recovering to do from his own injuries, but I hope he will come sometime, so I can settle his mind. No one picked the murderer, even when I had travelled with him to the farm, early in the case. I didn't sense that it was him.

I know that Matthew will need help in getting through these formative years, and I want to be that help, but for now, I need the sanctuary of these walls. I'm not ready to revisit the broken places.

THE END